PULSE

J Z YORK

ISBN 979-8-9864861-0-9

Visit jzyork.com

For Jenniva,

because I said so.

PULSE

Contents

1. Genesis 1

2. Oberon 17

3. Metamorphosis 25

4. Getting Acquainted 41

5. Mind-reading 49

6. Brothers 54

7. Personal 66

8. Blinded 73

9. Codes and Knives 87

10. First Aid 97

11. Dark Ops Down 113

12. Awakening 123

13. New Moon 135

14. Homing 149

15. Love and Healing 162

16. The Village 168

17. Hunter Rising 180

18. Towers 192

19. Slings and Arrows 201

20. Clear Sight 211

21. The Wall 216

22. Inside Out 228

23. Shattering 238

24. Battle Plans of the Heart 243

25. One 249
26. The Battle. 260
27. After. 278
28. Day of Grace 280
29. Renaissance 288
30. Asa. 300
31. Revelation 305
Epilogue. 314
New History 314
Acknowledgments 318
About the Author. 320

'We are not down to a single, unique universe, but our findings imply a significant reduction of the multiverse to a much smaller range of possible universes."

- STEPHEN HAWKING

TAMING THE MULTIVERSE, 2018

1.

GENESIS

NO STREET SIGNS marked the carefully neglected-looking lane. Turning onto the narrow drive, Grace slowed her car for surveillance cameras to read its encoded tags.

The bordering forest still held shadowed patches of snow. A half-mile into the wood, the first crocuses flung bits of spring along the drive's sun-dappled shoulders. Her twin, Ellie, had always won their game of spotting firsts: first robin, leaf bud, uncurling fern, firefly. Grace may have let her. *Ellie, I miss you.*

Noting slight movement in the tall undergrowth, her fingers tightened on the wheel.

That's unusual…

Rounding the lane's final curve revealed her favorite Security Police sergeant manning the gate. Battle fatigues and upgraded hardware replaced Sergeant McKinley's standard uniform and sidearm. His eyes flicked along the tree line before turning full attention to her approach.

Grace scanned for clues warranting the armed shadows drifting through the perimeter wood and the sergeant's uniform change.

This is a first. I've never seen an alert exercise spill onto external grounds.

Security was strict but discreet; this was Boston, not Baghdad.

She coasted to a halt atop the scanning pad. Covered Kevlar vests and a sidearm were normal at the gate; guards in body armor with MP5 submachine guns were not.

McKinley drew her focus back to routine procedure, accepting Grace's ID badge. She summoned their usual small talk, as both badge and car were scanned.

"Are you thawing? Thank God the snow has stopped," she said.

"Almost there, Sergeant Woods. I wait for full sensation to return before taking spring inventory."

Eyes crinkling at her laugh, he returned her badge as "STAFF SERGEANT GRACE WOODS—CLEARED—," flashed across his handheld screen. McKinley's nod released her to enter the grounds as steel pylons retracted into the ground.

Grace parked. Her questions and feet turned toward where the answers lay; underground, in the black ops site known as "the Bunker." The extensive, state-of-the-art facility lay far beneath her feet. Camouflaged from air traffic and satellites as a derelict Park and Ride lot, its entrance was disguised as snow-removal equipment storage, a familiar sight in New England. But this storage could withstand a direct hit from most non-nuclear weapons.

As she navigated the buckling asphalt's weed-filled

cracks, Grace nodded at two exiting day shift officers, right hand curled in her coat pocket. Three years assigned here and even with uniforms covered above ground, it was difficult to restrain a salute.

Grace paused at the entrance, face upturned for a last kiss of sun, curls ruffling in the briny breeze from the nearby salt marsh. Entering the tunnel her stride quickened. Life outside the gates vanished. Checklists and protocols dictated time here, her past firmly kept at bay.

The young security airman at Checkpoint One was missing his flirtatious smile. "Sergeant Woods," he said.

"Airman Kent. Working hard, or hardly working?"

Fidgeting, he gave her a nod.

Good grief, has he flunked an inspection?

With a sympathetic look she turned away, shrugging off the trench coat worn to cover her uniform outdoors.

Ellie would have chosen it for a cloak-and-dagger effect, so Grace had. Waiting for the X-rayed bin of her things, she finger-combed her windblown curls. Bypassing the escalators, Grace jogged down three flights of stairs, arriving a bit breathless at the one place in the facility her confident composure slipped.

The Door. An immense, round, nuclear bomb-proof steel hatch, latched open with enormous clamps. Its inescapability—once released, there was no stopping its closure—prompted her heart to sprint, her stomach to clench. Turning with relief to the familiar Intelligence officer joining her, she smiled.

He's in early—if anyone has a clue...

"Good afternoon, Major Rodriguez. Ready to rock and roll?"

A brief nod. "Sergeant Woods," he said.

His regular warm smile stopped short of his eyes. He softened at her questioning look. "I know. I'll update you after I check the boards and am sufficiently caffeinated," he said.

They crossed the Door's safety zone of broad, fluorescent yellow-and-black floor stripes and incline ramps bridging its elevated sill. Lockdown was an event. Warning sirens wailed; incline ramps dropped flush with the floor; strobe lights visually stuttered all motion as massive machinery groaned. The finality of the Door's thunderous closing—the repercussive boom of seating bolts—secretly terrified Grace.

Drills were run for high-level dignitaries. She escaped them whenever possible. She'd never been claustrophobic, so the increasingly intense panic frustrated her and was carefully hidden from coworkers.

With a parting nod, Major Rodriguez turned toward his wing. Grace entered the elevator to hers. Gauging the car's plummeting descent, she swallowed to comfortably pop her ears. The doors slid open with a soft chime. Equalizing air pressure brushed her skin. Grace answered the unspoken question from two airmen waiting to enter.

"It's gorgeous outside. Sunny."

Weather reports were a routine greeting for those working below ground.

"Thanks, Sarge."

Her break room locker was the final stop.

"What's the weather, Grace?" Meredith, a lieutenant from Logistics, put down her paperback to rub tired eyes. Her crumpled camos, energy drink, and stretching yawn suggested her flight was pulling 24-hour Alert shifts.

"Sunny. Spring's knocking."

"Thank God." Meredith's body sagged further into the uncomfortable plastic chair; feet propped on another.

"What's up with Alert levels?" Grace asked.

Meredith rolled her eyes. "Still need-to-know. Lots of visitors in the Wing Commander's office. No solid rumors in the mill."

She waved her book at Grace. "My sister's offensively into horoscopes, so I'm defensively learning her love language. Let me practice on you."

Grace's hands rose in surrender. "Have at it."

"I'm twenty-six, so you're—one year younger? We share our birth month, —hold on a sec—."

Waiting patiently, Grace leaned against her locker while Meredith flipped back a few chapters.

"Your birth sun dominates your personal strengths. As celestial paths converge, you grow stronger. You become who you are meant to be." Meredith looked up for Grace's reaction.

"So, the sun is in charge. Predestination." Grace made a wry face. "I'm not much of a fate person." Meredith scoffed. "I'm fated to wear at least one star."

"I believe you, but you're busting ass for them, no one's handing them to you. You'll own those stars."

She blew out a breath. "Personally, I can't believe in fate. If my birth sun dominates who I'm meant to be, you'll see my destiny as a catastrophe on network Breaking News."

Meredith waved off the remark. Pulling her feet from the chair, she rose to depart. "Outta here, girl! You'll leave us all behind."

Grace glanced over her shoulder as she turned to her locker, coquettishly fluttering her lashes.

"A kind thought no matter how misguided. May you find a quiet corner for a nap."

Laughter trailed Meredith's departure leaving Grace to the empty break room. Stowing her things, she paused to trail fingers over the yellowing photo taped inside the locker door. Grandmother Lilli in the porch swing with Grace and Ellie tucked into her embrace, proudly displaying gap-toothed smiles, and scraped, summertime knees.

Fate is a four-letter word. This job is the only fate I can control.

Closing the locker, she searched for a thought to lighten her mood. Her glance fell on the vending machines. She laughed into the empty room.

Who stocks black site vending machines?

Standing inside the entrance to the cavernous, two-story room of Central Command, Grace inhaled the scent of chill, scrubbed air. The darkened main floor, dubbed the Pit, made the most of huge, lit-glass Intelligence boards. Though currently not in use, the Wall, an IMAX-sized display screen, dominated the room.

Keyboards were clicking at a normal pace. Intel boards showed little overnight activity. There was nothing to explain the heightened security level at the gate, the jittery checkpoint airman, Major Rodriguez's poker face or Meredith's high alert shift.

Monitoring the interactive world map was like watching civilization breathe. Vertical bands highlighted zones in daylight hours. Synchronized dots in the thermosphere were satellites, the ISS, and military space activity. Air traffic, ground and sea action, color-coded overlays indicating active or impending threats. Grace had her fingers on the world's pulse.

Crossing the Pit floor to her terminal, she formally accepted control of her station fifteen minutes early, earning the gratitude of Sergeant Harrison, the departing cryptographer. Grace leaned in to question her, voice low.

"What's up with the alert status? No one seems to know."

Harrison shrugged. "There's some unusual brass in the Colonel's office, including NASA reps and weirdly, some astrophysicists. It can't be the usual suspects with them involved, it would be on the boards." Eyebrows waggling, Harrison suggested possibilities, "UFO's? Asteroids? Superheroes? I did see hypotheticals concerning civil unrest response, but it didn't specify where. As long as the world doesn't end before tonight's hot date, I'm good."

Grace laughed, straightening to initiate transfer protocol.

"Sergeant Woods, taking control of station," said Harrison.

"This is Sergeant Woods, taking control."

She ran her checklist, keeping an eye on the second-floor squadron and wing commanders' offices encircling the Pit. She plunged into the messaging stream, watching for critical-level FLASH message traffic.

An air-conditioning duct was positioned high above her station. Wonderful for keeping her cool when some inbred has his finger on a launch button; a stiff neck when things were minimally death-defying. It clicked on, cool air licking the nape of her neck.

Grace's fingers stuttered on her keyboard. Time lagged

for a single, slow-motion blink. Heart stalling, she fell into icy darkness that was more than lack of light. An orange slash of color moved in the angry blackness—all vanished with the completed blink. Time resumed at normal speed and the moment evaporated without a trace.

Colonel Jennings appeared in his second-floor office doorway; red Pentagon phone pressed to his ear. "Turn on the Wall to NASA live feed; cede control—Juliet-Mike-Tango-Zulu." Instantly on her feet, Grace acknowledged the order.

"Yes, sir."

Quickly keying the nearby control pad, she brought the huge screen to life. Before her hand left the keypad, DEFCON 3 began shrieking and flashing from all wall beacons. "Fuck!" Grace blurted, jumping back as though burned. Her glance darted up to Colonel Jennings, awaiting further commands. Strobe lights, in combination with klaxons, were nerve-shredding. Whoever thought this would sharpen people's response in times of emergency was a fool.

Within minutes, having garnered everyone's attention, the shrieking alarm was silenced. The flashing lamps efficiently continued to warn all personnel to remain on edge. Those who were able to leave their sections migrated toward Central for accurate intel over circulating rumors.

A sergeant drifting in with Logistics people scoped out the action in the Pit.

"What's up? A drill? Didn't we do this last month?" Meredith looked to Grace, who subtly shook her head indicating she had no explanation.

"Cool, they have the Wall on. I've never seen the whole thing lit, just sections," said an airman.

Grace also had never seen the entire Wall in use, nor noticed how nauseatingly close her terminal was. She pushed back from her station as a NASA satellite zoomed in on two turbulently swirling dark spots on the sun's surface. A second satellite stream joined, splitting the screen, covering a different angle.

Other departments moved into Central, smells of hot-plate coffee and microwaved lunches swirling in behind. Each wave of newcomers milled about questioning until caught up, joining the silently uncertain majority. No one had a clue, except perhaps Colonel Jennings. He stood gripping the railing above the Pit, flanked by brass and visitors. Those in the Pit monitored him. His eyes were glued to the Wall.

"What are we looking at?" a woman asked.

Her colleague's response was uncharacteristically sharp. "It's the sun."

Surprised at his tone, she elbowed him. "Don't be an asshole. Why are we at DEFCON 3 to look at the sun?"

He shrugged, eyes fixed on the screen.

Similar exchanges were echoing throughout the room with varied intensity, pitch, and volume.

Talking came to a halt as action exploded like a match strike into gasoline. The larger vortex decided its silence was not golden, erupting violently. The mother of all solar flares flung herself into magnificent, terrifying existence.

Grace felt the pulse of shocked energy from the watchers as though all were wired to the screen. Sound erupted from the crowded room in hard bursts. Profanity and startled cries littered the still-filling room. Many stumbled away from the screen, falling against those behind. Personnel lining the upper floor railings, including the brass, jumped back against the wall, dragging the nearest person with them.

"Fucking hell!" spit a master sergeant, pulling stunned people from the floor.

Disconnected voices, emotion-sharp, rose above the noise in the now milling crowd.

"Is that as huge as it looks?" asked an airman, frozen directly in front of the screen.

"What… how does that affect us?" called a voice summing up the question on everyone's mind.

Colonel Jennings simply stood, eyes darting over the displays, analyzing data, frightening many with his motionless, silent stance.

An airman tugged at his chief's sleeve. "How far away is that?"

A question cut through the noise.

"Why aren't they saying anything?"

"Because," Major Rodriguez said, "it's streaming from satellites. We're not watching a documentary." His voice was level, an attempt to calm the rising fear.

Multiple feeds were now streaming, fed by every NASA satellite turning to face the sun. The immense, fiery loop of hydrogen, helium, and plasma was now shown with a fly-speck sized Earth superimposed, showing scale and distance.

From the upper railing, an astrophysicist spoke. "Holy God, look at the size of the thing."

Noise levels began dropping from shock as the smell of acrid sweat and souring drugstore cologne rose.

Smaller, silent screens multiplied across the bottom of The Wall like manic post-its, showing every broadcast channel, each rapidly switching to live news. All showing carefully curated, time-lagged selections of the live feeds, likely without strictly accurate narration. Sitting arms crossed, hand to her mouth, Grace was taking in the room and screen, piecing together a picture.

This explains the large-scale crowd control hypotheticals.

Avoiding civil chaos was a high priority. They wanted civilians to understand what was coming, but not quite the full scale. The government was working to ascertain impact and prioritize high value assets to protect, which would not reassure the public.

The extra guards, the heightened security.

These events didn't happen without warning. Sunspots, like volcanos, were monitored. Government agencies had hypothetical models of such scenarios. But no one could accurately forecast catastrophic event size or impact.

In case those in the Bunker, Pentagon, and White House weren't panicked enough, NASA, frantic to impart the full significance of the event in motion, knew pictures were understood faster than words. They threw up a titled clip of the largest flare ever recorded, the July 23, 2012, Carrington Class flare. It had missed the planet by a safe margin, barely making two news cycles. Only astrophysicists had been disturbed, discussing the inevitability of worse outcomes.

A hopeful voice rose.

"I remember that! The news said it was interesting but no big deal."

The Carrington flare was superimposed over the live shot. The current flare was already ten times larger and growing, generating an enormous solar wind headed squarely at Earth. The room quieted as more were absorbing the visuals, struggling to understand the implications.

Two Master Sergeants versed in electromagnetic pulse generators quietly talked near Grace. Hands locked behind his neck, one spoke. "My family… it's fucking game over."

His friend leaned into him, forcibly whispering. "It *won't* be over. It'll set us back, maybe a century. We'll figure it out."

He shook his friend's shoulders. "This is not asteroid, dinosaur-extinction shit."

They fell silent, watching the screens. Grace knew electromagnetic pulse ramifications. The sun fascinated her. She'd done a science project on them in school.

NASA inserted a Time-To-Impact clock at the top of the frame, subdued time pip subtracting seconds. The solar wind was traveling the 92.9 million miles to Earth too fast for meaningful response. Frightened voices eddied through the room. Some personnel ran for the restrooms, trying not to lose control on the public side of the door. Many stood rooted to the spot, watching the countdown clock, literally wringing their hands.

Hearing muted to a hum, Grace processed what she knew to scale. When a solar wind hits Earth's atmosphere it generates an electromagnetic pulse, or EMP. Nukes detonated at the correct height have the same effect. The pulse would knock out everything electrical covering an area corresponding to pulse size. Small ones were fixable or seen as beautiful Aurora Borealis. A larger one could take down a sizable city power grid.

Due to her studies and the overheard doomsday conversation, Grace could extrapolate the effects from an electromagnetic pulse of this magnitude. Her mind played out horrifying scenarios of what was coming.

Every unshielded microchip would fry. Those chips were

in everything carrying electricity. Everything. Light bulbs. Nuclear power plant safeties. Planes would fall from the sky as flight controls died. Vehicles in motion would lose control. Everything that wasn't animal or people-powered would stop. Fires from blown transformers would burn unchecked.

Hospitals. Food transportation, water... even wells had electric pumps. Communication to connect, comfort and instruct populations would cease. Only those in specially-hardened shelters like this one would have any services at all.

Grace worked to control her breathing. Thinking of her family calmed her.

Thank God it's only me. You're all safe. Ellie, this once, I'm grateful...

A sergeant looked up at Colonel Jennings.

"What's the plan? There are protocols, right?"

Colonel Jennings looked to the low-voiced clusters of Generals behind him. None offered an answer to the room. Grace couldn't tear her gaze from the second sunspot. Though slightly smaller than the first, it swirled with the same intensity.

Why would NASA keep it in frame?

A politely insistent female voice initiated prerecorded PA announcements. "All personnel report to your duty stations immediately."

Training response broke passive observers free to do the one thing they could—their jobs. As the room emptied to Central Command personnel , Grace remained focused on the screen. If Earth rotated just enough and the second spot erupted on this trajectory it would hit the now dark side of the planet. The entirety of Earth would suffer the same fate. Her shaking hands didn't know where to settle.

"All personnel report to your duty stations immediately."

Attention dropping to her insistently beeping monitor, she reflexively resumed typing, processing the barrage of highest-level FLASH traffic. Her vision shook with each pounding heartbeat. Subject lines scrolled warnings to all governments of imminent total blackout.

"All personnel report to your duty stations immediately."

For the second time in history, shrieking wall beacons announced DEFCON 2 and lockdown protocol commenced. The Cuban Missile Crisis status as first was eclipsed. DEFCON 1 was now moot.

The Time-to-Impact clock dropped below fifteen minutes. Sweat ran down Grace's back as three years in terror of entrapment by the closing Door churned through her.

The solar wind's leading edge swept impersonally into the exosphere generating a cataclysmic Pulse. Earth's satellites lost function, and The Wall emptied to static.

The Door.

Adrenaline spiked into fight-or-flight territory. Scanning the room, she saw three recalled cryptographers hugging the wall nearby. Command would be fully staffed without her. Go, or be trapped. Grace flashed to her feet, summoning one of the dazed standby replacements.

"Sergeant Braun, take over this station," Grace said.

Leaving Braun no time to question, she initiated transfer. "Sergeant Braun, taking control of Station."

"This is Sergeant Braun, taking control."

Braun opened her mouth on a question, but Grace had already disappeared into the milling crowd. Time-To-Impact clock: 10 minutes.

Grace maneuvered through the flow of incoming

personnel, forced to pause at the elevators as they spilled streams of recalled personnel. Alone in the ascending car, panic rose as the elevator's normal swift speed seemed sluggish. Her watch ticked below eight minutes.

Please... I can't... I have to go...

The doors chimed, Grace already launching through them into the Door Security Zone. The monster was still in motion, moaning through its relentless, final yards. Grace's nightmares snapped at her heels as she sprinted into the yellow and black zone of the Door's path.

Strobes flashed, warning sirens wailed to stand clear, echoed by shouts to stop. One stride from the sill the incline ramps dropped beneath her feet, jolting her to her knees. Exploding adrenaline launched her upright.

Scrambling over the chest-high sill, Grace ducked under the Door, yanking herself clear as the trailing air wake brushed over her.

Racing up the escalators, she jerked as their movement stopped and lights began shutting down in segments of blackness, chasing her faster than she could run. She threw herself against the last set of doors at the abandoned Check Point One into the outside air a split second before their locking mechanisms slammed into place, falling silent. Lungs burning, her shaking legs moved her forward. Grace trailed a steadying hand along the cold tunnel wall, tasting the salt marsh air, cleanly fresh after the acrid air below.

I made it... I'm free...

Standing at the tunnel's entrance, Grace took in early evening's golden hour, and the world's last seconds of structured life. The seating Door bolts rumbled faintly beneath her feet. Balance wavering in adrenaline aftermath, she stepped out of the tunnel, instantly struck by the full force of the invisible Pulse. Her last thought was one of confusion as a firestorm of pain pushed her into blackness.

What—?

2.

OBERON

GRACE LAY ON her side, muscles convulsed, in a fetal position. Heart firing in erratic bursts, her shallow pants of air hissed between clenched teeth. Broader awareness crept in. Brackish grit was in her nostrils—on her tongue, pressed into her skin. Silent pressure waffled against her eardrums, giving way to a high-pitched tone, surging into a chaotic wall of sound. She struggled to comprehend… anything.

Where am I—what's wrong with me?

A hand tugged at her. Her cries of alarm and pain were echoed by voices in the surrounding uproar. She wasn't alone in her misery, others were suffering. The gripping fingers loosened and fell away. A heavy thud dusted her with dirt.

A new pair of hands took hold, dragging her. The dirt beneath her felt cooler, suggesting shade. Squinting through grimy tears, the blurry shapes surrounding her resolved into staggering soldiers in unfamiliar uniforms. More were on the ground.

An attack—can't smell chemicals—but why is everyone down? No arms fire—what language is that?

She latched onto a thought she knew was solid.

The Bunker is impenetrable…

Movement halted in a darker space. Grace felt smooth floor beneath her as she was pulled up to sit, propped against a wall. A large hand gripped her chin, lifting her gaze. Grabbing the wrist to stop the painful movement, Grace scowled into narrowed gray eyes, set in a stern, weathered face. A few cowlicks in close-cropped, dark hair belied his steely expression. Faint movement of clashing colors within the gray startled her.

She focused on his low-pitched, commanding voice. He wanted answers, but his questions ricocheted off the language barrier. Anger surged in her, voice rising above the surrounding chaos.

"Who the hell are you? What…"

Chin jerking from his grasp, Grace's defiance promptly lost its edge, as her traitorous body twisted in a violent spasm. Lifted to a standing position, her body rejected the vicious pain of additional movements, ripping consciousness away.

Body motionless, Grace became aware of motion.

Elevator, her grasping mind supplied.

Someone carried her. Modesty had the stupidity to suggest if this was correct; her skirt was not performing its job. She mentally snarled at it. *How the fuck did they run the entire security gauntlet?*

Long arms cradled her like a child. Blunt body armor edges pressed against her cheek and side; a holster of some sort near her head. Cautiously opening still-tearing eyes confirmed the elevator, but it was not the Bunker. Wood paneled the walls, edged with dark metal framing. No stainless-steel walls or armored doors.

Shifting her eyes to absorb these bewildering details, her gaze fell on Gray-eyed Guy, who was grimly studying her as though she were a weapon. She noted with surprise that his uniform was leather. It wasn't primitive in design or construction but there were no synthetic components. Heavier leather plating armored vital areas; it was a tactical uniform. No visible weapons—as though they'd been caught off guard. Gray-eyed Guy's uniform was black, the soldier carrying her, brown, so she renamed him Black Uniform.

Gritting her teeth, Grace painfully straightened her body, indicating her desire to stand. Black Uniform nodded permission to put her down. She acted as soon as her feet were planted. Taking advantage of the bent soldier's steadying hands, she grabbed for whatever the holster held. Almost before she'd moved Black Uniform caught her wrist in an excruciating grip. He eased his hold at her harsh cry.

His hard gaze suggested *No.* He examined her wrist and withdrew his hand. Grace's head spun from the effort. His speed, and her wrist… she'd thought her bones would snap. Now that she was mostly standing, she realized the soldiers were both really tall. Like, NBA tall. At five foot, eight inches, she felt like a child next to them.

I'm not in Kansas anymore.

She braced a shaking hand on the elevator wall. Her surge of defiance had drained any remaining adrenaline. She fought to stay upright as the elevator stopped. Air gently brushed her skin as the doors slid open.

Grace slid down the wall to her knees. Before her was an exact copy, in size and layout, of the Bunker. The floors were slate, not linoleum, The walls wood and brick, not cinderblock. But she knew each door location, each branching hallway. The corridor straight ahead was hers. Numbness spread under her skin as she scanned the impossible.

Her annoyed logic suggested that she find a different word. *Pulse.* That was a good one. Eyes closing, she jerked as memories flooded in from the start of her day until this moment.

She felt a hand lightly touch her cheek. As the thought stream slowed, awareness of the floor under her knees returned.

Black Uniform removed his hand from her face, dismissing the accompanying soldier. A hand to her back indicated he would help her up. Grace pulled away, swearing as she failed to regain her feet. Lifting her to stand, he withdrew one hand. Silent, he gave no direction or guidance of where to go.

Grace staggered forward. The man shifted slightly behind her, supporting her weight. She followed her normal path in *her* Bunker. She was immersed in differences of materials, fittings, and equipment overlaid onto her rooms and hallways.

Grace grunted with pain as another wave of spasms and nausea swept through her. Black Uniform bent, sliding an arm around her waist to hold her until she could stand. Breath rasping, she fought tears of misery and exhaustion.

How can I hallucinate in such detail?

With her captor's grip firmly under her forearms, she

moved on, cataloging detail as she passed. No scent of cleaners, coffee, floor wax. She hadn't realized the specific smell of tech until it was gone. A glance showed the break-room's sturdy wooden chairs hurriedly pushed back from tables littered with mugs. No lockers or vending machines. Apparently, they didn't grow to this size on corn chips and energy drinks.

At Central Command's doors, Grace startled as two brown uniformed soldiers gave Black Uniform angled fist-to-shoulder salutes before opening the double doors. He nodded in return, as his hands were occupied with her.

Pausing inside Central's doorway as she always did, Grace scanned the two-story room. Walls and railing were polished wood with dark metal supports. No darkened main floor. No Wall screen. Maps everywhere, but not back-lit, interactive displays. No worldwide Intel boards or time zone clocks.

She looked toward her desk. It was present but held no computer station. She could see no electronic tech of any kind. Fighting to stay focused and upright, she zeroed in on a group of people across the room.

It wasn't difficult to identify the commanding officer in the room. The man's stance, and hard planes of face and body, gave the impression of more than physical strength. She could hammer a nail with his presence. He listened as a civilian, waving hands for emphasis, describing something that seemed significant. The solar flare seemed a reason-able guess.

For the first time, Grace's shock faded enough for her to feel truly frightened. Somehow, standing in Not Central, she was reaching critical mass.

This is insane. Wake up! As though triggered by the thought, her sickness ramped up with a vengeance. Body falling, jackknifed with pain, sharp cries ripped from her as now familiar hands held her.

Turning to see her in Black Uniform's hands, the commander spoke to him, voice sharp. It seemed doubtful his answers contained much information. They seemed to be as stunned as she was. The commander spoke directly to Grace.

Attempting to unclench her jaw, she ground out one word, "No."

Her body contracted again, spine twisting.

Great time to pass out. Body? No?

The commander quickly cleared the room of all but a few people. A chair pressed against her calves. She dropped hard, elbows slamming into the wooden arms, head jerking up to see a huge world map opposite her. A geographically perfect match to those in her Central. All of its political boundary lines were wrong.

Black Uniform stood behind her, one hand keeping her in the chair. As his other touched her cheek, she feebly tried to pull away. Fight gone, she let her head drop to the chair back.

The room was silent as he began speaking in an even-voiced cadence, as though he were narrating her. Somehow, she knew—he was reading her mind. Out loud.

Sir Richard Attenborough narrates Grace. Good luck with whatever series I binge-watched last night.

Grace had reached her psychological limits. Due to much trauma in her past, her mind could reflexively dissociate under extreme stress. She thought of it as *ghosting,* watching herself from a distance. As she couldn't understand the language, his words receded into the background, allowing her to focus on details previously missed.

There were no visible light fixtures, yet the light was bright, even. There were no apparent vents or ducting, but the air smelled fresh. It was startling to see herself, so small and breakable, next to them. Grace studied Black Uniform's profile, bent above her. His hair looked brown beside her chestnut; the scar-flecked hand cupping her pale cheek, tanned. Her eyes moved past his moving lips, along his clean-shaven jaw, stopping at the slight point of his ear.

Seriously, Grandmother? You're part of this—mental hijacking—or whatever this is? Should it comfort me, or prove I'm insane? Because this could go either way…

Grandmother Lilli's foreshadowing hand in this detail shook Grace more than Not Central. Swallowed by loneliness with Ellie away at special schools, Grandmother Lilli had spun for Grace countless tales of a different world where gifted Fae had pointy ears, and Grace was needed. Her grandmother's stories bolstered Grace, insisting fate made the twins special, and Grace was no less special than Ellie. A few years after Grandmother Lilli's death, Ellie died, and with her Grace's belief in fate, or herself as special.

Studying his profile while she pondered these things, Grace saw surprise flicker across Black Uniform's face. He had become aware of her off to the side, watching, while physically under his hands. *You can see my thoughts in the present, as well as memories. Good to know.*

With these thoughts came images. Muscular movement under rippling patterns. They vanished as he abruptly removed his hand from her. Grace felt the chair under her, opening her eyes to the disconcerting wall map.

The room was silent. The commander signaled a woman nearby, while he held a brief discussion with Black Uniform. The woman gently put her hands over Grace's ears, then her throat. Grace startled when the next words spoken were in English. The woman withdrew her hands. "Is that better?" she asked.

"Yes, thank you," Grace said, voice rasping.

She could read the map in front of her. It was labeled "Oberon." She had not fully processed these revelations when she heard the commander speak to her.

"Sergeant Woods, I'm Commander Arundel. Operative Asa will take you to your quarters."

In all the strangeness, shock, and pain, they were welcome words. Grace made an aborted attempt to rise from the chair. Her mind and body were decisively done. The floor looked intimate. Cognitive time was up. Whatever held the full tide of sickness at bay for these moments of communication departed, as gravity became a black hole. Several hands caught her as she fell.

3.

METAMORPHOSIS

COMMANDER ARUNDEL WATCHED Operative Asa depart with Grace. He looked to Prefect Gunnar, his Black Unit Head of Intelligence; Grace's Black Uniform.

"A good fit?"

Facing his commander, the Prefect replied, "She's one of my best spies, well-suited for the task."

Arundel pondered the strangeness of the Human's appearance.

"We thought them extinct. I've never heard report of an occurrence such as this. She's a threat unless you deem otherwise," Arundel said. "A useful point—the terminology referencing this event seems concisely accurate—Pulse. This extreme physical response—pulse sickness."

Gunnar agreed. "Helpful for communication while we evaluate how widespread it is."

Arundel set the matter aside, turning to issue orders to his waiting Centurions, "Dispatch covert teams to assess impact to the territory and notify northern and southern strongholds to tighten border security."

With a nod, Gunnar released two Centurions commanding those units. Arundel ordered Medical Aid and Logistics Centuries to the Stronghold for assessment of supplies and aid needed.

Until it was certain the territory was secure, it was critical to protect Central Command, the seat of the Northeastern Territory's governance. More so if defensive guardians were incapacitated. As each Centurion departed to accomplish their tasks, Arundel returned his attention to his oldest friend. "Gunnar, seal the Keep."

Asa's diligent care was unable to prevent the painful extremes wracking Grace's mind and body. All those stricken with the illness had severe symptoms, but without Fae strength, Grace appeared to submerge almost past reaching. Even as her body suffered, her mind seemed torn loose from its moorings, adrift in eddies of time and place.

Setting the untouched cup of broth on the bedside table, Asa was surprised at her frustration. Her detached professionalism was softened by empathy for the small Human's plight. She'd read between the lines in Grace's relayed memories. Her family was safe. The only way to be safe from such a cataclysm was to already be dead. If she was truly from another world, she had been alone there. Now she was alone here.

"You cannot stay in this state and live," Asa said to her. "You must wake and drink."

Wiping sweat from Grace's face, she watched her slide deeper into restless dreams. Asa studied the female's body for answers of any kind. Grace's lack of muscle mass or battle scars left no doubt: she was not trained to fight. There were many small scrapes and bruises, stark against her pale skin. Fae, even while ill, would have quickly healed of such minor harm. Only pregnant females healed more slowly. Asa sent for a Healer.

Healer Ahma examined Grace's physical state with meticulous care. "Our bodies and bone structure appear proportionate, identical in all but heart and lung size," Ahma said. "I find no sign of pregnancy."

Ahma looked thoughtful. "Perhaps Humans have always healed slowly. In any case, there has been little we can do to ease Fae stricken with this sickness. The battle is hers to fight."

"Thank you, Ahma," Asa said. "I'll send word if she worsens."

Pulling the bed clothes over Grace, she ensured a fresh cup of broth was at hand. Moving her chair closer, Asa brushed Grace's damp hair from her face, monitoring her slow, uneven life signs and watched for indication she might rouse to swallow nourishment.

This Human was her assignment. Asa's every action was in pursuit of Intelligence, but these parameters did not rule out personal interest. Anything that deepened trust and relationship aided in her task. And Asa was undeniably fascinated.

"You must fight. You have many stories to tell. I would like to hear them."

Telepathic Black Unit Guardians monitored Grace's

dreams, searching for threat indications. The otherworldly content of her dreams proved difficult to analyze. But even more so, their unanimous impression that Sergeant Woods appeared to be dreaming past, present, and possibly future; a sign of Seer Gifting. But according to lore, prior to their extinction, Humans were not Gifted.

The ranking Guardian's report to Prefect Gunnar requested his greater Telepathic abilities.

With Grace deep in dream state, the Prefect sat beside her, hand lightly resting on her cheek. Eyes closed in concentration, he worked to understand the onslaught of images flooding through him. Cataloguing in his usual concise method was impossible. The absence of context made many events untranslatable. He focused on seeking insight into her psychological makeup.

Family memories were turbulent with loss. Mother, father, grandmother, and most recently, the fiery death of a twin sister.

Her emotions carry such extremes—sorrow, anger, fear— that they reach levels of physical pain. Is this a Human trait? Do we feel less intensely by nature—or choice?

Grace, restless under his hand as he passed through the loss of those she loved, quieted as he moved to areas touching her work. Gunnar observed no significant social interaction or relationships. She released emotion only in the context of work.

Focusing on dreams depicting scenes after her arrival brought up puzzling questions. Some involved personnel with whom she'd shared only moments of proximity in Central, present in locations she'd never seen. He and Commander Arundel were prominent in several shifting narratives of varying emotional states. She'd only been in their possession for a handful of hours, severely impacted by the sickness. *Was this a normal response in Humans?* Gunnar studied her face.

This female—she's more than an unexplored race. She's an unexplored world.

As days passed, his visits moved through a broader spectrum of emotions in memories and dreams. There were nightmares, set both here and in her place of origin. Gunnar was sifting through several reoccurring dreams of entrapment and loss when Grace went utterly still under his hand.

"Sergeant Woods."

Gunnar realized her skin was cold. He spoke louder.

"Sergeant Woods—can you hear me?"

Telepathic connection to Grace still open, his mind plunged with hers into darkness outside of time or place. A searching, twisting blackness—more than absence of light— enveloped them. A feeling of sentient death. A warrior, Gunnar had never feared death. This was something other. Grace's life signs staggered as her body's scent altered to terror. Gunnar wrenched his hand from her face, breaking their mental bond. He gripped her shoulders in a swift shake.

"Sergeant Woods—Grace, look at me."

Gasping a hitching breath, Grace's fevered gaze came directly to him—fingers dug into his wrist—panic eased from her face. Distracted by her eyes, he wondered if their coloring was common in Humans. Blue, flecked with amber, ringed in black.

Her heavy blink broke his musing as he realized Grace was not surprised to see him—a strange reaction. She'd had no waking contact with him since arriving. Gunnar listened to her life signs calm, watching as her eyes closed, body relaxing into sleep. He returned his hand to her cheek, searching for the malevolent darkness which had engulfed them. There was no trace of the episode. Gunnar monitored her throughout the night.

Days passed as Grace fought the sickness. Prefect Gunnar noted her dreams of home decreasing, and those of Oberon increasing. As she was primarily sleeping, confined to a small room without external stimuli, this was illogical. Though his instincts said otherwise, there were too many questionable elements and unquantifiable factors to rule her out as a threat. The Prefect brought in a Black Unit Seer who was unable to get a read on her, an occurrence he'd never encountered without Shield Gifting in the subject or one who held the Gift, actively Shielding them. The entire situation was frustrating. Could her appearance with the Pulse indicate she was a portent of events to come? Discussing the situation with Arundel, his agitation was apparent as he shifted papers on the table while expressing his concerns.

Arundel had never seen him fidget.

"The circumstances are too coincidental to be merely strange. First, she appears from an apparent duplicate of our Keep. Second, she exhibits characteristics and behavior that differ greatly from our histories of her race."

Gunnar drummed fingers on his notes.

"Third, our best Seer cannot see her in any capacity. Arundel, I'm concerned she may be a threat I cannot assess. I see no indicators of danger, but these unknowns are too great to be complacent."

Arundel watched Gunnar's body language. These reactions were uncharacteristic; something had rattled Gunnar.

He was always precise, concise, dispassionate. The situation needed to be brought into the open. If the entire Keep could not control one small Human, they deserved their fate.

"If she recovers, consider treating her as a monitored visitor. Operative Asa is with her at all times. The Keep is sealed; this is a unique opportunity."

Gunnar considered these points. "I appreciate your fresh eyes, brother. I can extract more information from a relaxed subject than a frightened one."

"If she is indeed a threat, we can contain it here. Run this as you see fit," Arundel said.

Pondering the amount of information he'd seen in her dreams, what would they learn of her once awakened?

The sickness ran its course. Asa's countless hours patiently bathing, coaxing her to eat, and comforting during tears of confusion and misery tacitly implied trust.

Grace spent waking hours silently observing Asa, absorbing details of the modest room, and transitioning to her new reality. She could not explain, even to herself, that despite the traumatic circumstance, the process felt organic—a stepping from one room to another. This dragged guilt in its wake at her release from the Pulse aftermath at home. It must be chaos. Here it was calm. At no time had Grace felt in jeopardy. No one had hurt her, or given reason to expect such a response.

Finally clearheaded, she realized the moment to move past the bare minimums of communication had come. Grace cleared her throat. Gesturing to the bedside chair, she got straight to the point, voice rasping from disuse, "Asa, thank you. Your care of me—thank you."

"Sergeant Woods, I'm pleased you're recovering. You have a strong will." Moving the breakfast tray aside, Asa handed Grace a cup of tea before settling into her chair. "You have questions, Sergeant Woods."

"Please, call me Grace. I owe you my life."

Asa accepted Grace's offer to begin their communication with informality.

Grace glanced away a moment as a smile slipped across her face. "We have a saying: a real friend will hold back your hair while you vomit." Her gaze returned to Asa, brows drawn. "I don't know where to start."

Asa patiently waited.

Grace noticed her uniform hanging on the wardrobe door, name tag and sergeant stripes visible.

"Asa is your name? There is nothing else, no rank I should call you?"

"Asa is enough, you will not need my title. I understand, everything is foreign to you. Ask anything you wish."

Grace released a deep breath. "Where am I?"

Asa sat back in her chair, stance relaxed, open. "You're in the Northeastern Protectorate of the Northern Territory under Commander Arundel. You met him briefly when you—arrived."

"But..." Grace gestured vaguely to herself, her ears and Asa's. "I'm from—somewhere else. Are you different? More than in size and... ears?"

Asa thought for a moment, hands quiet in her lap. "Our people are Fae. We have records of Humans similar to you but have presumed them extinct for some time."

Fixing upon the word Fae, in conjunction with the map's title, Oberon, Grace wondered why it felt familiar. Dismissing the thought, she pressed on. "You heard everything in… well, we call it Central Command?"

"We use the same term. Yes, I was present when Prefect Gunnar brought you in." Asa's mouth twitched. "To describe your arrival as a surprise is an understatement."

"The large wall map of your world, it's geographically identical to mine. But the political boundaries are different. I only had a glimpse, but my point of origin appears to correspond to your location. I recognized the smell of salt marshes, and your facility's underground structure and layout." Holding her elbows, she shivered at her memories. "I blacked out. I awakened here. I don't remember anything in between." She met Asa's gaze. "This is all so extreme, but it's a topic people discuss where I'm from. We've only theorized whether parallel planes exist. I'm struggling with the idea that this may be the reality. No one's ever moved between them—not that I'm aware of. Have you?"

There were additional questions she wasn't quite ready to put to Asa. *Can I go home? Am I alone here?*

"We are actively searching Archives but have found no records describing an appearance like yours," Asa said.

Grace tugged on a lock of hair, searching for precise words. "Expanding the parallel worlds idea… identical geography might suggest planes occupying the same space. We had a theoretical physicist, Stephen Hawking, who suggested similar possibilities." She gestured widely. "He'd have been thrilled by this entire situation."

Grace's ability to hypothesize such complex, abstract theory had Asa swiftly revising her preconceptions concerning Human intelligence. "These are fascinating theories to explore, Grace." Asa rose to refill Grace's tea, then resumed her seat. "Perhaps we should begin with our differences, then what we share in common."

Grace mused, "We have many myths and imagined versions of beings like you. Our current popular culture is quite obsessed. You mentioned Humans existed here but are believed extinct. Am I one-of-a-kind?"

"The short answer is we don't know," Asa said. "Our historical records are not precise, varying from region to region. But we've no current instances of Human existence. Humans were not feared," Asa stressed, "only different from Fae."

"In my world, Earth, most think Fae are myth. But Asa—Fae are woven through stories in history all over the world."

Asa thought this over. They had time to explore. "For clarity, shall we concentrate on current, basic facts?"

Grace smiled. "Yes, please."

"Our race is scattered over most viable areas of Oberon. We differ in area-centric physical characteristics: skin, eye, hair color, build, bone structure. Cultures, governance, and manner of living also vary by region."

Perhaps triggered by the word *culture*, Grace grasped the elusive thought from earlier.

The familiarity I felt: Oberon—he's Shakespeare's Faerie King. It's too coincidental. And...mind blowing. Did it derive from this world?

Asa watched Grace's face reflect her thoughts for anyone trained to see. She marked that point to address another time and brought Grace's attention back to their conversation.

"Healer Ahma examined you. She felt trace amounts of electricity present in your body."

"We do have tiny amounts," said Grace. "It enables our nervous system, organs, and brain to work together. Perhaps magic performs the same function in yours, and in your abilities."

And there it was. The M word. She'd thrown it out there to see if it was a word they used. *Magic.* Why not? Logically, from what she'd observed, magic was anything but a pixie scattering fairy dust or a bewhiskered wand-waver. It appeared to be a physiological attribute in Fae. Asa was marking signs of fatigue and body pain in Grace. "We'll explore these questions further, but you mustn't exhaust yourself. We have time."

Grace acknowledged that Asa was right. Exhaustion had swept in, along with a throbbing headache. So much information, so quickly. Finishing a cup of medicinal tea, Grace soon slept, continuing to search for answers in her dreams.

Back pressed to the corridor wall, Grace stood a few feet outside her room. It was the first time since her arrival. Face impassive, arms stiffly crossed, she forced herself to hold position. It had been easy to pretend a great many things within the small confines of her room. Discussion with Asa was also rather abstract inside those white walls, like watching a movie. Observing the few Guardians Prefect Gunnar allowed in her section pass by dragged fantasy from her surprisingly reluctant grasp.

Moving her gaze to the floor, concentrating on that one difference, slate, not linoleum, was a manageable step. There must be a quarry nearby. Her home in Boston had a slate fireplace hearth. Monitoring Grace's increased heart rate, Asa casually moved within touching distance, waiting for Grace to indicate her next action.

Grace's eyes lifted to those passing by, hungrily collecting details. Their varying ethnicities felt confusingly of home. There were no reasons to expect Fae to be different from Humans but somehow, she had. Two males deep in conversation passed without a glance toward her, allowing her to openly study them. The nearest, of medium build and olive skin, had mahogany-brown hair falling to midback. Leather cord knotted his hair with an intriguing design, restraining it neatly.

The heavier-muscled, Black guardian beside him had short, natural hair, twisted in broad rows clipped with silver rings. A short braid gathered them at the nape in an etched cuff. Both wore black uniforms. Asa's light skin and short, black hair emphasized variety as the common factor among the three.

Grace couldn't pull her gaze from these simple details; more than height or uniforms, the variance in hair was proof of how removed from Earth's military conformity she was.

So ridiculous. Surrounded by hundreds of details, and hair is my reality checkpoint?

Then there were the ears. The subtlest thing of all snagged her repeatedly. It brought a circular, dreamlike filter to her view of—everything.

Did I create this? All of this? Heartbeat rising, she pursued the thought. *It's a perfect combination of things I love from my childhood—possibly casting doubt on my mental stability…*

Something terrible had happened and she was creating a

false reality in her mind. It wasn't the first time. The flickering lights of the patrol car, coming to tell her of Ellie's death, had trigged a frozen, dissociative state as she fought the terrifying truth. There were levels in her, a doctor had explained, which wiped conscious recall, locking away extreme trauma.

Get a grip. Whatever this is—Oberon—these people, it's another chapter in my life. I'm not forgetting or denying past or present, I'm turning the page to a new one. I could never create such detail, even with these familiar ones...

Grace rubbed a hand over her face, sagging against the wall. Such a small leap of thought but she felt drained by the implied magnitude. Would it always feel like a dream—as though she would wake up? Asa's supportive arm swiftly caught her, guiding her back to bed.

Breakfast the next morning was almost silent. Grace's shadowed eyes proved sleep had been elusive. Asa, sensitive to Grace's mood, gave her space to accept what could only be staggering new realities. Concerned she might slip into depression from delayed shock, Asa offered an option.

"I've a suggestion that may help you process."

"I'm listening," Grace said.

"Every new sight or experience must feel jolting. Even waking from sleep," Asa said.

"It does," Grace admitted. "I don't understand why I have no difficulty with you, but leaving this room..."

Asa looked thoughtful. "It might relieve these feelings if answers were provided as swiftly as questions arise. You could have control of how much and the speed. If you're willing to try."

"That would be a welcome thing," Grace said.

"Prefect Gunnar has unmatched focus and specificity in using his Telepathy. You can direct him to any question, memory, or worrying thought you wish to address. He will not trespass beyond it. It would allow you to open dialogue from your own perspective. Will you try this?"

Putting her utensils down Grace sat back, considering. Access to her mind… Her first moment of contact with the Prefect had ignited questions, even while half-dead with sickness. He hadn't interrogated her. It appeared to have been only immediate, need-to-know information read in Central Command, under crisis conditions. No following actions had been aggressive. By anyone.

He could have interrogated her thoroughly while she was ill, but he hadn't. She could have been left in a cell to recover. It all could have gone much differently. They had treated her with dignity and kindness. More than she knew they'd receive if one of them appeared in her own command. She wanted to meet this new life.

"Yes. I'll try it," said Grace.

A few days later Grace was in Prefect Gunnar's office. They faced each other, seated in chairs before his desk, his hand lightly cupping her cheek. He efficiently answered Grace's questions as she thought of them, following wherever the thread took her. He was considerate of her emotional vulner-ability in the framing of his answers. After an initial period of adjustment, Grace found it amazing to communicate so easily, without struggling to express a question's nuance. The office door was open, and others moved through the hallway intent on their tasks. It felt reassuring.

"When you understood us in your language, it was due to the female who touched you. She has a Gift called Voice. It enabled you to hear, think, and speak our language as though in your native tongue. It is a permanent change, to have this ability."

Grace thought this over, wondering if it meant her brain synapses worked differently, or if it had affected other areas in her perception of reality.

"No, your brain functions normally. Voice leaves a beneficial result but only that specific one. Asa will cover Gifts. With your knowledge of intelligence work, you understand my own Gift is valuable to my position. But I don't rely solely on it to do my work; it's a tool. I will not invade another's privacy unless they are a harmful criminal or enemy. Then interrogation is justified. This is the opposite. It's cooperative communication, within parameters you define."

Grace considered information she would desire if positions were reversed. First was threat level. She innately knew there was no risk in sharing her work, even if travel between worlds were possible. The bunker and government, as she'd known them, no longer existed.

"I would like to show you the Bunker, Prefect. More than you saw the day I arrived, so you can see both where I came from and how identical the Keep is. Ask anything. Our technology is very different so details may take time..."

"I would like that, Sergeant Woods. From the moment

you began navigating the Keep upon your arrival to seeing your day leading up to the Pulse was fascinating."

Grace visualized the Bunker's orientation briefing and tour. She showed him every facet. She hadn't realized until this moment that she'd been unconscious when brought through their version of the Door, wondering what their equivalent was like… or if they needed one.

When she finished, the Prefect sat back, removing his hand. She couldn't imagine what he was thinking. He was quiet, sorting through what she had shown him. His gaze shifted to hers.

"You're correct, I have a multitude of questions. Looking at the differences in our political boundaries, I'm interested in why your populations settled where they did, where seats of power developed, and whether conflicts resulted from those choices." He surveyed the maps covering the office walls. "Perhaps we could move into sessions encompassing these things. Our races share similarities. Contrasting our positive and negative histories would also be invaluable."

Grace loosed a held breath. This process changed everything. Her job at home had become the lynchpin to her life, and his proposal accomplished more than easing her transition.

It gave her purpose.

4.

GETTING ACQUAINTED

PARADOXICALLY, BEING SHIELDED in the sealed Keep from the Pulse's devastating reality freed Grace. For the first time since childhood, she was released from the burden of responsibility. Asa's voice drew her focus back to their conversation. They were seated at a corner table in the dining hall where they could watch the rhythms of Keep personnel.

"Grace, this time is ours. We can discuss anything you wish. I may ask to address or expand topics, but it's unstructured."

Grace's mouth quirked. "I drove my grandmother and teachers crazy with endless questions…"

"As did I. Children ask from a hunger to understand. To engage with their surroundings. Your questions on every subject are important. Between us, there is nothing you cannot ask. I'll tell you when asking someone else is not polite or correct." Thinking of her torture-resistance training, Asa smiled. "I doubt you can disturb my mental equilibrium by asking questions."

Grace twirled a strand of hair, squinting at Asa. "I might consider that a challenge."

For almost three weeks Grace had been lost in illness and recovery. Asa's suggestions for Grace to work cooperatively with Prefect Gunnar had opened communication floodgates in both directions. Her time with Asa centered largely on Human and Fae cultural differences and practices. With the Prefect, geopolitics, and larger societal infrastructure.

Wryly, Asa began with the most basic Fae nomenclature. Pointing at herself: "Fae." Pointing at Grace: "Human. That covers the most important delineation."

Grace laughed. "Let me write that down."

Asa continued without missing a beat. "Male and female replace the terms man and woman. Family composition varies but family member designators are the same. My father, your daughter. Since it's sealed, we'll use the Keep as a sample microcosm. There are military, social, and personal or private relationships, but with limited representation. No children, of course. Do you have a particular questions to begin?" Asa asked.

Several guardians were leaving the hall. Grace noted a female's hand casually brushing another's.

"What are basic tenets for relationships?"

"In regard to official boundaries they concern age, consent, slander, violence, or any manner of willful harm. These things are not tolerated or negotiable and are swiftly handled if crossed. The dynamics of physical desire, or emotional affection and love, are fluid concepts shaped by the individual."

"That sounds—utopian. How do you hold people to such high standards?" Grace asked.

"It's what we strive for; it's not always achieved. There are territories which don't agree with these freedoms. But within our own, Commander Arundel is not forgiving of those who break these protections."

Grace pondered these rather mind-blowing points. "You don't have marriage, in the Human sense? An official union?"

Asa gestured to the scattered groups remaining in the hall. "We may commit to relationships with single or multiple others, or none. Remain in them a short time, or a lifetime. We see and feel how others respond to us. It engenders openness. But all societal boundaries apply, no matter the attraction, if it is not mutual and desired. On rare occasions, a deep connection triggers an involuntary biological change. The body creates a permanent scent marker denoting lifelong Mates. A serious thing with our lifespans."

Rare on Earth, too.

"And children?"

"Children are also rare. Estrus is unpredictable and can be absent for years. As a result, Fae reproduce at a much lower rate than Humans. An important societal element; all Fae can scent a pregnant female."

It's all about that scent, 'bout that scent, no trouble—

Grace almost kicked herself.

"Powers of rapid healing wane during pregnancy to prevent rejection of the fetus. As a result, those surrounding her will instinctively protect her."

So—no belly rubbing by strangers at the supermarket.

"May I ask about your family, Grace? You spoke of them briefly during your illness."

Sighing, Grace rubbed her eyes. "I'll give you the abbreviated version and we can talk more as it comes up." Lifting her brows in question to Asa, she continued at her nod. Her voice became monotone, no room for emotion or commentary.

"My mother died giving birth to me. I'm the eldest of twins. My father never got over my mother's death. He became ill. I helped my grandmother nurse him until he died."

Asa, studied Grace's face and almost angrily concise word choices, noting more than family dynamics.

"My twin, Ellie, was gifted. It became clear when she was four. By six she was going to special schools, and by eight she had gone away to very special schools. I missed her—very much.

Her tone lightened slightly. "My Grandmother Lilli provided love. She didn't just take care of me, she kept me company. It was my favorite time of life. Most of her stories were about me, and Fae were often in them."

Asa noticed her scent shifting toward stress, edging toward fear.

"She became seriously ill just before I turned fifteen. A month later I obtained emancipation papers. By our laws, they made me an adult. I could take care of her until she died. I managed our home and anything Ellie needed."

Grace's voice wavered, a crack in the emotionless wall. "I was seventeen when Ellie died." She said, her hands scrubbing her face. "It was—a burning crash. She was afraid of fire her entire life. We couldn't put candles on her birthday cake—as though she knew..."

Asa watched Grace calm her shaking breath, focused somewhere beyond the room's walls.

"I remember the flashing lights—the police coming to tell me Ellie had died." She paused, shifting back to a neutral tone. "I graduated school and joined our military the day after. Seven years later, here I am, with you." Grace sat, hands folded in her lap, face put back together. Asa let several beats of silence pass as the last sentence faded.

"Thank you for trusting me, Grace. I'm sorry. It says much of your character that you have a generous heart after so much pain." Asa changed topics, to one she believed would give Grace relief. "Before we stop for the day perhaps we might discuss Gifts."

Grace refocused on Asa. This was a critical step in her integration, proving she had passed the test of trust to hold this information.

"It's important to remember, Grace, it's impolite to ask the nature of someone's Gift. Most are classified. Because of the Keep's mission, there is heavier representation of Gifts here than in the civilian population. The desirability of certain types prompt many to volunteer in Oberon's protective forces." Asa noted Grace already scanning the room.

"I'll list the basics," Asa said. "There may be subtle variations, but most follow these definitions. Telepaths read minds. Strengths vary from of-the-moment thoughts to deep memory retrieval."

Yeah, regular dates with that one.

"Empaths accurately discern and sometimes affect emotion."

Have they used that on me? Haven't had any hysterics…

"Seers subjectively foresee the future along specific lines, shifting as contributing factors do."

That's just cool.

"Healers assist where self-healing wasn't enough, in serious injury."

The scientist in Ellie would have loved that.

"Shields block other Gifts from affecting themselves or others."

Badass.

"Travelers move unseen for varying distances."

Doctor You-know-Who, is that you?

"Possessors control others mentally or physically."

Possibly as scary as the name.

"Voices are universal translators."

Hey, I speak thirty-one languages!

"Shifters encompass the form of an animal native to a parent's birth location. A small percentage also encompass Fae form."

Ok, this one's to die for. But—Boston? A skunk?

"A dying Fae may pass Gifts to another. Additionally, they may pass their essential life spark, called a Life Strength, to another, extending the recipient's lifetime."

"Extending a lifetime—wow. I've met two Humans who were over a hundred years old— how old is Prefect Gunnar? He must be older than you, but younger than Commander Arundel."

"He's well beyond three hundred, perhaps four hundred by your aging. I'm not exactly certain." She was amused by the shocked look on Grace's face. "I'm past two hundred and I'm considered young for my position."

"I guess three hundred is the new thirty." Grace laughed, stretching in her chair.

On that note she bade Asa goodnight, ready to ponder the day's fascination points and add to her list of questions for tomorrow.

Asa sat in a Dark Unit debrief room composing her report for Prefect Gunnar and Commander Arundel.

Sergeant Woods is intelligent, honest, and compassionate, with a voracious appetite for knowledge. Regarding others highly, she appears to recognize few positive qualities in herself apart from her work ethic. I believe this originates from heavy personal loss in her turbulent formative years. Her low self-esteem has stunted her maturity in some areas, particularly social interaction.

The closed environment has undoubtedly aided her assimilation, as have the sessions with Prefect Gunnar.

Outstanding notes:

1. *Sergeant Woods was twin to a gifted sister.*

2. *Her maternal grandmother taught her stories of Fae, depicting her as actively engaged on our behalf.*

A few days later, while getting ready for bed, Grace replayed a discussion they'd had on spiritual beliefs. Oberon had a satisfying range of beliefs. Choices were personal and not considered a thing to be challenged. Grace's favorite was a widely held allegorical belief whose deities were often invoked linguistically as well as prayerfully, for emotional emphasis, though not typically in anger. Its simplicity spoke to her. The story calmed her mind while waiting for sleep.

The Mother and Father Above were stars in the Great Celestial Migration. As their paths drew them closer, their lights flared brightly. Paths shifting, they circled one another. Their movements fusing them into One, sending surging waves of Light into the furthest reaches of the Dark. The Father Above made Oberon, to circle them. The Mother Above created Children to enjoy and care for the new world. Together they created the Moon to mark Oberon's own migrations. Light illuminates Dark. Where Darkness overwhelms, the Mother and Father Above shall always send Light.

Grace burrowed into her pillow. Perhaps the Pulse was the light sent to illuminate the Dark. It had for her. She'd been unable to express to Asa or Prefect Gunnar that she didn't pine for Earth. She was happy here. If she hadn't left the Bunker, she would still be locked inside—on Earth.

The thought panicked her.

5.

MIND-READING

THE DAILY SESSIONS with Prefect Gunnar were a fascinating focal point for Grace. She never tired of the Prefect's personal opinions on any topic, firmly rooted as they were, in centuries of life.

His detailing of why they had chosen to maintain the level of weaponry used, rather than pursue those capable of wider harm from greater distance, brought up political philosophies of war. Gunnar in turn appreciated her own views and opinions, augmented by remembered bits from Sun Tzu's The Art of War, or the opinions of war veterans she had known.

His unobtrusive ability to pull her back to main points in their discussions after she rabbit-holed off on some tangent was miraculous to her. She never thought of it as part of an intelligence master's toolkit.

Prefect Gunnar found her nuanced knowledge in diverse areas extraordinary. She downplayed her intelligence, comparing herself to her twin, but he observed with every session how deeply she absorbed, analyzed, and cataloged detail. It took very little prompting to resurface old memories, which she elaborated upon as though they were freshly made.

Today Gunnar smoothed several crumpled sheets of paper, handing them to her with a lifted brow. Appalled by her underutilized handwriting, Grace had begun practicing her penmanship soon after recovering. Looking over her efforts, she mentally facepalmed. Of course, her trash was examined. Even the Amazing Kreskin Prefect couldn't read her thoughts while she was in her room. Looking them over, she considered that they could look—like many things. Code for instance. She realized afresh how little they knew of each other.

"Prefect, Humans have moved almost entirely away from writing by hand. We have machines with alphabets and punctuation pressure points we touch with fingertips."

Because any form of electric-run messaging was difficult to explain, she let him draw his own conclusions on how communications were exchanged, implying only that it was swift.

Grace sketched a keyboard on the back of her practice paper, then positioned it in front of her, fingers in proper placement, demonstrating how keystrokes were pressed. "It's ingrained from childhood, until we write much more swiftly than with pen and paper. It is also simpler to read as it has universal, clear print styles, like your printing presses, not affected by each individual's manner of writing."

Grace watched his expression, knowing he'd seen this in her memories, but without context or explanation.

"This is how the world communicates. A military code adaptation is how I performed my job. I could write code more quickly than you can speak."

Gunnar was silent while he considered these things. Even as an abstract concept, it was staggering to think of the amount of information passing through her hands.

"The strategic ramifications must be beyond anything I could imagine. It must greatly affect the outcome in conflicts," he said.

"It's a double-edged sword," said Grace. "Every major power has the same capabilities to use as they wish. Propaganda, misdirection, insurrection..."

Gunnar observed an abrupt shift in her body language toward tension. Not in the information shared, but something personal. He leaned back to give her space. "You have reservations about these things?"

Grace blew out a breath, plucking at a thread in her shirt hem. "Ironically, I found this manner of communication in personal life easily misunderstood without voice and body language. It was frustrating and exhausting. I shut much of it out, which was isolating."

"Without true understanding of the framework, you've communicated the essence well. I believe I would feel much the same."

Because their sessions were cooperative, not interrogational, the Prefect didn't dig deeper than the information freely given. Grace diverted her thoughts away from areas too complex to explain. Implications of modern tech, automotive dominance, or global reach through aviation were impossible to broach, and she doubted their usefulness.

Her eyes swept the wall maps. She couldn't imagine discussing how her global mapping knowledge derived from satellite imaging, or the truly unimaginable aspects of walking on the moon, the ISS, deep space probes and reaching for Mars. Grace never questioned how she was able to permanently wall those areas off; it was enough to be grateful.

It's as though I've left a noisily packed room and can breathe freely, hear myself think, focus on one thing at a time.

In descriptions of infrastructure, she kept to early versions of ships, steam-driven trains, and the like. Gunnar knew she was simplifying, but he understood it was not evasion. Trust was no longer an issue.

"I'm excited to see the surrounding territory once the Keep is reopened," said Grace. "I know it's odd, but I see it in my dreams: your village on Market Day."

The Prefect was silent, studying her face. Was it possible she had, or was it a simple turn of phrase? Asa's last report had raised several questions. He was certain evaluating her reactions upon emerging from the Keep would prove interesting. But he still awaited the return of dispatched covert assessment teams. They could only conjecture outside conditions, and whether other Humans had arrived. Was she the only one?

He gathered up his notes. "I understand your enthusiasm. It's a new world."

Grace laughed, "I'm not so sure it is."

He turned back to their mapping, instincts alert, but unable to define why.

With the Keep sealed and many duties curtailed, Prefect Gunnar and Grace found their time working together absorbing, and sessions lengthening. Gunnar's professional interest began a subtle shift toward fascination with Grace.

Not just a window into another world, but her way of framing, and processing information. It bore similarities to his own, trained over centuries.

"In retrospect the paradox drives me crazy," she said. "Battles lost when troops were sent in blind because Command held back accurate intel. History repeats itself, no matter the technology."

Grace brought his hand to her face and let him see heartbreaking battle summations of Napoleon's incompetent officers, the Charge of the Light Brigade and Gallipoli, with their horrendous loss of life. He could hear her heart racing, furious over the loss of life from stupidity. He would have been as outraged.

An underlying matter still waiting to surface concerned her Pulse sickness dreams. Particularly, the violent one which had pulled him in. He sensed no conscious effort to block him, but the strangeness of areas he could not access in their open communication was puzzling. It resembled the Gift called Shielding. He never prompted attempts to recall them, but he ceaselessly watched and listened.

6.

BROTHERS

ONE OF GRACE'S requests of Asa was to hear of Prefect Gunnar and Commander Arundel's histories. Past the knowledge they'd risen in rank together, the rest was conjecture.

Only Arundel and Gunnar knew each other's full stories. The bond between them was stronger than blood ties. Their goals, ethics, and priorities were the same. Only their pasts differed.

Arundel met the love of his life when they were children.

Etana came from a revered line of Seer-Gifted females, highly sought after and valued by the powerful around the world. Some were king-makers. A few brought empires to their knees. And some were quietly purposeful in their fulfillment of fate's plans.

Etana, and her oldest sister Luma, weren't attention

seekers. Sola, the middle sister, would openly pull down an entire dynasty, aiding a more just ruling party's ascension. With the rarity, and irregularity of birth in Fae children, the three sisters' ages covered almost a millennium.

Etana knew Arundel would be her world, at their childhood introduction. His family had traveled to meet with hers, needing guidance in managing a brewing conflict. Arundel was sent outside to explore the pleasant meadow behind the house.

Fragrantly warm with the summer sun, he contentedly explored. Hearing an eagle cry, Arundel squinted into the midday sun, watching it wheel above. His eyes dropped to meet those of a female child sitting in the tall grass, smiling as though she knew him. Honeyed hair cascaded in waves down her back, bits of bracken in it tattling of her lying in the grass, also watching the eagle. Arundel thought her young, perhaps eight to his mature ten-year-old eyes. She reached up to give him something she held, so he put out his hand. Tipping in a ring of braided grass divided in two by a golden-brown eagle feather, she said a thing he did not understand.

"Someday, I'll be your everything, and you'll be mine. I'll give you wings, and you'll keep watch."

She looked to the eagle, still soaring above and back to Arundel.

"Etana! Come here." A grown female, with the same smile and mysterious air about her, came to take Etana by the hand.

"You're like Luma," Sola admonished Etana, lifting her to her feet. "Giving words to strangers. And where is she now?"

"He is not a stranger," said Etana, as Sola led her toward

the house. "Someday he will see Luma, as we see. He'll know why she had to go."

Arundel seemed to awaken as they walked away. He'd been mesmerized by the child and her strange words. He held the ringed feather carefully, not knowing why. As he returned home, the confusing interlude faded, slipping into the future. He kept the talisman close, with no clear understanding to explain its importance to him.

On a chill rainy day, several decades later, Etana saw him passing through the nearby Stronghold. He was a young Guardian, barely out of recruit training. The grass talisman, which lived in his tunic pocket, gave a warm pulse, prompting him to look up. From across the road, Arundel met her eyes and the smile he knew. He dodged through the market vendors to stand looking down at her, hearing the eagle's cry, scenting the warm meadow grass.

"I've been waiting for you," she said lightly, putting her arm through his. He accepted her words without question.

After a courtship filled with breathless flirtation and an insistent, joyful pull between them, Arundel held her fast as their bodies recognized the shifting change marking them Mated.

Arundel, earnest in his desire to advance in rank, hoped to use his placement to better the plight of those in need. But when he came home, work vanished. Etana played with and soothed, discussed with and wooed, laughed and loved with him. She was the evening calm and passionate night's balm to the hard work that filled his days. They were happily occupied with each other for half a century when Etana became pregnant. Arundel was astonished and filled with joy. He threw himself into work, determined to secure a safe future for his family.

Brilliant in his ability to strategize victory from the poorest of positions, Arundel laughed with Etana in his arms, suggesting her Gift spilled over so he could see the outcomes. She nuzzled his neck, impudently suggesting she could see a rousing skirmish just ahead.

He drove himself harder as Etana's time to give birth approached, for he would stay with her and their child those first months. As deeply as Arundel loved and cherished her, Etana loved him more fiercely.

Her birthing time came early, but the Healer was not overly concerned. Etana's size was good, and dates were a calculated guess. Etana kissed the uneasy Arundel, who arrived at a run when called. She held his hands tightly in hers, as he sat beside her through the early stages, not letting go as she breathed through contractions. Etana cherished his hands in hers, holding his gaze as she spoke of their hearts first meeting in the meadow.

Her overlong hours laboring caused him increasing unease. Forced to release her hand, he paced out of the way, firmly ordered by the Healer. Etana turned to him often, and his eyes upon her missed nothing. As the baby's head appeared it was apparent on the Healer's face; something was wrong. Arundel took a step close behind her. The baby emerging was very small. Arundel's gaze rose to Etana, with a swift, reassuring smile.

The Healer, with a discreet gesture, sent for another assistant. There must be a twin. As she tied and clipped the cord, she examined the child. Twins were extremely rare. If they survived, they were always unusually Gifted. It was a boy, perfect and beautiful, but so tiny.

The Healer roughed him lightly in a linen cloth to stimulate circulation, put her mouth over his tiny nose and mouth and gently suctioned any substance blocking his airway and spat it to the side. His tiny wail at this indignity brought a smile to the Healer's face. She handed him to her assistant to clean and fold in a soft flannel.

As Etana lay back, for a moment's respite, Arundel looked at his son with absolute wonder. His entire body would fit neatly in Arundel's hand. The child's downy hair color and chin were hers. The infant's eyes opened, looking over the Healer's shoulder deeply into his. Arundel stilled at the connection. The assistant moved to wrap the baby in a flannel, breaking the tie.

Arundel turned to Etana just as the placenta came with a torrent of blood, and with that frightening tide an even smaller, second child. A girl, fragile as thistle down, with Arundel's features in a feminine mold. The Healer felt an unknown fear shiver up her spine. Perhaps it was the twin birth, or that she suddenly realized Etana asked no questions, nor was she frightened.

She handed the infant to her assistant and devoted herself to stemming Etana's bleeding. She called Arundel from the babies to Etana's side, concentrating her Healing Gift to constrict the hemorrhaging blood vessels, to bring oxygen to Etana's lungs, to stimulate her heart. The Healer assessed the wan and weakening mother.

"Fight, Etana! Pull on your strength, for your Mate, for your beautiful babies!" Her healing powers slowed at a time they must not.

Arundel took in the amount of blood on the floor, the two babies in the attendant's hands, and the waxen pallor and stillness on Etana's face. He knew that look from the battlefield.

Magic could not replace so much blood. He made the only possible decision.

The Healer looked up from her efforts to see Arundel, his hands on Etana's face, asking her, telling her...

"Take my strength—you must, for our children, Mate! They are beautiful, but so, so small. They need you."

The long-lived Healer had seen only a few males offer their life strength to their Mates dying on the birthing bed. None had been warriors. He would die so she could raise their children.

Arundel saw Etana's answer in her eyes, the lids drifting down.

He gently shook her shoulders and lifted her to him. "No—you will not go."

She forced her eyes open, short breaths pushing words out. "*Mate—I'm sorry...*"

Panic-struck, Arundel grew more forceful. "You must stay with them. I have never held anything from you, give me this."

Etana rallied, fought for him. She tried to breathe, to find strength. The babies were brought for her to see. Their breaths, as tiny as their bodies. She looked longingly at them, tears slipping to her pillow.

Her determined gaze came back to Arundel. For him, she was grappling with the darkness. Everything within her struggling.

Arundel's hand cupped the back of her head as he put his

forehead to hers and tried to will his life strength into her. But she would not pull it to her.

"Please, Etana, I cannot bear it. I will die, and they will have no one."

The Healer wondered that his Mate could resist such pleas. She was stemming the hemorrhage; it had significantly slowed. The Healer opened her mouth to encourage Arundel, then made a small sound.

Arundel's heart cried out as he saw the Healer holding the second placenta from the infant girl, releasing a crimson flood, and Etana's life strength from her body. As though still tied to her by their cords, the two babies sighed and followed her, final breaths as one.

The room was empty. Of his life. His joy. He could not move. He could not think. He could not breathe. It felt obscene that a moment ago three lifetimes were in his hands and now they were empty. He felt a golden thread of movement within himself. Then two more, twining with the first.

Etana had used their last breaths to push all three life strengths, and their Gifts into him. He had opened himself, when asking her to take his, and so their lives had flowed effortlessly into him.

He reacted with anger.

Arundel exploded through the door at a full run. Faster, past the Stronghold gates, past the roads, a blur to sentries, he plunged into the forest. Faster, lungs shredding, as the consequences chased him.

How could you leave me, then condemn me with so many lifetimes to bear it alone?

It was torture. His heart was screaming in rage, his body reacting to the grief that caused it. He felt the golden threads flowing through his muscles, bones, brain, and finally, his heart.

Images flashed through him. Etana looking at the babies, then him, with overwhelming love and purpose. A whisper of feeling brushed against his mind with what she had been unable to say.

Oberons, soon to come under his care, needed him. *All* of Oberon would need him.

More images came as he ran faster from these thoughts.

The three of them were there to give him what he needed, though not what his heart wanted. He could feel her sorrow cover him, but also her strength. Not the strength of her broken body, the strength of her entire bloodline. She had known this time was coming. She was born for it, and her line before her.

He felt the cliffs approaching before he saw them, too late to slow his momentum, too devastated to care.

The golden threads turned to steel, pulling him apart as he left the cliffs behind, sending him tumbling through the air.

Intuitively he threw his arms wide. Massive wings unfurled in their place, turning the tumbling fall into an unsteady glide. He looked down upon lion feet an instant before he crashed into the peninsula ahead, rolling to a stop among broken trees.

Etana, what have you done?

He felt the three golden threads pulse with reassurance.

He coughed at the dust in his throat from the trees and soil. A gout of flame roared from his mouth. A mouth which had no teeth. Leaping back, he pawed at his face, feeling razor claws, and stopped. There were feathers and fur in his claws. He lashed a tail in panic, hearing a hiss. Leaping forward he whirled sharply, catching sight of his tail. It was a viper.

Father Above.

He was a Chimera.

Not in several millennia had a Shift manifested a Chimera. They only appeared in times of dire need. They were a thing of legend, history books. Most had been female. Created to combat great evil, the Father and Mother Above chose the most worthy in the time of need. That Arundel was male did not matter; fate had fitted him for the task.

Three animals in one, breathing fire, with many Gifts.

As the sun set, he found a pond of still water and looked at himself. His head was a lion's, with a golden eagle face, feathers blending into fur. His leonine body was huge-pawed, bearing those massive eagle wings, his long tail, a viper.

There was no part of Arundel that was not pulled down into darkness, overwhelmed with shock, and grief. He felt the threads pulse. His body Shifted back to his Fae self. He sank to the ground, and for the last time in his life, Arundel wept.

Gunnar went through almost a century of Guardian training, then the interminable Civil War alongside Arundel. Mutual respect, the holding of themselves to a higher standard in service to their people, forged and solidified their bond. It was a brotherhood more profound than familial ties.

Neither made friends easily, both were grateful to have one unquestionably trustworthy confidant to lean on; from whom to seek counsel. After a century of friendship, fighting side-by-side, came a quiet night's lull in a seemingly endless siege. A night which cemented their friendship forever.

They were lounging on their cots in a rare moment of rest. Cold rain pelted their tent, stealing heat from their small fire. Gunnar closely examined, then continued to sharpen and polish the already flawless edge. He eyed Arundel, who returned an inquiring look. Gunnar sheathed his sword, pulling out a knife belt to look over as he spoke.

"I'd like you to know my story. More than of training and postings. Should I fall in this war, you'll be the only one to have it. You're the only one who knows me."

Arundel sat up, pulling a pack behind him, giving Gunnar his full attention.

"I would be honored to have it. We're a pair. I've always felt we were set apart by fate."

Gunnar was still as he contemplated the word *fate* to encompass their bond. He would not have dared frame it that way, but he accepted it as right.

"These are pieces I've put together from those who fought under my mother and the villagers near our home."

He settled, hands still, the fire's crackle and hiss, and drumming rain backdrop to his words.

"My warrior mother was focused solely on achieving rank as a leader. She rose to Centurion in little more than two hundred years. You know how rare that is."

Brow raised, Arundel nodded.

"Fighting on the southern continent during the first century of the war, she had a brief relationship with a Southern Allied commander before transferring with her legion to a new posting. Soon after, she was dismayed to find herself pregnant, making it impossible, of course, for her to continue fighting. All under her command fighting to protect her instead of addressing the battle? There was no concealing it. She resigned her position and returned to the north where she tracked news of the war, bitterly awaiting my birth. She would perform her duty in raising me until I could be surrendered to the training camps and return to the war." Gunnar looked to Arundel wryly.

"I arrived at the correct time, as she would not have allowed otherwise. My name is from her native language, the word for warrior. She said it would set the bar high, and there was no acceptable place under it. She knew how to hone a weapon. If I competed only with myself, the competition would never end."

Arundel leaned forward to add wood to the fire, thinking of his own family. Discipline could be harsh, and he was also trained young, but his mother's hand had been gentle, and affirmation swift where warranted.

"My Telepathy surfaced early in childhood, earning her approval as she shared the Gift. Shortly after, I was sparring with a friend. He struck me from behind. I whirled on him in anger. Before he could lower his sword, I'd Shifted into a snarling Jaguar cub. My mother watched me writhe in pain, until I managed to return to Fae form, calculating what impact having two Gifts would bring. Obviously, my father had Shifter bloodlines from the area this animal inhabited in the south. Training then included lessons in absolute control over the Shift. She drilled into me the necessity of keeping it hidden, in reserve for emergencies."

He could feel Arundel watching him with empathy.

"An attack by an infiltrating guerrilla group caught

our village by surprise. My mother sprinted to warn the Guardians at the Stronghold and was taken down by a spear as we were overrun. She made me pull the spear so they couldn't take her alive. I held her as she bled to death, passing her Telepathy and life strength to me." Gunnar looked up. "Now you know why my Telepathy is stronger than most. My mother's was already unusually strong, so mine became doubled. The rest you know. After the attack, I went to a first-level training ground. Two decades later, we were brought together, by fate it seems."

Arundel sat in silence, thinking through Gunnar's words. It was an honor to give one's life story. It happened more frequently in war, but neither Arundel or Gunnar felt the need for casual friendship, and therefore none before theirs had taken root. He shifted the head of his cot nearer Gunnar. Reaching for Gunnar's hand, he held it to his face— the manner Gunnar's Telepathy allowed him to read most clearly.

Arundel directed Gunnar to memories from the childhood meeting with Etana, until his first meeting with Gunnar.

He released Gunnar's hand. There was not another living soul on Oberon who knew of the Chimera. He silently sat back while Gunnar processed.

The immensity of Arundel's burden—and the sorrow creating it… Gunnar met Arundel's gaze.

"You were right, brother, it is fate. I'm beside you, to guard and ensure you are not alone in this. I'll give whatever is required."

It did not change their friendship as Arundel feared it might. He was intensely grateful. It was a relief to have Gunnar know his burden—and his grief.

Their bond was critical for the inferno ahead.

7.

PERSONAL

P REFECT GUNNAR'S OBSERVATIONS referenc-
ing his personal opinions on war fascinated Grace. It
was sometimes difficult for her geopolitics-geek self
not to fangirl, or conversely, frustrating that such wisdom
was heard only by her.

Today she'd been outlining the political background of
several war scenarios, both historic and currently playing
out on Earth. His beliefs conflicted with those endorsing
remotely directed, impersonal war.

"War is death and dying, warrior and civilian," said
Gunnar. "At its best, it's the terrible labor pains of freedoms
for those to come, at worst, senseless slaughter that robs the
future of priceless potential."

She was silent, turning this over, applying it to her
knowledge of the vast diversity of war. Its rightness reso-
nated deeply.

"You cannot convince your opponent to think the way
you do," Gunnar pointed out. "If that were possible, you

would not be facing them across the field. But it is critical to know for yourself why you stand there, and why you are willing to die for it."

As he finished speaking, a flash of fathomless pain in her eyes startled Gunnar. It vanished as quickly as it appeared. There was not a flicker of change in Grace's life signs. She was unaware—leaving him puzzled and disturbed.

The next morning was, for her, the extreme opposite of such profoundness. Over breakfast, Asa grilled Grace concerning Human personal relationships. Grace's in particular.

"I've told you of our relationship structures—many aspects," Asa said. "You've given me only broad references. Nothing personal."

Arms crossed, she leaned back in her chair, deliberately provoking Grace to note her response. These were fundamental societal markers. How Grace interpreted them, personally, added dimension to Asa's assessment.

"I've been forthcoming with personal examples to illustrate these points," Asa said evenly. Flustered, knowing an inevitable, mortifying personal moment had arrived, Grace fought the urge to slide down in her chair.

"Asa, relationships and sex are not as straightforward with many Humans. I think Fae have kept it simple, or you're further evolved."

She dodged Asa's directness with general observation.

"Intrinsic dignity issues concerning personal choice that should have been settled long ago are still a struggle. Maybe it's our short lifespans. Humans love prying into one another's personal lives," Grace said.

Asa thought this over. That Grace's scent and body language indicated stress over the topic was unexpected. "What do you search for in lovers? Intelligence? Skill? Power? Do you prefer males? Females? Either, as I do?"

Grace was caught off guard by Asa's directness. She didn't understand the reasoning behind her invasive persistence—that her answers could reveal exploitable weakness. Grace was untrained. If a spy knew her predilections, it gave possible access to whomever and whatever information Grace held. The Keep was as secret as Grace's Bunker.

Grace blurted out the truth, "I've—no real experience. With any of it."

Disbelief written on her face, Asa was blunt. "Why not? Were you not allowed? Are you unsure in your desires? Has someone hurt you?"

The purpose for the exercise disappeared as Asa lost focus, uncharacteristically indignant—as though it were a personal affront. Asa shifted in her chair. Her response was unprofessional, surprising even herself. She cared. Grace deserved love.

Grace's face heated, thrown off balance by Asa's intensity, unable to think of a noncommittal response. Swallowing, she scrambled for a neutral answer.

"It's not that. I've—always been taking care of someone or working. I had no real friends. When my family was gone, most people my age used socialization methods unappealing to me."

How do I explain dating apps? Or how loud, packed bars made me cringe, that I felt alone in a sea of strangers?

Grace shook her head. She'd never developed romantic friendships, or anything deeper than acquaintance with either sex.

"Several of my coworkers had relationships with someone at work which ended in anger or hurt. They were trapped, seeing one another daily. I've had enough pain in my life. I focused on work."

Asa studied Grace. Her flushed skin, and fluttering pulse indicated rising stress over the topic. Comprehension dawned. This wasn't an inability to find sexual attraction or love. The isolation and continual loss in her life had left her unable to emotionally connect at all.

"You're untouched."

"Asa! Hush," Grace hissed, hyperaware of surrounding Fae, able to hear just how backward she was.

Everyone she'd ever loved died. There had been no opportunity for experience, to separate romantic love from familial. Hand shading her eyes, Grace wiped away tears of humiliation. Asa immediately backed off, and took a sip of tea, giving her space to work through her feelings.

Grace had never analyzed her lonely state or questioned the absence of girlhood friendships discussing romance and sex. Her life had passed straight from childhood to adulthood. No adolescence. Just living between deaths, each subtracting more from her until she was grown and alone. Work had punctured the vacuum, pulling the passion and loneliness in her heart into relentless perfection in her work— something she could control. No one could hurt her through it. It wouldn't abandon her.

Until now.

An emotional wall began to crumble. Grace desperately

did not want to reach some world-shifting epiphany here in the dining hall.

"I can't talk about this," Grace said.

Observing how deep Grace's distress was, Asa pulled her into a hug, a gesture foreign to Asa that she had learned while Grace was ill and transitioning, needing comfort.

"Human senses must be grossly inferior," she whispered.

With a shaky breath Grace laughed at Asa in spite of herself. Glancing over Grace's shoulder as she released her, Asa noted Prefect Gunnar passing by. Her eyes narrowed. Grace straightened, changing the subject as abruptly as Asa had, by asking a question she knew could not be answered.

"Asa, I haven't guessed your Gift. You'd think I would have by now."

It was Asa's turn to scan the room. She wasn't allowed to show Grace her Gift. Prefect Gunnar was the only one in the Keep to openly display his Telepathy to her. And the Voice upon her arrival.

Mother Above, it was bound to come up sooner or later.

She trusted Grace, but as a Dark Unit spy, Asa was sworn to secrecy until the Prefect gave permission. Grace watched Asa's expression change, knowing why.

"I'm sorry. That was rude of me," said Grace, pushing away from the table. "I'd like to study. I'll see you tomorrow."

She missed Asa's hand lifting as she walked away.

Asa was quartered a few doors down from Grace. It was embarrassing, even to herself, that she was snuggling into the bed of her private room. It was much nicer and several pay grades softer than her normal bunk and quarters. As her body drifted toward sleep, she pondered Grace's heart.

Today was a startling glimpse into her psychological makeup. She'd been on the precipice of a major self-realization too private to share or have unfold in a public place. Provoked responses from Grace often surprised her. It was admirable that she'd turned the conversation by effectively ending it.

Grace would never guess Asa's Gifting. It was not something she could see or guess, as with some of the others. Rare and valued by the Dark Unit, it had brought her to Prefect Gunnar's attention at an early age.

Asa was a Traveler.

Asa's Gifting was not in her family line. Her endless curiosity had led to much familial speculation of what exactly her Gift might be. Asa remembered most of her childhood as a question preceding, and an exclamation point following her name like a tail.

"*Asa want why!*" was the refrain drifting behind her toddling steps.

She was continuously restless and watching, as though her mind battled stillness. She woke with questions, ate with them and wandered the village trailing them like a string teasing a kitten.

The village, after the first waves of deep sighs and eyerolling at her approach, made a game of answering her questions by turning them back to her.

"*Mama, why eat?*" prompted early talks of biology. The

village seamstress had a fascinating talent, turning cloth into many things. Pointing at neatly folded stacks of finished items, she looked up, brows drawn.

"How?"

Moments later Asa held a needle, learning her first stitches. The engineering of flat cloth into multidimensional shapes intrigued her baby logic.

Her demanding finger, pointing to the kitchen hearth fire, was beyond her mother Erla's abilities to explain. There were none in the family line with a Gift related to fire, thank the Mother Above. Asa's mother desperately hoped one related to it would not manifest. The curious child would burn things to see the results. Erla pushed the thought away.

"Come. Help me braid my hair, my love."

At the word "braid," Asa dropped her questions, following her mother. Dancing up the stairs, humming to herself, she tried to climb only alternate steps. Erla turned at the landing in time to see Asa lose her balance, falling backward. She snatched at her in a blur of speed, just as Asa disappeared, reappearing at the top of the stairs, still humming and dancing toward her mother's room.

Erla remained frozen, her hand tightly gripping the stair rail. Asa was a Traveler. It was a rare and respected Gift, but the thought of this precocious child appearing without warning in a dangerous place frightened her. As did Asa's lack of control.

Erla's work was clear. The entire family, the entire village, if needed, must help in training her to master this "why," which already appeared an unconscious reaction in the child.

"Mama! Come please," Asa demanded, waiting in her mother's room. Erla sighed heavily, continuing up the stairs.

8.

BLINDED

HEADING TO HER session with Prefect Gunnar, Grace studied wood grain in the hall paneling, and her fingernails, which she was tempted to bite. Anything to crowd out her conversation with Asa from Gunnar the Mind Melder.

I could strangle Asa. I've never hidden anything from him, —but his feet are propped on the seat at Grace's Multiplex, watching my home movies. Not that he's ever disrespectful. We've just become less formal, which has been wonderful.

Until now.

She had no landmarks to recognize her shifting emotions concerning Gunnar. His open honesty in discussions of any kind were as close to intimacy as she'd ever experienced. He responded with interest to her questions and thoughts, always asking for more.

He cares about what I think. I can ask anything and trust his answers.

She felt safe, emotionally unguarded. While he never

brought up personal details of his life, Grace never noticed. Her guileless interest allowed him to speak of things which mattered to him. She was unaware Gunnar had rarely discussed his philosophy of life and work — subjects important to him — with anyone.

An unprecedented mental bond formed between them. Grace could feel emotions from him as they spoke intensely of things that mattered. Sometimes visual flashes of his thoughts appeared when deep in discussion. Most passed so swiftly they barely registered.

Lying far beneath everything were flickers she didn't understand. Rippling patterns. A muscular, silent presence that felt—not strictly Fae. She never mentioned it to him, instinctually knowing he would withdraw.

Gunnar was treading a similar path, missing the obvious though he'd spent a lifetime reading others. It didn't occur to him that he was plunging to a much deeper level with Grace.

He never felt himself exceed normal limits in personal areas unrelated to their work, but unfamiliar with the open boundaries of Humans, even those light touches went deeper than recognized.

Grace sat in her chair before his desk, running her hand along its edge to avoid looking at him. He settled into the chair opposite her. Still ducking his gaze, she closed her eyes, inhaling deeply, exhaling slowly.

Gunnar held a partially-filled map and correlating notes for their current project. Though she stumbled over some of the locations, the information was clear when he looked at her memories.

"I apologize for the lapses."

"Sergeant Woods, this is unprecedented work. The

amount of information you recall is impressive. I would not have thought it possible to learn so much from a single source."

After they had names and borders, she covered political ideology, population centers, predominant cultural features. It was exacting and difficult, easiest when he Telepathically examined the areas he felt relevant.

At least the detailed ones take longer… If those who mocked me for my interests could see me now.

A quiet, derisive sound escaped her, drawing the Prefect's notice. Logic dryly suggested she redirect her thoughts elsewhere, while they were actually working. *Idiot.* She stumbled quite a bit, giving Gunnar an apologetic look.

"Don't be concerned, we'll fill in as we go," he said, hand resting lightly along her cheek.

For the first time, his touch flustered her. She concentrated on her breathing, thinking of the Intelligence boards and maps in Central, relaxing in relief when the image was clear.

Exhausted from the extreme emotions Asa had triggered, and her attempts to keep her underlying nerves from tattling, Grace worked to prevent trembling under his hand. There was no escape from herself, from him. Anxiety mounting, Grace found herself ghosting. She watched from a step away, studying Gunnar as he wrote. A strong impulse to touch him rolled through her. Without thinking, she laid her hand on his shoulder.

A clear stream of images flowed into her. Her eyes closed, seeing, feeling, a multifaceted sense of him, faintly underlined by the vaguely shifting, other she'd sensed before. The predominant images, sharply defined, were of the maps she was holding in mind for him, but also a less clear undercurrent of the week's embarrassing conversation with Asa.

Grace broke the connection, jolting back into her body, startling her eyes open. Gunnar was speechless. His hand had dropped away. He tried to carefully word the question to ask.

Sharp awareness of her presence in an impenetrably private place, shocked him. It was dangerous, an invasion of boundaries critical to his work. He lightly held her arm to keep her in place as he swiftly analyzed, at a loss for how to react.

She penetrated my guard—

He'd never been caught so unaware.

Grace burst into tears.

He couldn't have been more surprised if she'd hit him. She was blushing furiously, hand shielding her face. Gunnar released her, uncertain of what to say or do. Her desperation was clear.

"May I go—?"

"Grace…"

Not Sergeant Woods.

"I shouldn't have touched you!"

"You *read* me. How?"

"I was—ghosting. I touched your shoulder. I saw my—my personal memories below the map."

"Grace, those aren't in focus to me. They flow past like water. But I don't understand—"

He scented her distress. She was wringing her hands, trying to decide if she believed him. With her so distraught and without contact, he had only to form a question in his thoughts—and he was instantly in her mind.

Asa's conversation unspooled, underlined by Grace's cruelly negative view of herself. He also felt the depth of her growing feelings for him—now shaken awake by physical awareness—coursing through his mind and body with Human intensity.

Grace's calves knocked back the chair as she sprang up, tears streaming, breaking the connection. "I—I can't—" She almost ran, in her haste to leave the room.

Gunnar was at a total loss, a thing he had never experienced.

A Guardian passing in the corridor saw Grace fleeing in tears, turning to look with puzzlement at Gunnar. He rose from his chair and closed the door.

Gunnar found his well-organized, disciplined and efficient days, decades, centuries—disappearing into an unfamiliar, irritating and unpredictable shape.

If he had allowed himself to consider it, which he did not, he might have easily located the catalyst. Instead, he allowed no time for introspection, inflicting his frustration on subordinates, demanding precision, and as close to perfect performance as they could muster.

The Prefect was merciless with his warriors, judgmental gaze raking over them.

"Tessera Two and Four repeat flanking maneuvers drill. A quarter of you are leaving exploitable, potentially fatal gaps. While the enemy will thank you, your flanking warriors will not."

He ignored the muttered swearing before entering and upon leaving training sessions. While his warriors respected that he drove himself towards the same perfection, they deeply desired their Prefect to figure out what, exactly, was driving him. Before they dropped in their tracks.

They exchanged low-voiced theories over their ale in the canteen. Most ascribed to notions involving females.

"Father Above, what's dogging the Prefect? I thought I'd lost my sword arm today."

The male signaled for another round of ale. Shaking her head at the juvenile recruit, a more seasoned Tessera Guardian regarded him with annoyance.

"Suck it up. Maybe it's been too long since his last bed warming. It's not like he's got much choice, locked up down here. He's females only. Most of the time you have no idea who he's with. He's Spy Master for a reason, halfwit."

The male Guardian on his other side looked the promiscuous young male up and down with pointed disapproval at his whining.

"Not everyone grabs everything, and everybody."

They all scanned the room while sucking down another pint. It was true. Choices were limited. A battle-scarred veteran surveyed the room.

"There's maybe one of his former lovers here, as far as I can tell. The way he's pounding us shows he's shoving it into his work."

Several grunts of agreement echoed the sentiment. Bets were laid as to who might have attracted his attention, but not reached his bed. There were several females whose eyes followed him crossing a room. A surly young trainee who'd had his ass handed to him that day, muttered under his breath.

"I hope he gets someone soon. I'm sick of this."

Every older Guardian at the table pounded him with glares, fists to the shoulder, or knuckles to the back of the head. No matter what their Prefect did, they'd follow him anywhere.

"If you children can't take it, get out now, before a battle shows what you're made of," the ranking Guardian said. She rose to go, disgusted with the juveniles.

Gunnar would have been annoyed if he knew of their speculation and worked them harder until they were too exhausted to concern themselves with his personal matters. It would have further proven they were correct.

In the training room showers the following week, a juvenile Guardian unaware Gunnar was nearby, made an off-color remark concerning Grace.

"That Human female. Got a bit of a lost look. How different could she be? I'd give her directions."

Moving in a blur, Gunnar had the male by the neck in a crushing grip against the wall.

"*Fuck.*"

The Tessera leader spit the word, having never seen the Prefect react with such rage. Gunnar immediately dropped the offender. The surrounding Guardians had leapt back against the walls. Their leader stood his ground, hand raised to stop his Prefect if it looked like serious damage was imminent. For the Prefect's sake, not the offending juvenile.

The remark had been base, completely unbecoming of an on-duty Guardian, but sharp words and onerous duty would have been sufficient.

There could be no doubt now that it was personal.

Gunnar was wisely training by himself, pondering the internal disruption his time with Grace had created. Still reeling from her penetration of the one place he considered impregnable, he scrambled to check the erosion of his confidence and self-control. He was belatedly noticing peripheral thoughts or emotions underlying their sessions.

Am I blind? This didn't appear, fully formed. When did I allow myself to take her personal thoughts? Violating my principles—and her trust.

He shared fewer personal thoughts, in their time together, becoming tentative in their work, which irritated him.

Why do I care? Can I emotionally distance, or should I leave our work to one of my Centurions...

He dismissed the second idea before it was fully formed.

Retreating to superficial levels, he felt grieving pain in Grace, unconsciously blaming herself for his backing away. His withdrawal was another loss, in an endless progression. She began to mentally shut down, a self-effacing shadow of herself, even the color in her memories fading.

After two days of missed appointments, he sent for her. Grace had difficulty meeting his eyes. "I don't think— Prefect, I'm running dry of useful information. I'm sorry, I don't want to waste your time."

He couldn't bear it.

"Sergeant Woods, I believe it impossible to reach an end to your knowledge. You've taught me a different aspect of analyzing—so many things. Shall we finish this country you favor—Iceland?" He smiled. "The language is similar to my mother's native tongue."

Grace hesitated before cautiously placing his hand to her cheek, partially opening doors which had been wide. He gently moved forward in her thoughts, reassuring her without words that nothing had changed. He felt her involuntary sigh of relief, and they were back in sync.

That night he lay waiting for sleep to find him, pondering the situation.

Is this weakness a loss of perspective? Perhaps lines are blurred because this isn't threat work; Grace is not an enemy.

Feeling this to be shaky ground, he diverted his thoughts toward the mundane, falling into uneasy sleep.

Much of Gunnar's struggle was seeing but not identifying aspects of himself in such an extreme opposite. Grace competed with herself rather than others. She was not a warrior but had a warrior's heart concerning justice and the defense of others.

He was surprised at her lack of friends, not recognizing the same state in himself. Her drive and loneliness were very like his own. Such a thought was new to him. *I must find a way to shape this. It's already in motion.*

Gunnar finished his solo training session, having pushed himself well past his normal limits. His Guardians observed this and stayed out of his way as he showered and dressed.

"He's headed out, *move*," commanded the Century leader, wanting to keep her juvenile recruits out of harm's way.

Gunnar paced the outer corridors of the Training facility, seeking a logical resolution. Grace loved the high-performance level of her former work. It was her companion.

With it gone, their time had become common ground, filling the need.

*She understands and provides counterpoint views I value.
I haven't felt the pleasure of such a thing since—the early days
with Arundel. I could talk to her for hours—but I do...*

Forcing honesty within himself, there was the factor of
Grace's physical loneliness to consider. He was surprised she
was untouched. He'd seen her orientation toward males in
memories and had not gone further. Upon reflection, he
realized her thoughts pertaining to sex were all in the context
of books she'd read or forms of imaging she'd explained. No
physical interaction.

She'd had no affirmation. Sexual or otherwise. She was
able to generate pride through work proficiency but not intimate affirmation for herself. It was an unopened door.

*That's where my logic fails. I'm applying my standards of
self-worth to hers. I keep emotion and lovers separate from my
identity. She's never had that choice to make; all who cared for
her left.*

Gunnar saw nothing to account for the deficit of male
attention. She was small and vulnerable compared to Fae
females but held unique appeal. Her unusual eyes were beautiful, her smile never failed to draw his attention, her *laugh.*
He enjoyed the dry wit running through her thoughts. Her
nicknames for him made it difficult not to laugh outright.

Mother Above, when had humor last played a role in
his life? His warriors would never recover from the shock of
seeing him laugh, much less smile.

Her lush figure—Gunnar instantly tried to shut the line
of thought down. But his traitorous physical response gave
evidence of his thoughts.

I'm a fool. How can I examine other's body language and tells and not notice how I respond to her?

Gunnar stopped pacing at the dead-end wall of the corridor. He leaned a palm against it, gazing unseeingly at the floor while his mind coalesced the now unavoidable facts. The result hit him like a club. He swore.

The door was open now.

Gunnar woke with a start, heart pounding. He flung his arm over his eyes, shutting out the dim light, struggling to control his breathing. His pulse slowed, and his thoughts reordered as he examined this new facet of attraction to Grace.

It frustrated him. It wasn't the uncomplicated immediacy of lust. He understood the sudden urge for the heat of skin and slickness. Giving and taking satisfaction, with no vulnerability of emotions. He never chose partners who would ask for more than he desired to give.

Intimacy was a vulnerability Gunnar did not allow. An exploitable threat to his position. His work was everything: his identity, purpose, life. His mother had set the tone with her cold disdain of affection. Feelings were an interference to strength and duty.

He wouldn't allow himself to act on the desire but couldn't prevent the hunger. She was a first for him. Never had he failed in controlling his mind and body. He was unsettled at the change, and therefore angry with himself. He wanted her.

Swearing, Gunnar swung his legs over the edge of his bed, stretching to loosen his tight muscles then headed to shower the sweat from his body, and the lingering feeling of Grace.

I must do something about this.

He tilted his head back in the chill spray.

I'm not a juvenile in the throes of my first infatuation. She's a grown female.

He could think of no official objection to taking Grace as a lover. Arundel would accept his decision without question, knowing he had thought through all ramifications. She would need to be cared for while she found a purpose once the Keep reopened.

He scrubbed himself while carefully considering the monumental significance of Grace's innocence. He had seen no shame concerning her desires, only worry over her appeal, and personal ignorance of her role in participation. She was afraid to do something *wrong*. That she might not please him.

Gunnar shook his head over the disgusting mess Humans had tangled around the simplicity and affirmation in pleasuring a desired partner. Frustrated that in her ignorance, she thought herself less worthy of his attention because she was not hardened of muscle, thinner here, bigger there.

He sighed in exasperation shutting off the water, vigorously drying himself as though it could remove the difficulties.

We must talk outside our sessions. Intimate things can't stay in the mind. They must be spoken. I need them to be spoken.

His thoughts drifted toward the dream that awakened him.

Is anything more erotic than expressing what one desires?

Gunnar finished dressing, sitting to pull on his boots.

His hands wrapped around the laces as he considered consequences.

How would this impact—everything? Particularly, if she declined.

He knew Grace was innately predisposed to regard this as an important relationship declaration. But she must also realize he would not be a fickle lover. He was monogamous.

She's safe with me. I know her. Mother Above—I've never known anyone as deeply as her.

He finished rapidly lacing his boots, yet paused, tilting his head back against the wall, eyes closed, chasing the dream moment that had awakened him.

Grace woke with a start at Asa's knock, sweating, muscles tight, heart racing. She called through the door.

"Asa. I overslept. I need to shower. I'll meet you in the dining hall."

Asa paused at the door, listening to Grace's audibly pounding heart, scenting what was already obvious to her. She headed to breakfast, preparing for what was unfolding.

Grace dropped back on her pillow. Throwing the damp sheet from her, she swore.

"What is wrong with me? I'm losing my mind."

Rubbing her hands over her face, she dropped an arm over her eyes, keeping the light at bay. The persistent dreams were making it hard to sleep. After facing her physical attraction to Gunnar, she had no idea what to do next. The vividly erotic dreams—the frustration in awakening on a physical precipice. She wasn't a child; she'd been immersed in explicit information about sex for half her lifetime. But Ms. Frawley's sex ed class didn't deal with crushes on four-hundred-year-old Telepathic Fae Intelligence officers.

Talk to him. You know him. It's a natural, open topic.

She forced herself up and headed for the shower.

Would he be put off if I simply asked—by the way, would you help me with my virginity problem?

Asa had mentioned his lovers in passing, but never knew with certainty who they were. He was thoroughly private.

He can take his pick, from what I've seen in the dining hall.

Standing in the cold shower, she killed her impossible hopes. These females who openly wanted him were fierce warriors.

What I wouldn't give to see a roomful of supermodels go toe-to-toe with these females… I don't have a chance.

But then, Fae didn't worry over physical attractiveness. They paired off whenever they found someone they desired, who reciprocated.

Maybe it wouldn't work in the sealed Keep. Perhaps there would be fraternization problems with his rank. It gets fuzzy when everyone is a warrior. But really, that logic doesn't apply because—I'm not in their military.

She finished showering, shutting off the water harder than strictly necessary, and dressed.

It's not complicated. I'll never find someone I feel this way about again. It's safe here. I know him, more deeply than I've known anyone. If he says no, he won't hurt me. He'll be kind. And I'll still see him… If he says yes, I trust him, with everything, anything.

She was ready to head out. She rested her back against the door, closing her eyes a moment, trying to recapture her favorite part of the dream.

9.

CODES AND KNIVES

GRACE APPROACHED COMMANDER Arundel during breakfast in the dining hall, choosing the public location to ensure nerves wouldn't allow her to abort. *Clear and concise, Grace. Calm. Stop with the alliteration!*

It was the first time she'd sought the Commander out since arriving. Their occasional encounters were in debrief Q & A.

The weight of his presence never lessened. She'd thought of a request which might help preserve her sanity.

Arundel watched her approach while sipping his tea.

Bold move, seeking me out with an audience. Not what I would expect. Perhaps that's the point. No retreat. Whatever it concerns, it's important to her.

Commander Arundel's table sat to one side of the hall, where he could observe the room without making those present overly self-conscious.

She gripped her plate and mug firmly to hide her nerves.

Arundel eased Grace's fear by indicating the seat directly in front of him, effectively putting her back to the room. A kindness.

"Sergeant Woods."

He put his cup down and folded his hands in front of him, giving her his full attention. Meeting Grace's eyes, a vague memory stirred. It disappeared when she spoke.

"Commander Arundel," she said with a nod, taking the seat.

Clear. Concise.

"Commander, I have a two-point proposal to offer. I've learned of your astronomy/weather communication towers. I assume they are—multitasking."

Observant, discrete with security, thought Arundel.

"You know of my work in cryptography. With your permission, I would like to attempt a backup encryption code as standby, if yours were ever compromised."

Interesting offer. Has she discussed it with Gunnar? No. He would report.

"It could be used point-to-point in the field so your primary communication network would not be compromised from field ops if the key were captured."

A sound idea.

"I don't need access to classified information. I can study the towers and how you operate in the field. Commander, when it's finished, one sequence change would render even me unable to break it. I think it necessary in light of my physical limitations."

Wise, understanding how easily she could be broken.

His relaxed attention encouraged her.

"The second point, Commander; I did well in code

breaking. We had methods to speed the process, but I have a solid base in patterns and cyphers. I could employ that knowledge wherever you wished. For misdirection, propaganda. The unrest to the South—if you haven't already broken their encryption, I would like to try." Grace's speech slowed to a halt, waiting for a response.

She knows where her strengths lie, understands high level security...

Arundel let her request hang in the air a long moment, giving it due consideration.

"Sergeant Woods, you cooperate fully with our requests. You have an excellent tutor who speaks well of your progress. Why do you wish to add this task?"

"Because I respect you, Commander. Your methods of leadership. I've never felt a prisoner, have always been treated with kindness and dignity. I'm grateful. Offering my skills is my contribution to your mission." Grace paused, looking past him to the blank wall.

"Commander, my twin and I pushed ourselves to excel. I miss that challenge."

Arundel scanned the room.

Direct answers. Consistent with Asa and Gunnar's reports. I doubt she offers her allegiance lightly.

His gaze returned to her.

"You're a twin?" he asked.

"Yes, Commander. My sister was extraordinary—a genius. I'm not so impressive, but I excel at these things."

Gifted twins... But she's Human...

Arundel studied his hands a moment, then looked at her. The full weight of his gaze caused Grace to lift her chin. She had nothing to conceal from him.

"Sergeant Woods, your desire is admirable. I have no answer at the moment, but I will consider your proposal."

Grace waited. There was something more.

"Prefect Gunnar mentioned basic defense training. You may report to Weapons Master Oran."

Arundel nodded to indicate dismissal.

"Thank you, Commander." Rising, Grace returned his nod, crossing the hall to sit with Asa.

Asa had the decency to wait until later to ask what that was about. Grace did not offer an answer, even to her.

Arundel needed to know she was trustworthy.

Reporting to the training facility, she found the Weapons Master in session with a Guardian unit. *Damn*, they were *fast*. Weapons could be secondary in importance when a body that strong could move with such speed.

Easing in quietly to watch, she stood against a wall displaying an impressive array of weapons. She was having second thoughts about the wisdom of training.

How could I ever get on the mats with one of them?

How could the Prefect and Commander think it possible to defend herself from Fae?

The finishing group took up formation with the Weapons Master walking in review, giving correction—praise where warranted. She heard very little praise. Grace realized the warriors might not appreciate her observing this part, so she turned to examine the weapons wall. Absorbed in a knife's design, it was an effort not to jump when a voice like gravel spoke over her shoulder.

"Turning your back to a roomful of warriors indicates you do not consider them a threat."

Grace wiped all facial expressions as she turned. It was such a commander thing to say. The scarred, older male maintained steady eye contact. Her first test.

"Weapons Master Oran, I apologize; I meant no disrespect."

"Commander Arundel sent you for basic strength and protection training."

His wiry, evenly-muscled frame looked arrow fast. "Yes, Master Oran. Perhaps a student could teach me?"

The Weapons Master raised an eyebrow. Thinking honesty not only wise policy but likely to save much pain, she elaborated.

"I have no rapid healing ability and weaker bones. I lack strength, muscle-mass, and speed. The first two can't be changed but the rest could improve with work."

The Training Master's eyes narrowed as he looked her over. "You are honest in recognizing your limitations and what can be improved. You were not a warrior in your Human command."

"No, Master Oran."

Grace's pride would not allow her country's military to be judged by her appearance. "We had strong fighting legions, but my position was processing intelligence in a fortified Keep such as this. No self-protection training beyond minimums was required."

He circled her, correcting her posture, allowing her to kick her useless, heeled shoes to the near wall, widening her foot stance.

"Prefect Gunnar has also spoken of this need for training.

It is wrong to leave anyone without basic ability to protect themselves." He walked to the weapons board selecting several size knives and a bow with quiver.

This is more than training. His assessment may affect my placement here. I'm the only one in this Keep with no fighting skills.

He wouldn't be asking for anything too difficult in these clothes. With the Keep sealed, Asa was having difficulty finding clothing to fit her small, curvier form. She wore the Air Force blue skirt and blouse she'd arrived in.

Master Oran handed her a twenty-five-centimeter knife, indicating a line before a target ten meters away. She'd seen people throw knives but had personally thrown only darts. She gauged the target distance, hefting the long knife.

Much too heavy for me to throw so far…

She looked to him for permission, moving closer to the target. At half the distance Grace stood in an open stance, grateful no one else was watching. She examined the grip, made to fit a much larger hand.

It was too big, too long; the handle too heavy. She shook her head. She'd never be able to throw it. It would slide out of her grasp before the correct moment to release.

Ah. It's a test. It's a close-in fighting knife.

She turned back to him, surveying the knives he now held fanned across his large palms. There were a range of sizes and handles. She returned the knife, evaluating the others.

Size and weight matter. I can't try to manhandle these hefty ones with any kind of accuracy. Those. They're small.

Picking up a stack of three fifteen-centimeter knives with only thicker steel for a handle, she squeezed one, hand molding comfortably around the handle. She looked up at Oran. He nodded.

She glanced at the target. It still looked too far away.

I wouldn't throw a knife at that distance; I'd use the bow.

She paced toward the target until it was the size of a live threat, five meters away.

Her first throw bounced off the wall half a meter to the right of the target. The Weapons Master turned her shoulders to line up her throwing side with the target, nudging her feet into the correct stance.

Grace marked these things. Raising her eyes, she used less of a windmilling motion, throwing harder. The knife spun this time, hitting the lower part of the target, clattering to the floor.

She felt the Weapons Master's hand on her shoulder, guiding her a short distance closer to the target. He stood back, still silent. She closed her eyes, picturing the rotation of the knife as she mimicked the motion of letting go.

It had spun past where the point could stick, hitting the board flat. He moved her closer, so if she threw it with the same amount of force it should hit earlier in the spin, and stick.

She pictured a Bad Guy running toward her. When he was even with the target, she threw the knife, trying to release at the same place, as though she were merely letting go. The knife struck point-first near the bottom of the target, sticking for a moment, then falling to the floor with a clatter.

She faced the Weapons Master, red-faced.

"Master Oran, the attacker would have been unhappy before he killed me."

He nodded, expressionless.

He gave her the bow and a standing quiver of arrows and indicated the original line. At least she'd done well in archery at summer camp.

But shit, *that was with a plastic bow and blunt arrows into hay bales. This compound bow and arrows—could take down a grizzly.*

Grace knew from rifle training, to treat practice weapons with respect. Walking back to line she put them down. Eyes closed, she mimicked the motions she remembered. Front foot pointing at target, back foot perpendicular. Bow arm straight. Nock arrow, three fingers on string. Begin draw, raise on inhale, sight target, release.

She picked up the bow. Once again, the weapon was much too large and heavy for her. Thumbing the immovably taut bowstring, she scanned the wall for a smaller bow. None.

Use your wits, Grace. Make it work.

As she took up her stance, she noticed a knob for relaxing the bowstring when stored. She loosened it a bit, then tested the draw. It didn't help with the weight, but hopefully she could manage some level of propulsion.

Gripping as hard as she could, Grace nocked an arrow, raising the bow at the top of the breath. She drew, grunting with effort, and released. The arrow made it less than two meters before nosediving.

Shit.

She'd leaned forward struggling to grip the bow. She quickly pulled another arrow from the standing quiver, nocked, drew, and released. It dropped just short of the target.

Stupid, stupid, stupid.

She plucked the string. By loosening the bow string, she'd considerably shortened propelling force. She grabbed the quiver, glancing over her shoulder at Master Oran.

He was observing, expressionless.

He knows the bow is impossible. He's evaluating my determination to do well with what's at hand.

She paced forward three meters and tried again.

Hit the damn target, Grace. Even if you shove the arrow in with your hand.

The next arrow hit the wall to the side of the target. She continued shooting until the standing quiver was almost empty, hitting an outer edge of the target twice. She grabbed the remaining arrows and a shoulder quiver from the stand. She shot the last five arrows while walking toward the target.

Hit the fucking thing, Grace!

Her last two arrows, fired at eight meters, hit inside the third ring of the target. Grace realized she had forgotten to correct her bow-arm position, compensating for the bow's weight. The result became apparent the moment her adrenaline slowed as she finished shooting.

She looked down at her inside forearm. There was a ten centimeter long, broad welt of angry red, bowstring burn. Deep enough for stripes of slowly bleeding scrapes. She laughed.

I deserve that.

It stung sharply but not as much as her pride. Grace looked up at Weapons Master Oran, ready for whatever criticism he would dish out to someone so inept.

The Weapons Master looked pointedly at the weapons strewn about her. Grace bowed her head once in acknowledgement and went to retrieve her arrows and knives. She checked over all of her equipment, wiping them down, testing edges, looking for damage she might have caused, then carefully put everything in its proper place on the weapons wall.

She removed the bloodied bowstring. Seeing no replacement strings, she laid it on a table next to the board rather than rehanging it.

Grace took up a spot two paces in front of the Weapons Master, gazing past him to the wall beyond, waiting until he was ready to speak.

"I will send training gear and a schedule."

"Thank you, Master Oran."

Taking a step back, Grace turned, picking up her shoes as she departed. She felt exhilarated.

He must think there's some potential.

Or a dangerously weak link.

10.

FIRST AID

MILITARY DECORUM DID not permit sprinting down hallways. For the first time since her arrival, Grace was going to be late, a disrespectful thing she loathed. Threading her way through a forest of Guardians she felt like a child on bring-your-kid-to-work day. It would have been funny if so many hadn't turned at the scent of her arm wound.

Thinking of anything other than her dreams and the worsening effects of physical proximity to Gunnar was proving futile. Their sessions had been put on hold due to his duties, giving them both too much time to think.

It had been a thing to hide behind, as well as contribute— offering the code work to Commander Arundel. Her gut seemed to feel everything was about to change.

Distracting muscle aches were blooming everywhere. The injured arm burned badly enough to make her eyes tear.

Grace hissed to herself, "Suck it up, it's a scrape."

Gunnar looked up from his papers as she appeared,

gripping the door frame, catching her breath. A slight breeze wafted in behind her rushed entrance. Gunnar's nostrils flared.

Grace opened her mouth to apologize, "I'm—"

Crossing the room in a blur, Gunnar startled her into swearing. Holding her wrist firmly, he closely examined her arm, which looked impressive in a minor way, having had time to swell, purple, and bleed.

"What happened?"

Grace's nerves prompted a flippant response, hoping to hide her heart's pounding at his dramatic reaction.

"I'm fine. I'm sure amputation won't be necessary for several hours."

Gunnar was not amused; a growl-like rumble emanated from deep in his chest. She wisely adjusted her response. "I had my first training session with Weapons Master Oran. I didn't have enough strength, or vambraces using the bow."

"Come with me," he said.

Gunnar silently led her from his office down two floors to a supply room, mentally struggling with the intensity of his response.

Alongside writing supplies and maintenance items were cabinets of simple remedies for the few minor discomforts Fae were vulnerable to. Too much alcohol. Gas. Splinters. There were no tables or chairs in the small space. A cabinet next to a wall with charts of remedy dosages had a narrow counter.

Grace surveyed the small space while Gunnar scrutinized an inventory list, a valid excuse to avoid looking at her. There were pleasant scents of herbal unguent and powdered tinctures.

Desperate to break the silence, Grace looked along the shelves.

"I should check these for human-friendly remedies."

"That's wise, Grace. A Healer from the medical unit should discuss them with you."

She'd been remarkably lucky not to have needed so much as an aspirin. Asa had supplied any routine necessities. A large medical unit at the Stronghold handled battle and other serious injuries which rapid healing alone couldn't fix. There were Healers in the Keep Med Unit, but this was a small thing to care for.

Her tough had run out and Grace wanted to sit. She kicked her shoes out of the way, put her hands up on the Fae-height counter behind her, and jumped, scrabbling up with her heels to sit on it. It was much harder than she'd estimated. Hissing, she pushed back from the edge.

"Ow."

Gunnar glanced over to make sure she wasn't really hurt. Grace blew out a breath. Her arm, shoulders, and back protested strongly, suggesting how much pain a full-on training schedule would bring. Gunnar's mind was on more than the supply cupboards.

This is a minor wound, but eventually an injury will come...

A pang of protectiveness shot through him, underlining the direction his thoughts had traveled. A reminder of the difficulties involved.

She's so fragile.

"Grace, let me see it."

The counter height assisted his examination. The intimacy of the space, his touch, and the relaxed use of her name spurred her heart rate. She suddenly remembered he could hear her heartbeat…

Studying his face, realization came.

He takes it seriously. This injury, less significant than a paper cut for them.

Feeling brave, she tugged his sleeve.

"It's minor. Really. A little soap and water, and a kiss to make it well will fix it perfectly."

Good grief, do they kiss boo-boos here?

She watched his hands, waiting to see his response to the kiss remark.

Gunnar briefly smiled, concentrating on laying out supplies to prevent himself from intrusively reading her.

Grace sat on her hands.

This would be so much simpler if you read my mind.

Gunnar hadn't experienced casual mental boundary issues until now. His lovers had never been this close.

Even Arundel doesn't fall into this depth. We've never needed it. I've never allowed it with anyone else.

Strange terrain, this crossing of line between work and private. Between private and—this.

She understands separation of duty and—personal context—but—she's lost her framework of existence.

The unexpected twist at the end of the thought, and the magnitude of its truth caught him deeply by surprise, though Father Above, it shouldn't have. Unbelievably, he'd never considered his own response if he'd appeared on Earth. It was terrifying. The realization cut him.

Pouring water into a bowl, he surreptitiously watched her, considering. He'd fallen into the habit of focusing on who she was, rather than what. Astonishingly brave in the face of such staggering circumstance, she'd transitioned so swiftly he'd lost sight of the enormity. Her world, gone in an instant.

Mother Above—how do I forget she has absolutely no one? Nothing familiar.

Grace was poking at her wound.

"Stop that, Grace. I need to find salve, then I'll tend to it."

She sighed dramatically.

He had chosen over centuries, to be alone. She'd had it forcefully imposed in an instant. Asa was becoming a friend but she was a spy, doing her duty, fitting herself to a task.

Who would I be if I didn't have my work?

This reversal of awareness, again to something so obvious, knocked him off balance.

Grace leaned to look at the supplies.

"May I provide assistance? I can start a fire by rubbing two pieces of wood together. You can sterilize whatever instruments of torture you're using."

"You sterilize items used for torture?"

She fought the urge to laugh at his deadpanned humor. The first, ever.

"We're not utter barbarians."

Gunnar fumbled for his thread of thought.

Are we alike, fear needing what may be lost?

Gunnar had been staring at a label too long. He forced his hands to continue moving. He commanded legions yet couldn't keep it together in this tiny room with her.

His heartbeat hadn't fully slowed from its violent surge at scenting her wound, now for a different reason. The danger here was in having nowhere to hide, no witness to their interaction.

He might allow his self-control to slip.

This—this is untenable.

He mentally swore, trying to ignore the effect of Grace, inches away. Grasping for what needed to be said. Grace sat looking at the supplies on the counter, afraid he would move them to a more public area.

Speak up, you coward! He needs to know.

She straightened as he spoke.

"Pardon me."

Leaning sideways to open a cabinet above her head, his chest angled across her. She did not lean back from his closeness, inhaling the scent of his leathers, his skin. Her heart leapt into a sprint.

Enough.

Ducking under his arm Grace grabbed his belt, tugging hard into his lean, pulling him off-balance. She swiftly yanked again, forcing him to step between her knees, trusting him not to resist lest he injure her. Gunnar steadied himself then stood silently looking down, one hand braced on the cabinet overhead, the other on the counter beside her.

Raising her chin, she gravely met his eyes, searching. Grace's hand slid through his tunic closures, resting over his erratically beating heart.

She pulled his hand down from the cabinet above to cup her throat, fingers resting over her pounding pulse. Gunnar's world narrowed to her soft throat, the beautiful, depthless eyes he willingly fell into. In his world one did not offer such utterly vulnerable touch. Her life, under his hand. Everything it implied. His heart staggered. This wasn't flirting.

It was communion.

Gunnar was still.

Grace was not.

She hooked her calves behind Gunnar's legs, pulling him against her. He was wrapped in the same limbs he'd awakened to in this morning's dream.

Enough.

Bending to kiss her, he moved slowly against the softness of her lips, tasting.

Finally.

He paused, resting his cheek against hers, breath warm against her ear, a tightness within him easing. Her soft sounds at his ear returned him hungrily to her mouth.

Grace's legs tightened, breath hitching at the feel of him warm against her. His lips, breath, body.

Finally.

Grace pulled his hand up from her neck, breaking the kiss, nestling her cheek in his palm, eyes asking him in.

"Please…" she said.

Gunnar felt her soul sigh as his eyes closed. Mother Above. Her heart was completely open. She awakened, like him, in the same state, from the same dream.

He felt—everything. Grace wanted him as she wanted air. Past every fear, insecurity, self-doubt. She'd been waiting for him. She brought his hand to her breast. He was the first to sensually touch her, an echo of their dream.

Gunnar's primal response to her sharp, physical desire was an impulse to pull her from the counter and take her against the wall, as with Fae lovers past. Her skirt had rucked up her thighs when she pulled him against her. His iron-willed control, always steady under fire, was paper thin before this fire.

He knew lust. He knew infatuation. The shape and depth of this, he didn't know. He *wanted*.

Grace was starved not just for the affirming physicality of sex; she wanted his thoughts, his scent, to taste his skin. She wanted his laugh. Her listening ear pressed over his heart. To give him everything he needed. She couldn't form thoughts fast enough.

Her body wrapped tightly around Gunnar. The intensity of her mind and body's yearning rolled through him, sparking deeper response, igniting a storm of wanting—all of it.

He kissed her fiercely, stroking her cheek, neck, breast, stealing her breath, nipping her earlobes, biting her neck. She yielded, head thrown back to gasp for breath, her hands twisting in his hair, his clothing, bringing his mouth back to hers.

Crushing her to him, Gunnar's hand dropped from her breast, sliding down their bodies to squeeze and stroke her soft inner thigh, sliding it higher until he stroked against her thin undergarment, pressing harder as liquid warmth dampened the fabric.

Her response was instant and electric. Grace moaned into his mouth, vibration thrumming against him, reflexively rocking hard against his hand, arms sliding to lock around his neck. Gunnar rubbed his cheekbone along hers, hot breath on wet kisses against her throat darting throbbing sensation to his coaxing fingers.

Grace inhaled sharply, as his fingers pushed damp fabric

aside, slipping in to stroke and explore, pausing to let fingertips rest against her, barely moving.

Gunnar's thumb gently caressed, feeling the sensitive
flesh rise under his touch. His consuming kiss took her gasping, ragged breaths, the backs of his fingers pressing firmly,
against her softness. Grace's legs trembled in their grip—
struggling on the narrow counter as her body sought his.

Thwarted by her inexperience, and these unexpected,
awkward surroundings, Grace was near sobbing with escalating need and frustration as his fingers pressed, his mouth
cherishing her neck. The intensity of her emotions pierced
Gunnar, pulling him into focus to feel the rising sharpness
of her distress in not knowing how to culminate her desire
for him in this uncooperative place.

Angry with himself, he paused, holding her tightly. On
the heels of his decision to be careful with her, he'd let his
selfish want pull her to this state in this thoughtless place.
His eyes swept the narrow counter, the cold, dusty stone
floor. He had to get her away from here, somewhere safe,
and soft...

Grace's hands on his face brought him back to her. She
poured her desire into him, all remaining slender tethers of
self-doubt snapped, along with his logic.

Holding his eyes, her hand dropped to cover his, pressing
it against her, willing him to continue, injured arm sliding
between their bodies toward his lower clothing—prompting
her involuntary small sound of pain.

Gunnar stopped breathing. Withdrawing his hand from
her, he stepped back, breaking the grip of Grace's encircling
legs, and their mutual connection as cool air rushed between
their bodies.

"Grace, you're hurt…"

He'd lost his reason. He shakily exhaled a long breath, reaching for the injured arm. But Grace had bent, face in her hands, quivering in silent tears of humiliation at her ineptness, her assumption of his rejection.

Gunnar touched her face. "Grace—."

Insight flashed through him. He'd pulled away after she'd utterly opened her heart—everyone she loves, leaves. Gunnar felt the pain slicing through her and understood. The arm was nothing compared to this. He could feel her begin to ghost…

"'Grace. Look at me."

His demanding yet gentle tone drew her back to him.

"No," he said.

Rather than use words she refused to hear, Gunnar cupped her chin, intention clear in his eyes. Everything she offered, clear in hers. Her emotions shifted to align with his, easing her distress. Dim surprise at this tugged at Gunnar, then was swept aside.

He kissed her, hard, swiftly opening her shirt. Tearing the thread of ribbon clasping her bra, Gunnar slipped the garments off her shoulders. His hands moved under her thighs, lifting her against him, her legs wrapping his waist.

Grace pulled her body tightly against him, caring only that he held her, wanted her. Turning, he raised her to settle against the wall, breasts near his mouth.

After a warning glance toward her injured arm, Gunnar leaned into her, tasting her skin, reveling in her scent, mouth savoring her breasts. He sucked and softly nipped, traveling between them.

Head back, fingers in his hair, Grace surrendered to this

new pleasure, her small cries and breathless sounds spurring him on. His pressing chest further spread her legs, his hands beneath kneading her cheeks. The thin undergarment, rent by his strong, careful fingers, drifted in fragments to the floor.

Stroking the tender hollows where cheek joined thigh, he parted her gently, fingertips flirting in liquid arousal. Buzzing heat shot through her, beckoned to his touch.

Gunnar's lips pressed her skin, reveling in her responsiveness as Grace used her feet on the wall at her back to push her body into his hands and mouth. Shifting, he supported her with a single arm, hand cupping her bottom.

Grace was beyond shyness in his arms, pulling at his hair, tugging at his shoulders, breath ragged from his touch. Her eyes closed as he stroked her cheek, hand smoothing down her body until it rested between her thighs. She was swollen and hot, pressing wetly against his hand.

Resting his forehead against her a long moment, Gunnar struggled for control where none had ever been required. He could barely breathe, in his overwhelming want of her. He refused to betray her trust and desire for him with careless haste.

He would wait. He wanted only to take care of her.

He pressed and circled more insistently. She needed to cry out and would not; hand held hard against her mouth.

Writhing, spread thighs unable to grasp him, her body was forced to direct the energy to his touch. Clutching at his tunic, she moaned, muscles quivering, urgently gathering. Gunnar drew in her breast, sucking hard, teeth lightly scraping the nipple. With a gasping intake of breath, Grace's body stretched into a powerful push against him as she fell into overtaking sensation.

Gunnar quickly pinned her shoulder with his, holding her safe from bruising movement against the wall, cheek against hers. Grace's groaning cries at his ear as her hips bucked hard against him nearly pulled him into climax with her.

He listened to her heart. Coaxing, stroking, marveling at her intensity, her shaking body given over to response, until his hand rested quietly against her, feeling her throb against him in waning tremors.

His hands drenched in her scent, Gunnar turned his face into her throat, drawing deep breaths. *Mother Above*, he thought, *what a gift to share*. Then, selfishly—to have been inside her…

Grace shivered through several aftershocks before her body released her and she melted into him. Turning from the wall, he cradled her against him, sliding down the wall to sit on the floor. He brought his knees up, his face settled next to hers, sharing breath for long moments.

He was calm, settled. Fae, Human. He knew the consequences of her humanity. It didn't matter. He had long since fallen in love with every other part of Grace, her sharp intelligence, strength, humor; the list was long.

Here was the missing piece which he'd refused to acknowledge as more than fantasy. Their mutual, consuming sexual desire clicked into place, and he recognized the wholeness of Grace within him.

He would not take her as his lover. To take more from her than any lover had ever given, for he knew she would give him all. He had been waiting for her. He was unsurprised as the involuntary Shift began. The change permeated his being, marking him as Mated.

His Mate. Prefect of Intelligence, and he had not seen. His irritability when he did not see her, knowing she was near. Overreaction to perceived threats, their identical dreams. His restlessness and aggression towards his warriors.

Gunnar had seen and felt how she saw him, thought of him, loved him. Grace poured it into him, wrapped it around him like a shield. Her courage in this overwhelmed and humbled him. He pressed his forehead to hers.

"Grace, listen to me. I love you. You're my Mate."

She knew. Rising from afterglow as the words left his lips, a fierceness of heart overtook her, swept through her, changed her. She gave him her lips, saying into his breath, "Until my heart stops beating, I will love you. Mate."

She would have continued without it, but rich, decadent, joy grew, filling every empty space, healing, renewing. Gunnar, feeling the reflection of this in himself, silently agreed. His blind, punishing, warrior heart would never have recognized the state of its narrow existence, or the answer to filling it. She supplied the cause, effect, and response in language he understood.

The aftermath must be numbing her pain.

"Endorphins," Grace supplied.

Startled, he looked at her. She laughed.

"You must have known. When you're emotional, I catch glimpses of your thoughts."

He tilted his head against the wall, eyes closed. They'd keep that bit of information from Arundel for now. Grace breathed another laugh. Glimpses indeed.

Carefully pushing himself up the wall to stand without jostling her, he turned back to the counter. Slowly he lowered her onto it, hands giving a final caressing squeeze as they slid down to her calves, reluctantly bringing them up to draw on and close her shirt. There was no help for the undergarments.

Her swollen mouth, flushed cheeks, and disheveled hair nearly undid him. Forehead dropping to rest on her shoulder, his hands gripped the counter until it creaked.

"So," she said softly. "What are you doing tomorrow night?"

He laughed.

She had never heard him laugh.

Grace leaned into him, delightedly nestling. A change in the scent of his heated skin triggered an inexplicable response in her. Rubbing her cheekbone hard along his, Grace pressed in to groan a chuffing sound against his ear.

Gunnar instantly gripped her hard against him, a deep, open-mouthed growl rumbled through him, into her. Grace felt his sharp intake and exhaling whuff of hot breath against her throat, her heart thrilling in recognition. She waited unafraid, allowing him to dictate her response.

Gunnar moved slightly back, still holding her shoulders, eyes closed in concentration, breath tightly controlled. Muscle and bone Shifted under her hands, whispering of another shape, then calmed. Quiet words came from Gunnar.

"Mate... Not here—not now."

His eyes opened a hands-breadth from hers, irises vivid gold with tightly contracted pupils; fading to slate gray, pupils expanding.

He exhaled an endless breath, releasing his hold to stroke her face.

"Grace—I promise we will talk of this soon."

She nodded, feeling no need to ask more. He had

answered her subconscious question, latent from his first touch on her arrival. She let the moment slip into their future.

Gunnar turned to wash his hands in the basin of water he'd poured… a century ago?

Reaching above her for a jar of numbing salve, he felt her hands slide under his tunic. He snatched the injured arm before the leather of his tunic could rub against it but left the other free to roam. His sanity truly appeared to have vanished.

While the wound was cleaned, salved, and bandaged, Grace cursorily explored her new territory between ouches and hisses of pain. Some of them, his.

After fending off the wandering hand, Gunnar lifted her chin.

"Your arm will be painful when the salve wears off." He closed her fingers around a small vial. "Put a few drops in your tea or water. Drink it every few hours. Asa will help you."

"We'll ask the Healer to come tomorrow."

We'll. What a jewel of a word, each silently observed.

He gave her a cup of water, soothing tincture added in, then held her while her pulse slowed to normal. Drowsy, the entirety of her world centered on his encircling body's warmth, the thud of his heart under her ear, motion of his breathing against her cheek, his lips pressed to her hair.

He would carry her to her room, ordering Asa to guard her door, caring for her while he put things in order.

"I'm relieved our talk has resolved the tension between us," he said.

Grace smiled against him. Her brows knit at a new thought. "Will there be trouble?" she asked.

"All kinds of it."

She made an observation. "I don't seem to be sorry."

He laughed again.

"My uniform is toast. I'm going to live naked in your bed."

Gunnar groaned. With all his professional acuity, he would not have thought her capable of torture. Thank the Father Above he had the night to prepare. She would sleep soundly that night. He would not.

Tomorrow the entire Keep would scent them, the mark of the Mating claim. Bets would be collected. Shocked looks cast. Gunnar watched her as she was lulled to sleep by his heartbeat, unafraid of all that he was. His Mate. He'd be waiting outside Arundel's door before breakfast.

11.

Dark Ops Down

THE NEXT MORNING, Arundel opened his door to find Gunnar pacing the hallway. Hearing footsteps, he'd hoped to see the night watch with red-flagged reports on the scouts dispatched as the Keep was sealed.

"Have scouts returned?"

Uncharacteristically restless, Gunnar looked away. "I haven't checked Central yet."

For the first time, Arundel didn't know how to interpret his behavior. "What, then?" Gunnar stalled. "It can wait. Let's check the reports."

Arundel's brows raised at this awkward exchange. His nostrils flared as he scented Gunnar, studying his face.

Ah. Sergeant Woods. Becoming lovers after such intense contact is no surprise, nor is it enough to warrant this behavior...

Arundel's mind caught up with his body's senses. He was—more than shocked. Stunned. Gunnar was marked as Mated.

Arundel stepped back as the ramifications slammed into him.

Gunnar's *Mate* was a mortal Human who would die in a handful of years. At risk of death even sooner from injury, illness, or childbirth, if the latter were even possible. His heart wrenched, thinking of his personal pain. She would be his vulnerability, his liability, his necessary focus.

What has he done? How is the bond even possible? Why did I not see—prevent this?

Arundel swore.

He had noted the deepening attraction, deeming it a harmless byproduct of their prolonged Telepathic contact. He would not have spoken against them as lovers. There were no doubts concerning her allegiance to Oberon. She was a trustworthy asset, not a threat. But Mate to his spy master, his Prefect of Intelligence was another matter. He'd considered Gunnar immune to relationships which could render him tactically vulnerable.

He didn't know what to say. He put his hand on Gunnar's shoulder, then withdrew. Gunnar turned away, having watched all of this play out on Arundel's face. He didn't need Telepathy. He walked ahead of, instead of next to, Arundel through the halls to Central, giving him space to think.

Arundel couldn't remember the last time Gunnar had been involved with a female, beyond periodic, temporary lovers. His first love, though much different than Arundel's, had appeared to be his last. Gunnar's youthful foray had begun shortly after Arundel befriended him, almost two hundred years after Etana's death—Father Above, more than three hundred years ago…

Her name was Aalia. A Shield and fellow Guardian, already building a reputation on the field of battle for her faultless swordplay and bravado. After fighting side-by-side in several skirmishes with rebel factions, they fell into a rough-and-tumble relationship as lovers. Gunnar, with the inexperience of youth and the cold example of his mother, had further to fall, thinking the heat of infatuation love.

Arundel shook his head. Perversely, Gunnar had chosen a volatile female with the only Gift able to block his. Gunnar was never quite certain where he stood in their mercurial relationship.

At the time, the Northern Territory was still fighting to secede from the Southern. Gunnar and Aalia, distinguished warriors, were respected within their ranks. A short decade later the relationship had faltered and fallen when she was offered a Junior Centurion posting in the Central Protectorate. Gunnar was out on patrol when she left a note detailing her posting alongside a cherished dagger. From her, a warm goodbye.

Gunnar sucked up the pain and became his work, volunteering for the most difficult assignments, not out of despair, but to focus. Honing himself like a blade on a whetstone, he picked up intel in areas others found barren, sourcing information from impossibly sparse grounds.

Observing a crowd, he knew where the hidden danger lay, who to question for reliable information. All before he touched his Telepathy. Gunnar believed relying too heavily on one weapon was a mistake. With nothing to hold him back, he rose quickly in rank. Arundel was more than pleased to have his valued friend, also the most Gifted Prefect of Intelligence in the Territories.

Now Gunnar had undertaken the most impossible responsibility of his life, albeit for an admittedly short time. For the physical bond of Mate to have triggered was indeed puzzling. Gunnar could not be faulted for the response. What he would face when she died—Arundel could see no happy outcome. But he would not turn on his closest friend for something he did not understand.

Father Above, aid him.

Outside the door to Central, Gunnar felt Arundel's hand stop him. He turned to face his brother and Commander. He had spoken a dozen words, Arundel, less.

Arundel squeezed his shoulder.

"Brother, I'm at your side, always."

They turned to enter Central Command to find it adrenalized with a hushed buzz. Arundel put Gunnar's matter aside. The adjutant did indeed have fresh, red-flagged reports.

He handed them to Arundel.

"I was just coming to you, Commander. For immediate debrief. I thought you and Prefect Gunnar would want to run it," he said, tacitly implying it was Dark Unit spies who had returned, not Guardian scouts.

And the news was bad.

The two gaunt Dark Unit Operatives were part of two units dispatched to sweep the southern half of the territory, while two more had covered the north. They began a first-pass, oral report of their two-month mission, a command recorder swiftly transcribing. There were four Operatives in each unit.

Their bone-deep exhaustion, thinness and hollow eyes told Gunnar the cost of their intel. Lead Operative Fina began the debrief.

"We covered the first leg of surveillance in Raptor form, crisscrossing the breadth of the territory. All Shifters were downed by the Pulse sickness, allowing us to observe, dismissed as wild. The sickness caused extensive harm. Every village and town we surveilled was stricken, without exception. Many of the elderly, smaller Shifters caught in animal form, and the very young, died from its effects, or from complications afterward."

Clearing her throat, Fina continued, "In the second week, makeshift mourning streamers and cairns appeared. We began checking Tessera outposts for area reports. All Guardians were impaired to some degree. Many lay suffering where they dropped, taking days before they crawled to shelter."

Forehead now resting against a tight fist, Arundel extrapolated this scenario across the many millions of Fae likely to have been affected.

If Grace's reports are correct, the entirety of Oberon may have been struck by this devastation.

Nothing could have prevented the suffering of so many against the sun's power, but logic did nothing to ease the vast pain of his people enduring such horror. Arundel's magic clawed to get out. Shutting down the response with iron control, he focused on the operative's words.

Gunnar surreptitiously watched Arundel, calculating his own actions in the event a Shift occurred within the small space.

Fina continued, "Almost three weeks into the mission,

we observed the strongest Guardians recovering, organizing healers in mobile med units. Some were regaining use of their Gifts, but progress was slow. We recognized an emerging pattern with unusual missing Fae reports. Five stood out in their lack of detail. In each case, individuals were near others when the Pulse occurred. When victims were once again cognizant, the individuals were gone, no one saw them depart. There was no evidence of where they'd gone."

Operative Brant picked up the narrative.

"Commander, when we departed the Keep, we were traveling swiftly, covering as much territory as possible. Near the midpoint of our sweep southward, we slowed, studying details more closely and searching for evidence explaining disappearances. We discovered tracks with footwear soles, unknown to us. We heard scattered accounts of strangers who were not Fae. These strangers were alone, dispersed over broad areas of territory. All were traveling while populations were still down with sickness. Descriptions of size and physical characteristics suggest they were Human. I take full responsibility for lapses which may have led to earlier discovery."

Arundel dismissed the idea, with a motion to continue. "No training could have prepared you for this."

Looking puzzled over the next point, Brant looked to Gunnar, while addressing Arundel. "Commander, significance is unknown, but in the collection of these reports there were none mentioning Humans suffering from Pulse sickness. There were two reports of Humans who entered downed villages attempting to give aid, caring for livestock then departing with food."

Brandt's voice broke in a fit of coughing. Touching his shoulder, Fina took over the report.

"Reports emerged as more recovered mobility, of strange Fae in the Territory. Different vocalizations, manner of dress, most were evasive in their behavior. At the three-quarter point of our sweep, we were assessing Pulse impact, tracking missing Fae, searching for Humans, and investigating a potential security threat emerging from the south. We discussed whether our unit of four would be more effective as two units, to widen our sweep into overlapping patrols. No area would be left uncovered. We had seen no other operatives or scouts. Information gathering was shifting from passive assessment to defensive surveillance."

Fina straightened, addressing Arundel. "Commander, on my authority, we split. Operatives Valdis and Adana headed on an agreed route south, while we continued on our original course, our plan was to meet as we turned northward."

Fina inhaled deeply, exhaling slowly to steady her thoughts and voice.

Arundel waited patiently for her to continue.

"We spent the next two days sweeping every village and farm we passed. The further south we traveled, the fewer fresh encounters with Humans or strangers were reported, until there were none. We found cold trail evidence of their passage, but they were gone. We reached the southern border of the Protectorate, where we came across a small fishing village."

Fina looked to Arundel.

"We found a male with a very young child crawling through a woody area nearby. The male's legs were broken. Both had been beaten. He told us a heavily scarred male of unfamiliar ethnicity came to their village with a group of rebel warriors. Several were not Fae. They were torturing and slaughtering with no apparent goal."

Her voice became detached, a training reflex.

"Shifting to raptor form, we entered the village to assess whether action could be taken. We found the invaders in the village square. The male leader's features were similar to those in the extreme Northwestern Wastes. Straight black hair, ruddy brown skin, dark eyes, heavily built frame. He had severe scarring about the face and ears. His followers called him Morse or Mors. There were two villagers left alive and thirty-eight hostiles."

Arundel looked to Gunnar, his rage mirrored by his brother.

"The Gifted female he tortured longer, coercing her into giving him her Gift. He left the other to his followers; one of whom told the dying male it was an honor to die for the most powerful male in history, he would conquer Oberon. He appeared to have said too much. Mors stared at him— the follower drove his fist through his own rib cage, pulling out his heart."

Fina blinked in slow-motion.

Brandt turned to them, relieving her.

"The entire village had been slaughtered and left where they fell. Operatives Valdis and Adana were there. Dead. Flayed and nailed to a wall. We returned to the injured male and child. He had succumbed to blood loss. The child followed him after our attempts to aid her failed."

Arundel and Gunnar sat processing what they had heard. Gunnar looked to Arundel, silently asking for the Operatives to rest before debriefing the return trip. If there were events of major significance, they would have continued directly into them. Arundel nodded.

The recorder finished writing. Rising, Arundel went to the Operatives, a few quiet words to each. The adjutant stood ready to take them to food and rest.

Arundel studied the wall maps while the room cleared. Rubbing his jaw, he turned to Gunnar.

"Clearly this is not a case of rebels with a despotic leader. Whoever this Mors is, he's a different sort of being. To have multiple Gifts… I've never seen the ability to destroy a body in such a way, nor a tyrant who would slaughter an entire village while taking time to torture innocents. This is not simple barbarism. Preliminary analysis?"

Gunnar's thoughts were grim.

"I agree, Mors is something new. His butchery announces his arrival, who and what he is. And as the dead follower suggested, he's come to rule." He gripped the back of his neck. "His Gifts—the threat appears unquantifiable. How has he broken natural law? Assessment of the breadth and strength of his arsenal must be our primary focus. Are there others like him?"

Rocking forward, Gunnar rose to trace fingers over their scouts' routes on the map. Meeting Arundel's eyes, he nodded to their mutual unspoken thought.

"The scouts. Until now, I thought it possible they were assisting in the aftermath. Mors may have captured them. It's likely he left Fina and Brant alive to report back to us."

Gunnar tapped the symbols denoting strongholds.

"The southernmost Strongholds; we must brief them immediately, and the others in quick succession. If we lose a

Stronghold to him, the base and the resources it would give him could be catastrophic."

He turned back to Arundel. "Our knowledge of Humans – we need to issue protocols, sending them to all Protectorates. They're likely experiencing fear and confusion and do not have our in-depth knowledge. Sharing intelligence with leadership we trust may be crucial. The Humans won't know who to trust."

Gunnar sat heavily, spreading his hands on the table in front of him.

"What is it?" asked Arundel sharply. "There's more."

Gunnar met Arundel's eyes. "Brother. The missing Fae. They may be on Earth."

12.

AWAKENING

THE NEXT MORNING Grace awakened slightly disoriented. She looked at the plain walls of her room. Nothing had changed. Muscles were stiff, her injured arm burned, but her heart was also somehow involved. She tried to stretch.

Her body gave a strong response.

Um, no.

If there had been dreams, they must have been nice. There was unfamiliar euphoria kicking around inside. She lay still, trying to orient herself. There was a light rap on the door.

"Come," she said, pulling the sheet up to her neck.

Asa entered, dropping into the chair she'd drawn next to the bed. She extended a cup of morning tea. Grace waited for an explanation. As a general rule, Asa didn't provide room service. They met in the dining hall.

"Good morning," Asa said.

Grace accepted the tea, sipping loudly.

"Am I late? I'm still waking up."

Asa reached to brush Grace's hair out of her eyes.

"Prefect Gunnar said you might be a little fuzzy this morning."

Her lips pressed in a smile that appeared to have several hours of talk behind it. Her eyes scanned Grace, stopping on the bandaged arm.

"Let me help you sit up so you can drink your tea."

Puzzled by Asa's uncharacteristic behavior, Grace began to scoot upright for a game of Twenty Questions, then hissed at her burning arm, some moderate complaining in her joints, and sudden notice of mild, but odd soreness in unusual places.

Memory suddenly remembered its job and the previous day flashed through her mind, start to finish. Beginning with finish.

Her hands flew to cover her face, then slid down far enough to look at Asa, eyes huge.

Asa let her smile grow a tiny bit larger. "Drink this, Grace, or I'll be in serious trouble."

Pain meds first, answers after. Grace drained the cup, recognizing the slight tang of tincture.

"What time is it?" asked Grace.

"Midmorning."

"Where is he?"

It felt a daring thing to ask. No name or titles.

"Unlike you, he had work waiting for him this morning. You're not getting out of bed except for necessity breaks."

Grace lifted her arm to examine the bandage. It would need changing soon, but she'd never been so happy to have an injury in her life. Omniscient Asa obviously knew everything, but Grace needed a private moment for more than use of the washroom. Standing, she tried to stretch again. Her body allowed it but sharpened the edge of muscles she hadn't known existed. She looked down at a linen shift she didn't recognize.

"Need help?" Asa asked.

"No. Thank you."

Grace gently closed the washroom door behind her, leaning against it as a tidal wave of emotion flooded her. Forcing herself to put the things of deepest importance to her away for the moment, she thought over the previous day. A few blushes came and went.

She studied herself in the mirror. There was a light rub burn along one cheekbone and a raspberry shaded bite mark on her neck, with a few lighter ones trailing downward. Her jaw dropped.

Really? Hickeys?

She removed the shift, letting her eyes drift over the rest of her. Her nipples were particularly rosy. The left, lightly scraped. She felt a thread of electricity shoot southward at that one. She was holding her breath by the time she noticed the light finger bruises on her thighs.

She turned the shower on, took care of necessities, and stepped under the water with a hiss. Her back felt slightly sunburned. None of these things were remotely serious or uncomfortable. They were just new. Not only newly made, but a new experience. Some parts were washed more gently than others.

After she dried off, untangled her hair, and brushed her teeth, she realized she was tired, ready to climb back into bed and nap. Embarrassing, if you thought about it.

Asa was waiting, watching Grace cross the room, ready to help if she wobbled the slightest bit. She'd changed the bedclothes while Grace showered, shaking and piling the pillows so she could sit up.

Grace gave her a startled look. "Are you my nursemaid this morning?"

"Just following orders," Asa sighed.

Grace, remembering who she worked for, covered her mouth and laughed.

"Seriously?"

"Seriously."

Both of them laughed. Asa hovered while Grace got back in bed. "I wonder if we should remove that now that it's wet," she said, nodding toward the bandage.

Waiting until Grace pulled the covers back up, Asa opened the door just enough to tell the Guardian, *the Guardian*, to send for a Healer.

She reseated herself next to Grace. "May I ask?"

"Well, who else am I going to talk to? My personal spy won't tell anyone but her boss." She squeezed Asa's hand. She knew their friendship was genuine. "Most of it is above your pay grade," Grace teased.

Asa's face had run through several expressions as Grace said this. Unexpected from a spy, thought Grace.

"Mated."

"He told you?" Grace asked.

Asa raised her brows.

"He didn't have to. It changes our scent. It's permanent, until we die."

Grace pondered this as though it were fresh news,

shaking her heart, telling it to *believe*… waiting for another question or teasing remark.

Asa's focus had drifted from Grace's face. She'd been assessing what this meant since Prefect Gunnar sent for her last night, issuing several orders in his usual stern manner. Until shock had registered on Asa's face. He had paused, studying her.

"Operative Asa, are you going to have difficulty with this? Your assignment remains the same; the priority shifts to guarding Grace."

Grace, Asa had noted, not Sergeant Woods. Her stunned senses were correct. *Answer now*, she thought.

"Prefect Gunnar, there are no problems. I would have and *will* guard her with my life."

He saw that she meant it, not only because of his order, which would have been enough, but she truly cared for Grace. Next to Gunnar, she was the closest to her. Their friendship was genuine.

"Asa." Grace brought Asa's attention back to her. "I have so many questions."

"Yes. As do I," Asa replied.

Her lips parted on a teasing remark. She stopped, tilting her head, rising from the chair to face the door. When a light knock came, she opened it, ushering in an older female with a kind face. She set her bag down on the bedside table and nodded to Grace.

"I'm Ahma, Grace. May I look at your wound?"

Startled by the familiarity at using her first name, but charmed by the warmth of the female, she nodded. "Of course, Ahma, thank you."

She turned toward her, extending her arm. Ahma cradled

Grace's arm, her touch light as she undid Gunnar's bandaging of her arm.

"I must ask a few questions about your physiology."

"Of course," said Grace.

"You have no self-healing ability? How would you care for this injury?"

Grace looked it over before answering.

"Since a bowstring was the cause, debris is unlikely. I'd flush it with clean water and soap. I'm healthy and well cared for, so it should heal quickly. Perhaps a week to ten days. There may be light scarring."

Grace turned over her other wrist, holding it out to show a scar.

"This was cleanly broken; the bones properly set within a few hours. It healed in just under two months and was weak for two weeks after."

Ahma examined the break, gently probing where the bones met and healed.

Nodding, Ahma replied, "We heal in a similar manner. The difference is time. It would be wise for me to learn all you will share."

"Infection is our greatest enemy," Grace said. "A small wound like this, perhaps not, but a few millimeters deeper; if I could not clean it, could become infected and eventually poison my blood." Grace paused. "I agree, it would be good to discuss more when you've time. It's possible there are more Humans here."

"I would be honored, Grace. Now, allow me to care for your arm."

She opened her case. Thoroughly swabbing Grace's wound with boiled linen, she reapplied the numbing salve.

"We should bandage this until tomorrow, to prevent rubbing against clothing or bed linens; then leave it off to dry the wound." Noting Grace's cup of tea next to the bed, as she wrapped a new bandage, Ahma inquired, "Is the tincture working? Prefect Gunnar's basic medicine appears well remembered."

Grace knew better than to look at Asa.

She had a question for Ahma but debated asking with Asa present. Ahma saw the question cross her face and patiently waited. If Grace asked Asa to step outside, she'd hear anyway. She might as well abandon her inhibitions. This concerned not only her, but Gunnar.

"I'm not familiar with your methods to prevent pregnancy. I'm assuming we are enough alike that I should take precautions."

Ahma looked thoughtful. "It would be wise to examine any differences in your cycle, fertility, gestation, and childbirth. Our self-healing wanes in pregnancy so a child may grow without the body rejecting it. That may make our pregnancies more alike. I would like to be thoroughly familiar with these things long before you need assistance."

Ahma nodded. "Perhaps we should give your Mate the contraceptive. We do not know enough yet, if it will affect you correctly, or if ingredients are safe for you. Do you desire a tincture I have for yesterday? I think it safe."

"There is no need, thank you, and for your care of my arm."

Ahma repacked her bag and rose, looking down at Grace with a smile. "I look forward to speaking with you again."

Ahma departed, softly closing the door behind her. Asa resumed her seat, obviously struggling to hold her tongue.

Grace examined the method of Ahma's bandage wrapping. Then smoothed her bedcovers.

"Honestly Asa, for a spy you need to work on your poker face."

Asa choked out a laugh. "Grace! Prefect Gunnar sent for me last evening; you were sleeping in your bed, and he was marked as Mated. You have pleasure marks on you, but you don't need the tonic. I'm more surprised and confused than at any point of my existence."

Grace burst out laughing, causing several muscle twinges.

"Do you want to talk? If not, I will leave you to rest."

Grace loosed a deep sigh.

"Yes, I need some female time. Then I could use a nap. My mind is spinning as much as yours."

Leaning forward, Asa picked up Grace's hand.

"This changes nothing in our relationship. As for my work, I'll be a bit closer, physically. You'll need to check with me before you run off beyond—a certain distance. Once the Keep is opened, I'll always be close by. Not stepping on your heels, but—near."

Grace's brows rose. "That sounds as though you're my guard."

"I'm your Personal Guard, Grace. It's protective, not containment or—intelligence gathering."

Her mouth quirked imagining the moment Grace would discover Asa had been assigned to her since the day she arrived.

"Why is that necessary? It feels excessive," Grace said.

"You're the Prefect of Intelligence's Mate. It's not my place to explain all this entails, but he wants you safe. It is a wonderful and Mother Above blessed thing that we are friends. I would have taken this position regardless, but I personally care that you are safe, and to be ordered to spend time as your shadow is no hardship for me." She squeezed Grace's hand.

Thinking this over, Grace raised troubled eyes to Asa.

"I make him vulnerable, don't I? My inability to protect myself… I never thought of how this would impact his position." She put a hand to her mouth. "I never thought—"

Asa gently pulled Grace's hand away.

"He knew every possible aspect concerning his decision. Think of who he is. And his body reacted involuntarily. If I were you, I would take that as the clearest demonstration of love he could possibly make. He has never been known to have even a long-term relationship. Not that we openly discuss the topic. But Mated, Grace, it's a precious thing."

Grace let it sink in. There was no bottom to that well.

"Why did Ahma call me by my first name?"

"When you become Mated, if you do not hold other titles, your other names are left behind. You are Grace. Prefect Gunnar's Mate, or his other rank and titles in public, where appropriate." Thinking of Grace's military rank, she elaborated. "If you acquire titles, they will precede your name. Though your Human rank is gone it is not a lessening of who you are. Does it make you uncomfortable? You are the first of your kind. I'm certain changes would not be an outstanding thing."

"There is nothing difficult about this arrangement. I'm the first—that's a staggering thought."

"No one really knows what happened to the Human lines in our histories. The stories diverged and disappeared between centuries."

Grace considered this, contrasting it with current pop culture on earth.

"Humans have innumerable legends, varying in type from one continent and culture to another. There are festivals where people pretend to be Fae, have magic, dress up as them." Grace giggled. "I hope that's not offensive. You're very swoon-worthy. I'll confess, I've read—more than a few, very smutty books set in Fae worlds."

Laughter faded.

"My Grandmother Lilli gave me the idea of you. It was an escape from the complexity of my life."

Asa listened carefully throughout these revelations, marking several points for questions, and one or two to keep to herself. "Pretend to be Fae? How? How would they know what Fae look like? What magic is? What is swoon-worthy? And what is a smutty book?"

Grace laughingly explained. Asa thought the details funny, but her analytical mind was interested in why the idea of Fae was so deeply embedded and fresh on Earth—indeed, at all— down to their ear shape and certain Gifts, whereas Humans were distant and imprecise memories on Oberon.

While Grace slept, she would be on duty outside her door. She would send the Guardian to the Document Archive to gather anything the keeper could find on Human legends.

"Perhaps you should rest a while. Do you need anything? You slept through breakfast, are you hungry?"

"I *am* tired. I'm sure I'll be hungry later, but a nap sounds perfect."

Grace slid down under the covers, adjusting the pillows. She shook her head.

"What?" Asa asked.

"I can't get used to the idea of you guarding me."

Asa rose to leave, rolling her eyes. A gesture learned from Grace. Gently closing the door, she scanned the hallway for anything unusual, then took up position before the door, dispatching the Guardian to put in her Human histories request, and a second thread that had occurred to her; a search for epidemics similar to Pulse sickness, around times of human sightings.

Asa resumed her position. She didn't understand how things had escalated to this point so quickly, or indeed at all. She had suspected Grace and Gunnar would become lovers, happy for her if they did, knowing he would be careful with her. But this—this was unheard of, even with Fae. There were a few scattered instances of instantaneous attraction turning to love, but making the Mating bond so quickly…

She would not tell Grace how dangerous it was for the Prefect to have such a vulnerable Mate. Unable to protect herself. Unable to heal. Asa had become increasingly disturbed as she listened to Grace detailing human reactions to injuries with Ahma.

She needed to learn every aspect of Grace's vulnerabilities. She would speak to Healer Ahma privately, as Grace's Personal Guard. Her life depended upon Asa when not with Gunnar. Assessing external threats would require her absolute focus.

Grace will be a target for every enemy who knows of her existence.

Asa's work was now all-consuming, if only for a handful of years. Her empathy for Prefect Gunnar also ran deep. He had faced this with full knowledge that it would not be long until the time of losing her, before his body had responded.

She shook her head, tears pricking her eyes. They needed their Lover's Moon before all else.

Asa closed her eyes, thinking of her dead and missing fellow Operatives. Sorrow came too quickly, and in unpredictable circumstance. She hoped Grace and Gunnar would have their time before he must leave to oversee the trouble brewing in the south.

Asa would protect Grace, but she could not shield her heart.

13.

New Moon

"THE MISSING FAE, they may be on Earth."

Gunnar's agonized summation of the situation bit sharply into Arundel. The pieces fell together.

"Of course. Father Above. It's logical that whatever this is, it's not one-way. There's no way to reach them, rescue or help them. They may as well be in the Mother's arms." *It might be better if they were.*

Arundel's hands, gripping the edge of the table, appeared to flicker, his body rising out of the chair as a wave moved down his spine, distorting bone and muscle as it passed through him.

He felt Gunnar's hands on his shoulders, steadying him.

Gunnar said nothing, his presence giving Arundel an anchor to his Fae body as he again calculated the room space, should his brother lose control of the Shift.

After a time, Arundel's breathing evened out, a sheen of sweat over his skin. He was endlessly grateful that Gunnar understood. Preventing a Shift was becoming more difficult with every disturbing new piece of intelligence. To witness the devastation of his people, unable to help them. On the heels of the Dark Ops report, he was close to losing control.

"Tomorrow, we open the Keep. We cannot wait for scouts or Dark Ops any longer. It's time I visit the strongholds. I'll take four Dark Unit who are swift enough to keep up. You choose." Gunnar understood the ramifications of Arundel's words.

"Arundel, allow me to go. It's too soon for you to risk exposure."

"Brother, I'll Shift only to travel at night. No one knows to look; the Chimera is Shielded, and a Seer to see the way."

Arundel rested a hand on Gunnar's shoulder. "The people need reassurance their Protectorate stands, that I care for them. I *must* see them, share their grief, give comfort. Their pain is tearing me apart. I cannot stop the Shift much longer."

"I understand, brother. I will do whatever you ask," Gunnar said.

Arundel squeezed his shoulder, eyes shifting to the large Territory wall map.

"I'll leave late tonight. Thank the Father Above, there's a new moon."

Gunnar agreed. They needed the concealing darkness. "All will be ready."

They rose from the table to leave. Arundel met his brother's eyes, squeezing his shoulder.

"To new moons and dark nights. The Lover's Moon. I suggest you make use of it."

Inclining his head, a corner of his mouth lifted. As

Arundel left the room Gunnar glanced back at the table, verifying no reports had been left.

There were two sets of five, deep gouges in the edge of the table. He'd been so focused on how to contain Arundel if he Shifted, he hadn't heard them made.

He sent two Dark Unit Centurions who quietly destroyed and replaced the table. No questions were asked.

Grace slept until early evening. As she began to stir, Asa knocked, entering with a tray wafting mouth-watering scents.

"I would kiss you, but I think I'm drooling."

"Will you forever provide opportunity for me to mock you?" Asa asked.

Laughing, Grace went to wash the sleep from her eyes. Asa pulled a table from the corner, and another chair. After carefully scenting everything, she set out the food and drink, then sat with her back to the wall, facing the door. Grace emerged from the washroom to see Asa leaning back in her chair, laughter in her eyes.

"Nice nap?"

"Yes."

She didn't admit what had awakened her. Reconsidering, she rolled her eyes with a sigh, realizing she was never going to have any privacy with Asa. *Scent is everything,* should be a Fae motto. It probably was.

She tried not to wolf down bites of stewed chicken and bread while questioning Asa.

"What am I going to do for clothes? My uniform is no longer appropriate. Or useable," she teased.

"I'll have something very soon. I've finally found someone in the Keep with seamstress skills. Clothing should arrive shortly."

Asa wiped gravy from Grace's chin before she could jerk away.

"After dinner we'll pack your things and move you home to Prefect Gunnar's rooms. We can get you settled before sleep time."

Putting down her spoon, Grace realized it was a ridiculously obvious thing, which hadn't yet occurred to her. Her heart thrilled.

"Oh!"

"Yes, oh."

Asa's grin was wicked.

"Brat, this is new to me!"

Asa teased. "Not for long."

More than ever, Grace was grateful their easy familiarity. Because it was awkward when your dreams come true. And wonderful to have a friend to share it with.

Asa observed the emotions rippling across Grace's expressive face. She was so easy to read. Asa hoped it was only because of their close friendship. Grace must eventually keep her emotional tells in check. When she emerged back into the Keep, she'd be facing astonished and curious Fae. There was no reason to tell her now. Let her enjoy the Lover's Moon. Such a propitious thing. If their coupling weren't so strange, she would have said the celestial bodies had aligned for them.

"Eat. You missed breakfast and lunch. It's better to have food in your stomach with your tea if you don't want to be sleepy while we pack, and I'm sure your arm is painful."

Grace flexed her injured arm and winced. She blew a razzberry at Asa, who never having seen this gesture, burst out laughing.

"What is that? It's like an infant noise."

"I never thought about it, but that's likely where it came from." Grace laughed. "We use it to tell someone they're annoying."

"Brat? Also, a child's expression?"

The more Grace thought about it, the more she realized how many gestures or reactions originated with babies and toddlers. She was hiccupping with laughter when she heard firm knocking on the door.

Asa flashed to the door, a hand indicating Grace was to stay still before Grace heard the final knock. She opened it carefully and was handed a neatly folded stack of clothing and a pair of low boots.

"Must you do that?" asked Grace, wide-eyed. "You scared the shit out of me."

"Now there's a nice expression. I didn't recognize their scent. I'm sorry I startled you. They're from a part of the Keep I rarely go."

Grace must get used to it; this was as mild as her defensive posture would be. Soon she would train Grace in active engagement with her in times of danger. When to drop flat while Asa assessed a threat, to follow directions without question, hand signals. She would have a thorough brief with Prefect Gunnar before then. They would work up to Asa finally showing Grace the Gift she was so curious about. Asa could Travel a fair distance carrying one passenger, shorter with two, but Grace would always be her first priority. She was grateful it was a strong Gift to aid in keeping Grace safe.

Asa returned to her seat, pointing at the food to encourage Grace to eat while she went over each article of clothing, feeling edges and seams for anything sharp that could be poisoned, scenting for anything dangerous on the fabric. She covered her actions by appearing to check the cut and quality of the workmanship, then showing them to Grace.

There was a light-gray tunic, made of kitten-soft wool. Loosely cut with a softly cowled neck, which Asa demonstrated could be wrapped around the neck if cold. Thick but soft, narrow leather pants, with seaming and reinforcement in the knees to make it easy to move and softer to kneel. Grace thought of being able to shoot a bow from one knee. Much more stable. They had a simple closure at the waist.

Socks of the same wool as the tunic, but finer knit, and the supple leather boots, rising just above her ankle. The underclothes consisted of linen camisoles and brief shorts, the material soft and breathable under the more substantial overclothes. Simple. Comfortable, Durable. Perfect. No elastic, spandex, tight bands, or high heels in sight.

Grace finished eating and washed her hands before examining the clothing. The tincture had eased her arm pain. She stretched luxuriously.

"I feel like Cinderella, only better. I'll tell you her story when we're lazing about."

Asa smiled indulgently.

"Shall I pack? It's not much, mostly papers."

Bringing her few belongings to the table and a basket from the wardrobe, Grace looked over several filled journals, a thick sheaf of notes from her tutoring with Asa, maps and information she jotted down to think through for her sessions with Gunnar. Those sessions were likely to be a bit different now. Perhaps difficult to stay on task.

Gunnar had placed her sergeant stripe patches, name tag, and ribbons on the corner table. There were no other signs of her uniform. The back of the shirt, and some of the seams must have come apart against the wall. She held the small handful of insignia close, deeply touched that he would think to save these things for her. She had to sit down for a moment with a hand shielding her face as the full impact of the past few days shocked, then warmed her blood.

Oberon's form of married, to someone she deeply loved. A handsome, Telepathic Fae, who miraculously felt the same about her, even while knowing her better than she knew herself. It seemed impossible.

Overwhelmed with the significance of it all, she wrapped arms about herself, drawing a few deep breaths to bring her back to Asa.

Asa's heart tweaked, to see Grace's happiness. Few things were as joy-filled as watching new love opening. Asa gave her a moment to recover, then pointed at the sheaf of papers.

"Are these private? May I look at them while you're dressing?"

Grace looked them over as she put the diaries and the saved bits of military past into the basket.

"Certainly. They're not an exciting read. They'll put you to sleep before I'm done and back."

Grace padded off to the washroom with her armful of clothes. Asa heard faucets running as she examined the stack of papers, scanning each one and setting them aside. By the third page she felt a growing conviction that Grace had the sharp attention to detail one would want in a person training for Intelligence work. She retained almost every word heard.

Asa flipped through several sketches, until one brought her to a halt. She drew a sharp breath. Grace had sketched the Bunker. The hair stood up on the back of her neck as she studied the drawing and the map below it. It was identical to the Keep in layout and size.

Even the entirety of Dark Unit Command was accurately depicted. Those not assigned there were unaware of its size, beyond a few offices along several corridors separating it from mainstream areas. She must suggest Prefect Gunnar classify that one.

The sketch of Central Command was detailed with much Asa didn't understand, but she recognized everything Grace had attempted to describe. Grace's desk, the Wall, the commanders' offices upstairs, the hallways leading to the tunnel, security checkpoints, and where she'd been standing when the Pulse hit. Her stomach clenched. The enormity of what had staggered Gunnar, now hit Asa. How would she have reacted in the same circumstances? To find herself there? It was staggering.

She flipped to another. It was Grace's home. Tall, narrow, stone-sheathed homes with flowers in boxes beneath windows. People walked by with small, personal animals on tethers. That must be Ellie sitting on the stairs.

Asa felt her throat tighten at Grace's uncomplaining loss of her sister. The next page was a head-and-shoulders portrait of Ellie, looking over her shoulder at the viewer. Curling hair, in a fat braid over her shoulder. Their unique eyes. A dusting of freckles on her nose, a sweet smile.

Though they were twins, Grace had mothered this girl

from an early age, with a maturity forced by repeated tragedy. Grace's love could be felt in every line. Grace's description of those arriving with notification of her death was devastating. Yet Asa had only sensed her grief a few times.

There was so much here. Grace's intense emotions ran deep, while Asa had considered them too easily read on her face. The analytical side of Asa saw the tactical use for everything.

Many of these traits also made her a good and fit Mate for Gunnar. She instinctively knew Grace would show no fear when he left for dangerous missions or battlefields, facing her fears in private.

Asa was adding depth and definition to the Grace she knew. Her work, her home, her family. So much information in six sheets of paper. She flipped another two, hearing Grace finishing up in the washroom.

The last one was Gunnar. She had caught him looking at a wall map, a report in hand, his mind obviously not on his work. In the margins of the sketch were quick studies of his hands, him glancing at her, and one of his hands cupping her cheek while reading her. Asa quickly covered the picture with the others, in original order and placed them back in the stack exactly in place. The picture was too private for her to view.

The washroom door opened to Grace in her new clothes, grinning. "I love them. Asa they're so comfortable!"

She bounced on her toes.

"I can't believe the boots fit so perfectly! If you knew what women go through to find shoes that fit! Now that I think of it" —she laughed— "these are the only custom footwear I've ever had." She spun around, modeling her outfit.

"One more thing," Asa said. She held up a belt.

A light harness. It crossed front to back, angled over one shoulder between her breasts, clipping to a ring on the waist belt at her hip. It was made to attach any number of things she might need. It spread the weight of whatever was carried.

Grace watched Asa adjust the straps and buckles until it fit perfectly, running her fingers over the precisely stitched, supple leather.

"This is beautiful work. It's a utility belt? A civilian version of yours and Gunnar's?"

"Yes. We'll talk of its many uses soon."

"I love it. It makes me look tough," Grace said.

"*I* certainly wouldn't take you on."

Grace would have lessons in defending herself with a dagger, which would live in a scabbard at her hip. The dagger would likely be from Gunnar's mother and would have his sigil on it. The first of many actions to keep Grace safe, by visibly identifying her as Gunnar's Mate. This added protection as well as risk. Pragmatically, Grace's size, build and round ears would be a fairly loud indicator of who and what she was.

As Grace packed the last of her things, Asa stepped out, ordering the nearby Guardian to the door. Then Asa swiftly walked to Gunnar's rooms and thoroughly searched them. Returning for Grace, she notified Guardians to keep the way clear.

Asa insisted she stay outside while Grace explored her new home, immediately dispatching a Guardian with a one-word message to Gunnar—*Home.*

Grace slowly turned in the center of the main room, taking everything in. Cocooned in the warm light was a very large bed, which looked surprisingly luxurious. In addition to the fine linen sheets and wealth of pillows, was a fluffy duvet, with furs spilling across it. She forced her eyes to keep moving before she could stop to dive in.

It was quite cool in temperature, which delighted Grace, coming from a colder climate. She hadn't realized until now; they must have heated her room to accommodate her light uniform. There were wall hangings woven with beautiful designs. Some were stories, and one jewel-toned tapestry she recognized as the emblem of the Northeastern Protectorate.

A pair of inviting upholstered chairs and footstools stood in one corner, a table between them, holding a small stack of books. An open door next to them revealed a study. Large maps covered the walls with bookcases below, and a heavy desk facing outward toward the bed. She didn't go in. She'd rather Gunnar showed it to her. A thick, woolen rug covered most of the main room's stone floor.

A large wardrobe had shelves of neatly folded clothes. Gunnar's dress uniform, several everyday uniforms, personal items, another outfit for Grace. A match to the one she wore with a bluish gray tunic, and a night shift hung neatly from a rod. Underthings were in drawers below. A pair of knee boots with heavier treads, suggested winter treks.

More books and a water carafe sat on a small table next to the bed. Grace was drawn to a valet dummy wearing Gunnar's well-worn battle armor. It was similar to tactical body armor, but there were steel deflection reinforcements in critical areas. Several swords and other weapons hung or stood on a rack near it. Some of the deep scars in the leather made her shiver. She ran a hand over the steel shoulder guard.

Her Mate was a warrior. She accepted that he would fight. Grace knew to show him pride and courage, never weakness when she saw him off. Veterans at home had spoken of how their loved ones weeping, begging them not to go could sap their resolve and focus needed to fight.

Her feet carried her to the washroom doorway, where she stood in delight. Centered on the long wall was a large bathtub, big enough to accommodate his height, perhaps both of them? Piles of towels and another rug lay next to it. An open shower stood just beyond, the fragrance of his soap present on a wooden bench against its wall. The commode sat in the corner.

Opposite the tub was the sink, and a mirror with small shelves below holding toothbrushes, hairbrushes, soap, a razor, and Gunnar's contraceptive tonic. Grace's eyes lingered on the bottle, a flush of warmth spreading to appropriate places. It suggested their future together, a thing she struggled to fully grasp.

This is home.

Butterflies in her chest settled.

She returned to sit in a reading chair and began looking over books until Asa's distinctive knock.

Grace responded, "Come."

"What do you think? You've prowled through everything?"

"Not his study, but yes, everything! It's lovely. Who knew warriors were so pampered?" Grace said.

Asa's mind flashed through four centuries of lying injured in cold mud, scouting territory thick in ice and snow, fighting in a melee, in rain, on a bloody battlefield. His regular quarters were spartan. These rooms were among those set aside for visiting dignitaries and had been carefully made over through the night and morning for his Mate. Her logic softened its grip. She must make allowances for Grace's innocence.

"Asa, thank you. I see your thoughtful touches everywhere. And you had more clothes made!"

"You couldn't have only one set. After the Keep opens, we'll have a seamstress and cobbler in to fit you with a proper wardrobe."

"I can't wait to see the villages and countryside. I've dreamed of them."

Asa knew the Prefect would assess conditions outside the Keep with a thorough security sweep before Grace was allowed outside.

"We're all looking forward to it. In the meantime, there's much to do."

She gestured to a nightstand on the far side of the bed, which held books Grace had been studying, and a lovely writing desk she'd missed on the far wall. It faced outward, toward Gunnar's in his office. She loved the thoughtfulness behind the placement. If he were working, she could watch him from her desk or the bed. She could not think of a more intimate touch. She never wanted to take her eyes from him if he were home.

Asa took Grace's hands in hers. "There's a New Moon tonight. We call it the Lover's Moon. It's unusual to have a Mating occur that falls exactly on this time. Fate has given you a special gift."

Kissing Grace's forehead, Asa turned to leave. She paused at the door.

"Prefect Gunnar may be very late tonight. You might consider resting."

She had the tact and affection not to take the comment further. "I'll be here if you need me."

She softly closed the door behind her.

Closing her eyes, Grace pinched herself, then laughed at the ridiculous gesture. Truth be told, it was hard not to squeal. Taking Asa's advice, she unclipped the knife belt, undressing to slip on a night shift, neatly putting the new clothes away.

She examined her reflection while brushing her hair. It was easier to be objective after months away from all forms of media—but what did Gunnar see when he looked at her? She'd hardly thought about beauty since her arrival, other than admiring others. He didn't seem to mind her outward differences any more than those of her mind. He'd responded with pleasure to her softness, her shape, just as she was. It made her feel beautiful.

The thoughts prompted her back to the bedroom, setting the lights to soft dimness. Grace climbed into the high bed, giggling at her inability to resist rolling in the silky furs, before slipping under the duvet. Feeling a featherbed on top of the firm mattress, she wondered if it was for her. She was unable to picture him using one. She nestled into it, her eyes roaming the room. A pang of anxiety hit her stomach, suggesting that at any moment she would awaken to her alarm, alone in her grandmother's handed-down bed. How could such happiness come to her? Maybe it was time to give fate another chance.

At this time yesterday she'd been alone with Gunnar, and her world had shifted on its axis. She pointedly removed her shift and dropped it on the floor. A promise fulfilled. Grace snuggled deep into the wonderful bed. As she eased into sleep, she pulled Gunnar's pillow against her.

This is real.

14.

HOMING

ENTERING HIS OFFICE, Gunnar closed the door, resting against it. Breathing deeply, he allowed his muscles to relax by degrees. Two hours minutely sifting through mission-specific personnel records, followed by another four interviewing eight Dark Unit Operatives. He'd selected four. Two females, two males. Formidable, gifted warriors.

His best.

They would cover the entire Protectorate at high speed, from the frozen Northern Sea to the warmth of the Southern Ocean. Every Keep and Stronghold would be inspected.

Traveling at night, their days would be spent guarding their Commander as he reassured, comforted and mourned with his people.

Gunnar briefed his warriors on route structure and operation protocols. He fell silent, choosing his next words with care.

"You have the mission's parameters, now the reason you

four are here. Legend speaks of a Protector created when great need arises; the Chimera. Though no one can claim to have seen one for several thousand years, you will."

The four Guardians were perfectly still, eyes locked on Gunnar.

"Commander Arundel has been watching over the Protectorate, waiting for his time, the Chimera's time. You will escort him as he tends to our people and inspects our defenses. You will fly at night with the Chimera, keeping his existence hidden. You will guard the Commander in his Fae form during the day. You were carefully chosen. I believe you are worthy of it."

Gunnar was proud of his Guardians. They displayed little of the shock he knew coursed through them. They knew the legends. They looked to one another. For this to be true, here, now… the burning gleam in their eyes told him enough. They would willingly give their lives for Arundel, in any circumstance. But this. This was the stuff of a warrior's dreams.

Gunnar gripped Arundel's forearms in farewell. He felt the wildness of the Chimera stirring under his hands, finally able to Shift.

"Fly swiftly, brother. May the Father and Mother Above aid your task." Arundel gave him the fierce smile no one else had seen.

"I beg they keep watch over you, brother, and the command in your charge."

Arundel swiftly departed, his four Guardians following him into the night.

The Chimera's time had begun.

Gunnar set aside the last file on his desk, glancing at the note near his hand with its single word message. He rose, pocketing it. His heart and stride lightened as he returned the Guardians fist-to-shoulder salutes, doors opening before him into the main keep for the short walk—*home*.

As he turned the corner to his quarters, Asa came to attention. With a nod, she departed. Gunnar stood at the door for a split second, hand resting on the handle; feeling an unreasonable flash of fear that he would open it to an empty room. But her scent was here, spurring him to enter.

Grace asleep in his bed was the most beautiful thing he'd ever seen. Quietly closing the door, Gunnar watched her soft breathing. He moved closer, boots soundless on the thick rug. She lay stretched on her side, facing away, nestled into the snowy linens of the four poster.

The bedclothes had fallen away, down to the small of her back. He realized with a pang that she held his pillow to her, a leg flung over, pulling it close.

Gunnar stood silently, his day receding. He took in the night shift on the floor, Grace's words echoing through him. *I'm going to live naked in your bed.*

His heart knew the hardest decision he now faced was whether to shower and risk waking her, or to kiss the nape of her neck, ensuring it.

Gunnar sighed deeply, tight muscle easing, eyes touching tender places to explore. He needed to hear her voice.

Breath deepening as though scenting him, Grace curved into a stretch, bare torso twisting toward him. Her drowsy eyes opened to scan the room, stopping on him. She came fully awake, a slow smile aiding the hesitant decision to leave her arms overhead, rather than draw them down to cover herself.

"Welcome home."

Two words filled with understanding.

Turning fully toward him to her stomach lost the rest of the bedclothes. She rested her chin in her hands, pointedly looking him over.

"Your uniform looks exhausted."

A faint note of nerves underlined her voice, but no fear. He bent to breathe in her ear.

"So it does."

He tracked the shiver down her spine. Crossing to the wardrobe, he stripped with a soldier's efficiency, removing more of the day with his uniform.

Grace studied the shifting muscle beneath his skin as he approached the bed. He was beautiful.

She turned to her back, looking up at him. Catching his hand, she pressed it to her cheek. Slight tension in his body suggested work had been demanding. Pressing lips to his hand, she released it.

"Shower, if only to remove the day. You would already be in this bed if you didn't need a moment."

His eyes came back from roaming to hers, pleased, grateful she understood. He wanted to be fully here, no remnants of the harrowing day. He leaned in for a searching, hungry kiss, hand tangling in her hair, whispering against her lips.

"Think of when I return."

Gunnar stood motionless under the water, feeling everything recede but her. He wanted only Grace and himself in their bed. He began washing, feeling a flutter of—anticipatory wonder.

Vigorously toweling dry he returned to her, roughing his damp hair. Towel discarded, he prowled over her, dropping kisses to mark later targets.

When their eyes met, he lowered to forearms, weight warm against her. His fingers brushed her cheekbones.

"Grace, I love you. *Mate*, I will love you for the length of my life, and all that comes after."

Grace pulled his hand to her throat, fingers to her pulse. "Until my heart stops beating, Mate, I will love you, and for all that comes after."

Gunnar's hand moved to cradle her neck. He kissed the hollow of her throat. Inhaling deeply against her skin, he skimmed a path to her ear, exhaling against the tongue-traced shell, rubbing his cheekbone against hers.

Breath hitching, she gave him her mouth. Gunnar groaned at the taste of her mingling with desire-perfumed skin. His hand slipped from her neck, dropping to find the small of her back, pulling her hard against him. Grace's body flushed with heat.

She gasped into his breath. "Tell me what to do."

"Tell me what you need," he whispered.

"I—I need—" Her hips shifted. "Everything…"

Drawing a deep breath, Gunnar reined in instinct, retrieving control. He eased his hold on her hip, smoothing fingers down to raise her knee, opening her legs so he could settle his body between them. Grace felt urgency shift to something slower, her eyes darting to his face.

"Did I do something wrong?"

"You can do nothing wrong." Gunnar kissed her collarbone. "I'm reminding myself."

"Of what?"

"That the world has vanished, and you are mine to cherish."

He returned to her mouth, coaxing her to lead, teaching her to take, deepening until she raised her chin, chasing her breath. He drifted downward with licking, soft bites and hot breath against her throat. Her fingers tugged his hair, tightening as he sent tingling darts through her.

Not knowing what to do with her hands, Grace set them free. The luxury of freely touching him was intoxicating. Learning the muscles of his back, shape of his shoulders, and planes of his chest. What an intimate thing it was, to feel his life, vibrant beneath his skin. Grace ran her hands over his lean, muscled ribs, stretching to dip under, feeling his swift inhale.

Her soft laughter paused Gunnar's exploration. He marked his place with a gentle nip that zinged through her, lifting his head to look a question.

"You're so tall. I can't reach very far."

"I'll help you."

A faint blush tinted Grace's cheeks. Gunnar drew her hand to him, kissing her palm. He lifted himself, settling onto his side next to her, gently keeping her on her back. She hesitated, uncertain what to do. Gunnar guided her arms to comfortably fold and rest above her head. Caressing her face, he spoke against her lips, "Breathe."

Content to have him lead her, she pulled the pillow from beneath her head, tossing it aside. Stretching, she relaxed into the bed, returning her folded arms above, smiling at his pleased sound of approval.

His gaze returned to her lushly soft body, running fingertips along the dips and curves, deepening to firm palm strokes and squeezes here and there. He paused to catch her with a look.

"You're very beautiful, Grace."

"I'm—I'm not—."

A rare, slow smile challenged her. He kissed her, pulling away too soon, sliding his hand downward. A pleasure then, affirming how uniquely appealing her body was to him. Fae bodies differed, but none had this richness.

Cupping her breast, he brushed his unshaved chin across the nipple, laving away the roughness with his tongue. Grace twisted, urging equal attention to both breasts.

Gunnar moved on, flattening his palm to smooth over her velvet belly, callouses trailing tiny fires. Body shifting downward, he lay his head on the gentle rise of it. Arm hugging her hip, he breathed deeply. Her scent shook every sense awake.

His hand followed the beautiful curve of her hip, gliding along the dip from belly to thigh, slipping between her legs. Fingertips trailing, he let them rest a moment.

Hips shifting at the memory of his hands, Grace nestled into the bed, opening her legs as he squeezed a cheek, dragging fingers up to dip into wetness. Teasingly they slid further up, circling once, triggering a targeted rush of heat.

She almost seized his hand with a breathy cry when he continued on, smoothing over her thigh, down to her calf.

Returning upward, he paused to nudge under her knees, further raising them.

Pausing at the top of her thighs, Gunnar's fingers stroked through soft curls before slipping back into silken wet softness. He turned his face into her belly, lips pressed to feel muscles beneath quivering as his wet fingers circled with exquisite precision before withdrawing to rest on her hip.

Grace's breathless sounds of protest and rising hips asked for more. Gunnar smiled against her skin at what she did not say.

Rising, he shifted over her body, knees between hers, their eyes holding as his mouth lowered to her breasts.

Drawing a nipple in with slow, strong pulls, brought Grace's hands, tightly gripping his hair, moving quickly to a firmer grip of his shoulders, arching into his mouth. Gunnar gently rolled the other nipple, traveling between them, massaging, suckling, teeth lightly scraping.

Fiercely pulling him up to kiss her between panting breaths, Grace bit his lower lip, rubbing her cheek hard along his, legs sliding around his waist. He felt her intention to repeat yesterday's reaction, hoping to move him past self-control.

Gunnar cupped her nape, tipping her head back before she could reach his ear. He nipped her throat, growling against the curve where neck met shoulder. The sound and vibration thrilled sharply through her, legs tightening in quick response, hips lifting to find him warm and hard above her.

The tables swiftly turned from gentle foreplay to serious intent. Gunnar's breath caught harshly as she moved, urgently sliding along the now slippery underside of him, attempting to position him with her body.

Gunnar's head dropped against her, muscles locked to prevent thrusting into her.

"Grace—stop! Talk to me!"

Gunnar swiftly rolled to one side, firmly holding her still. Grace relaxed her grip, hands guiding his face toward hers, wanting him to read her thoughts, wanting him to hurry. With a steadying breath, he brushed her hair from her face.

"Tell me in words, Grace, not thoughts. I need to hear your voice. There is nothing that cannot be said. If you have no words for what you want, guide me there. Trust me."

Magic words.

"I want you. I've waited. Show me I'm not dreaming."

Gunnar made a soft sound in the back of his throat. Turning her to her back, he kissed her, his heart on her lips.

"You've never been more awake."

Guiding her bent knees further apart. He settled his body between them, kissing his way down until her thighs rested on his shoulders. Hands splayed over her hips, he pressed her to the bed, exhaling hot breath against slick skin. His tongue passed firmly over peaked flesh, once, twice, slowly a third time.

Grace bucked against his restraining hands, breath speeding, fists twisting in the bedclothes. Gunnar paused, lifting his head. "Hold onto the bed post above if you need it. Breathe."

She grabbed the post.

Keeping one hand flat on her stomach, his mouth continued caressing as he eased a finger inside. Gunnar's hands were of a size to match his six-foot seven height, as was the rest of his body. He would take the utmost care with Grace.

Even flooded with arousal, her body's grip was tight. He was right to wait. He would have hurt her. He continued firm movements with his tongue as a second finger joined the first, pressing, stroking.

Panting, Grace pushed against the post, muscles quivering, grasping at his touch. A third finger joined, stretching, moving more deeply inward. She twisted against his hold of her—his mouth—it was too much—.

He eased in with four, carefully stroking, relaxing tight muscles—she was opening enough to ease his concern, but Mother Above…

Grace was losing her mind. She felt her body would pull itself apart. She was done waiting. Hesitation fled.

"*Mate*," she implored. "Please…"

Gunnar slid a pillow beneath her hips. Gently sucking as his tongue stroked, his fingers sliding deep, he pulled her to the edge. Grace's entire body stretched hard, then muscles surged as she pushed against him. Rising quickly, he stroked himself against her wet softness and pressed in, slowing for her body to allow him in.

Grace was having none of that. Her hips lurched upward, drawing him further in, gasping sharply, unprepared for her body's pained response. Now she understood his gentle pace, his care of her. Closing her eyes, she focused on calming her body, to relax around him.

Gunnar dropped lightly over her onto one hand, not allowing his weight to affect his movements. He placed a hand over her racing heart, drawing her focus.

"Grace, look at me…"

Meeting his eyes, she finally followed his instructions to breathe.

Moving with care, he felt a barrier and stopped. He searched her flushed face. Were their bodies incompatible? His eyes closed briefly. He would take no risks with her but would please her in every way he knew. He moved to withdraw.

"No!"

Grace pushed off the bedpost, curling upward for a grip under his arms and shoulders, pulling him with her, into her, as she fell back. Gunnar felt the thin barrier give way, her small cry stilling him.

At the concern and hesitation on his face, Grace pressed her lips to his, breathless.

"It's normal… it will pass."

The discomfort eased with each small push and retreat. Her hands and hips encouraged him, but he refused to hurry. Pausing to feel her pulse pounding around him, he groaned against her lips. Her body heat was higher than his, further igniting his senses. He held her eyes in the final slow press until they were fully joined.

Grace caught up to the heart-stopping sensation of Gunnar in her. He was hers. Was her. Eyes closing, her hands explored the physical connection of their bodies, feeling a tremor in him at her touch.

Gunnar rose to sit back on his knees, keeping her hips against him, her thighs gripping his hips, head and shoulders resting on the bed. The pillow beneath her hips kept them fully joined, his body weightless against her.

"Grace," he said softly, again drawing her focus to him.

His body's small movements in her, and his skillful

fingers against her slippery flesh narrowed her world to the rising, thrumming heat he summoned from her shaking body, and her cries of response. Adrift, anchored only by his gaze, she was unaware of the cresting wave until it swept over her.

Gunnar leaned into her. "Mate, let go."

Her eyes closed, head turning sharply to the side as nerve endings vibrated into soft explosion, intensifying, sharpening, spreading like wildfire. Grace grasped his wrists, forcefully pulling herself onto him, her sensuous groan, as she contracted hard around him brought him swiftly down to cover her body with his, sliding an arm under her to pull her detonating body against him.

Her tight hold of him expanded as muscles pulsed, freeing him to move. Gunnar rubbed his cheekbone hard against hers with a harsh exhale. Hand in her hair, his rough breath against her ear added fuel to the flames as he stroked deeply into her.

Having no breath for words, Grace gave an upward glance, asking him to slide her toward the bedpost.

Using it to push her body harder against him as he moved in her, her guttural sounds elicited instant response as his body surged in answer, driving her to near frenzy.

Back arched, she ferociously pulled their bodies flush—Gunnar fused with her—as she took him to the edge of pain in an iron grip—intensity wringing a scream through her clenched teeth.

Her quivering body relaxed its hold in spasming degrees, Gunnar's hands and body stroking, holding, moving her into gentler pulses. As she softened, Gunnar finally let go, lost in the lush, pounding heat of her. Driving in hard, energy from every point of his body pulled into his spine, culminating deeply inside Grace.

Grace cradled him to her, softly surrounding him as he came, their sweat-slick bodies rocking against each other in small, urgent movements. She did not let go until he quieted.

After long breaths, Gunnar carefully lifted himself to lie next to her, pulling her into his arms.

Father Above.

Neither of them spoke or moved while waves of sensation receded, their bodies bonelessly sinking into the bed. It became chill as their damp bodies dried. Gunnar turned Grace, nestling her body into the curve of his, pulling the bedclothes over them. His hands smoothed her trembling muscles, easing her into sleep. Head resting on a raised hand, he looked down at her.

Never had he experienced such utter contentment.

Home.

15.

LOVE AND HEALING

AWAKENING A FEW hours later Grace knew, if Gunnar hadn't been spooning her, she would have thought the night before a dream. It took a moment, naming her unfamiliar state. Loved. Sated. Safe.

Needing to slip out of bed for use of the washroom, she reluctantly eased out of Gunnar's arms. She washed her hands and brushed her teeth, laughing softly at remembered tales of lovers sneaking to do so, concerned with morning breath.

Beginning a luxurious stretch, prepared for an onslaught of sore muscles—she stopped, mid-stretch. There were none. No pain or soreness—anywhere.

It wasn't possible. She should have been sharply sore, at least some pain. Never had any part of her body worked as intensely as every muscle had last night. She should feel stiff, bruised. These things were expected, not feared.

Grace examined her face in the mirror, tilting from side to side. Where were the stubble burns? She remembered— her hickeys were gone. She looked down at her body. There were no marks. None such as were visible from their first encounter. Last night was incomparably stronger.

There was no evidence of their lovemaking. She met her eyes in the mirror. Overpowering dread; the ever-present fear that Oberon, Gunnar, their love, were merely dreams, gripped her like a vise as shock triggered her.

Grace bent, nearly dropping to her knees. She was still on Earth, about to wake to her alarm.

Her heart kicked like a panicked creature, her face numb. She'd thought nothing could be worse than patrol car lights and a knock at the door. Until now.

Knees folding, her forehead pressed the cold floor. Shards of pain sliced her heart, filled her lungs. Grace began to ghost.

A low-pitched snarl and heavy thud pierced the paralyzing vacuum of fear. Grace watched from a distance as an enormous, stunning Jaguar leapt to stand over her. She felt the floor again under her as a roughly-drawn breath exhaled, gusting against her skin; Whuff. His heavy warmth, close above her, vanished in an instant.

Awakened by the knife-sharp scent of Grace's fear, Gunnar's involuntary Shift into his Jaguar had taken less than a second. Three seconds to cover the distance, assess Grace, and look for danger, one to Shift back. Gunnar lifted her, cradled tightly against him.

"Mate! What's happened?"

Choking sobs of relief tore from her. She frantically pressed into him, as though to merge, hands fiercely gripping the arms locked around her.

"Grace, tell me…"

Seeing that she couldn't yet manage words, he cupped her face, reading her last thoughts.

Trapped in her worst nightmare. Gunnar was gone. Abandoned.

Gunnar felt her intense fear. The physical pain.

"Mate—look at me—"

He returned to sit on the bed, completely enfolding her. The scent of fear waned but was still sharp enough to sting his senses. This was no small thing, not just a nightmare. Gunnar kept her tight against him, her ear pressed over his heartbeat.

She was calming, able to breathe.

"Tell me what caused this. Are you hurt?"

Grace put a hand to her face. "No—I'm not hurt…"

Gunnar slid back, revealing minor blood stains on the bed linens. He was concerned he'd hurt her. She grasped at the need to reassure him. The reality of it swiftly calming her.

"I should have thought to tell you." Grace's voice calmed. "The first time—women—we may bleed. It's normal." Gunnar's arms tightened.

"The first time left you marked. Last night I was not always gentle."

Grace turned in his arms, hands firmly holding his face. "You did not hurt me. I felt desired, loved—I don't have the words—I never thought to have or feel such things."

His worry eased. They matched in these things.

Gunnar kept her against him, patiently waiting to understand what created the terror still echoing through him. Answering his unspoken question, she brought his hand to cup her cheek.

"It would help if you saw what happened; it's hard to explain."

She pulled him into her engulfing pleasure because of his care and passion, moving to her expectation of physical aftermath. The surprise, followed by shock in the washroom causing her extreme distress. Letting his hand drop away, she asked her pressing question.

"Do you understand? This is impossible."

Analyzing, sorting evidence from her memories, Gunnar turned to lay her down. He carefully searched her body for marks, knowing he had repeatedly rubbed her with his unshaved face, sucked and nipped, fiercely held her at the height of passion. These things had left marks before. There was the blood on the linens. There were no marks on her. No scent of blood or injury. He was as puzzled as she. A thought crossed her face.

"What is it?" Gunnar asked.

"A— possibility? Ellie studied applied science. She would say this was a case of Occam's razor. A philosopher wrote that all things considered, the simplest answer tends to be correct."

Gunnar nodded in agreement with this, waiting for her to go on.

Grace glanced at the small bloodstain. "We have illnesses that can pass through the tiniest wound." She blew out a breath. "What if your ability to heal is transferable? I had a small wound; you came in me. I healed."

Her eyes narrowed at a new thought. Before he guessed her intent, she ripped away the arm bandage. There was no wound. They sat in stunned silence.

Gunnar studied her face. He could find no fault in her

reasoning. His first thought had been the same. Healing was impossible. But the evidence of her body, her arm, pointed to the contrary. He could find no other conclusion.

Grace's eyes searched the room for something clean and sharp. He took her hands in his.

"No. We will not test this by wounding you. It may be a temporary thing. We must think this through, speak with Healer Ahma… It is too soon to hope for a miraculous, permanent answer."

His hands came up to cradle her face.

"Mate, I wish for it with all my heart, and hope the Mother Above will let it be so. But we cannot let our hopes go to that place until we know more. It would be crushing if we believe, then found it was not so."

Even while he said this to forestall her, he wondered if they made blood to blood contact through a wound, would it heal her? At the very least, he would hope for that. It would be a miraculous thing for him. If she were wounded, or had some illness…

He laid his cheek against her hair. These concerns were the price he willingly paid in responding to the undeniable pull for them to be Mated. Grace's lifespan was short. The worst pain in his existence lay not far ahead.

While he pondered these things, Grace straightened to look at him.

"Do you think this could be influenced by our Mating bond? Asa said it was a first."

His eyes came back to hers. He considered this aspect. It *was* a first. Even he didn't understand the Mated bond forming when she was not Fae. It was physiological. Every Fae could see it. How had it triggered?

With the same blindness that had delayed recognition of his love for her, he had simply passed over the logic of the bond and considered his love for her the cause.

Could her loving him bring her closer to self-healing? It was beyond his ability to answer. He could scent no Mated mark, but now this. Asa most certainly would have noted it, and Healer Ahma. But they had seen her before she healed.

"I'm not certain. Another factor to consider. I have much research to do. Mate, you have a brilliant mind. You take my breath away."

"Speaking of taking your breath away…"

He smiled. "Let's shower."

16.

THE VILLAGE

EXECUTING ARUNDEL'S ORDER to open the Keep, Gunnar assigned half his Dark Unit Legion and a full Stronghold Legion to sweep the area a hundred kilometers out. Forces from every Stronghold in the Northeastern Protectorate expanded searches outward to overlap, until the entirety of the territory had been covered. Regular patrols were set, and his warriors were allowed rest-leave in shifts to see to their families.

The Commander of the Stronghold Aid Century desperately needed relief troops. The Aid warriors were exhausted after three months of constant labor. It was bittersweet for the Keep Guardians. Joyfully reunited with their loved ones, they also faced revelations of those who had died. A skeleton crew of Guardians who had no local family volunteered in staffing the Keep.

For Gunnar, it was the dreaded first time Grace would leave his protection, albeit for only a few hours. She had dreamt of seeing the village for so long. Five Humans were now settled there, two of them children. If he accompanied her, their attention would be pulled to him. His position and rank would also draw Centurions from the Stronghold, ruining her experience.

He briefed Asa on things she already knew, but she listened and responded with sharp focus. She sympathetically understood and was realistically aware of the risks. He knew she would note every detail, reporting back with precision. Feigning a casualness he did not feel, he left Grace with Asa.

"I look forward to hearing of your day. Enjoy exploring."

He turned towards Central, a last glance over Grace's head to Asa.

Three Dark Ops circled them, undetected by Grace. Asa tracked them with ease. She inwardly smiled; she could make quite a dent in a Stronghold with three Dark Ops. But better to be over-safe than unprepared. They left the Keep, heading East through dense trees. They skirted a series of fallow fields and outbuildings from a long-abandoned farm.

These vacant lands provided an easily surveilled perimeter around the wood secreting the Keep. Grace snorted quietly.

What a coincidence…

Sun kissing her face, Grace spun in a circle, the briny scent of nearby marshland teasing her senses. Pausing to pinch pine needles from a branch, she crushed them between her fingers, inhaling their pungent, memory-laden fragrance.

"I've known exactly where I am," she said to Asa, "but to smell home—as though my two homes merged, or this were the first…"

Asa accepted and scented the offered pine, smiling at Grace's joy. Continuing to scan past the location of each Operative, she marked that Grace had said *or this were the first.*

They came out of the forest near a dirt track, Operatives stealthily out of sight, and walked the half-mile to the Stronghold's lands. Grace could see it squatting on a rise near the bay, looking rather like a Norman castle. There was an orchard sloping down its south side, and a patchwork of farms stretching past a river to the west.

"If only I could fly, I'd love to see this land as it is, untouched by the changes we've made to ours. But today—I'm grateful to walk."

Asa paused her scanning to smile at Grace.

"It's a beautiful day to see the village."

Though mentally preparing from the first report of other humans, Grace was unsure how to greet them. Their arrival and lives afterward had been dramatically different. Information of her existence spread soon after the Keep opened, but the Keep was classified, so details and her location were unspecified. Since no local had seen her, she'd acquired somewhat mythic proportions.

Moving through the village outskirts, Asa pointed out the marketplace not far ahead. A small girl, perhaps four years old, chased a very annoyed, bedraggled chicken across their path. A word from a young woman nearby, hanging laundry in the breezy sunshine, sent her to collapse giggling on a blanket under a tree. An older woman sat there with a young boy, teaching him to patch clothing—until they noticed Grace.

There was no ducking it now. She paused, waiting for them to make the first move. Grace knew her appearance would set her apart. She wore different clothing, was well-cared for. She was also accompanied by a female Guardian.

Palms sweating, heart skipping like a jump rope, Grace

fumbled for the right words. Regular greetings felt out of place. Thinking of all these people had been through spurred her to close the gap, extending her hand.

"I'm Grace. I lived in Boston."

The younger woman reached for her hand with a cautious grasp, but then did not let go.

"I'm Dawn, from Portsmouth."

She pulled Grace in for a hug, eyes filling with tears. "You're real. We kept hearing talk about you, but didn't know if you were a story, or…"

The older woman trembled as she shook hands, offering a tentative smile.

"I'm Meg, from Stowe. How 'bout those Red Sox?"

"Right?" Grace said. "And the Bruins. I mean, come on."

All three laughed.

Asa slipped back a few paces behind Grace, so she could clearly see everyone.

It felt foreign looking at Humans. Grace realized they were the first she'd seen since narrowly escaping the Door. She was failing in her effort not to stare. Fortunately, all three were.

Grace again broke the silence. "Meg, your lovely accent—are you French?"

"French-Swiss, from Geneva. I married a businessman from Vermont. We're quite the scattered bunch here."

Dawn was looking speculatively at Grace.

"I think once the locals heard about you, soldiers from the fort began watching for us, bringing us here. You can imagine our relief—seeing normal people. The boy over there—that Meg's teaching to patch clothes? He hasn't spoken at all, so we call him Sweetheart. First hoping to annoy him into talking, then because he is one."

A disgruntled male voice startled Grace. "They're herding us like cattle."

A man had approached from behind, though he kept a safe distance from Asa, whom he warily eyed. He'd been eavesdropping rather than openly listening. Meg and Dawn ignored him.

"We think the kids are from furthest away," Meg said. "It's hard to tell. The little girl speaks a few words of English, but I don't recognize her real language. We ran through a lot of names, and she perked up at Marie, so that's what we call her. She was clinging to her rescue guy for dear life. Lots of tears when he had to go. We had a time, getting her to trust us."

Dawn's eyes followed the child, who was again chasing the chicken.

"He visits her once in a while. But they all seem pretty busy helping their own people. A lot of them died."

They were silent a moment, air thick with unasked questions.

"What's your story?" Meg asked.

Their expectant faces encouraged Grace as she explained her arrival in broad strokes.

"I worked in a government job just north of Boston. I lived in the Back Bay."

"So you should know—what the fuck happened?" The surly man glared at Grace. "Why are we here?"

He had not allowed a Voice to help him, but his body language and speech patterns told Asa everything. She adjusted her stance toward him. Grace saw him flinch away from her toward the women.

"What's your name?" Grace asked.

He rapid-fired words. "Derek—why are you living somewhere else? Who's Army Barb?" His eyes narrowed. "She's with you. And you sure don't look like you missed any meals."

Grace extended her hand, waiting patiently until he crossed his arms, refusing to shake.

"Derek, I live where I appeared. Asa is my friend."

Grace had forgotten how tall Fae were until Asa was standing among Humans. She was intimidating. But the little girl moved closer to Asa at Derek's anger.

"I realize how fortunate I was in arriving among people. I was very ill when I got here. They took care of me."

Meg's brows knit. "You were sick? Like they were?"

Grace glanced round their circle. "Yes—were none of you sick?"

"Not like that," Dawn said. "Meg and Derek were banged up, and we were all half-starved before they brought us here."

"That's for sure," Derek said, "We had it tough. Nobody was in charge."

Dawn frowned at him, waving a dismissive hand.

"Yeah, well, anyone who tried, figured out most of these people are friendly. Pointy-ears or not." She glanced at Asa, embarrassed, before continuing. "I'm sure they were just as shocked by us. Meg and I got translated, or whatever it is they do. Things got easier…"

Meg cast a pointed look to Derek as she emphasized Dawn's words.

"You must admit, they've been good to us through all of this—craziness. There's been a couple of people who've passed through—searching for someone or someplace they recognize— but we five are pretty much settled for now."

Grace was feeling survivor's guilt. Asa's care and friendship—her safety and comfort—all weighed heavily. The miracle of Gunnar felt separate, not something she wanted to share.

"It must be difficult, knowing my circumstances were different…" Grace left the statement open-ended.

"Now why would you think that?" Derek snapped. "Just because I mostly starved for weeks and weeks, and it was freezing at night. You were cozying up to them at the first opportunity. Bet you didn't even know if they were enemies or not."

Asa was now directly behind Grace, though no one had seen her move.

Meeting his hostile gaze, Grace mildly pointed out the obvious. "I would have died if they hadn't taken me in. I regret that you had a very different experience. But like you, I had no control over these bizarre circumstances. They obviously were not the cause, how could they be enemies?"

She turned to listen attentively as the women spoke of family and friends left behind. A weary-looking transient lingered at a distance, watching but not approaching. Asa had spotted the Human when he first appeared, signaling a Dark Op to monitor him; directing a second to sweep the immediate area.

The drifter looked the group over, then shook his head, turning toward the market. There he sat quietly drinking a mug of kindly offered tea until the tailing Operative turned his head to scan the surroundings in Grace's direction. Swiftly maneuvering into a shadowed niche of the Stronghold wall, he sat motionless, watching Asa and the Operatives guarding Grace.

When focus had fully returned to Grace and her immediate surroundings, the man took a circuitous route through the village, slipping out the far side to head south.

Tired of being ignored, and the general lack of complaining among the women, Derek examined Grace's appearance more closely. He loudly cleared his throat.

"You don't look like you're bathing in a bucket."

Irritated, Dawn turned on him.

"Derek, several homes offer to let us use their bathrooms."

"Like I'd go in their house," he said. Gesturing to Grace's clothes and boots, he continued. "You have new clothes, and shoes for Christ's sake. Who'd you sleep with to get those?" His voice had grown louder with every remark.

Grace signaled asking Asa to hold her position, scooping up the now whimpering child who was nearly clinging to Asa's leg. The child was repeating words which sounded vaguely familiar to Grace—perhaps Portuguese, common in some fishing ports not far from home. Grace stroked the child's hair.

"Hi there, beautiful girl."

The child patted her face.

"No man. No. Eat? Mama, food?" she said.

Grace turned to the angry man. Asa stayed within arm's reach, ready to Travel her out. The child would come with them; Asa could easily carry them both a safe distance.

Grace gently replied to the man. "Have these people hurt or threatened you? Have they forced you to do something against your will? Have you received medical care, shelter, food?"

She waited for him to meet her eyes, carefully reaching to lightly touch his arm.

"Would you expect them to be treated the same if they appeared back home?" Grace said. "I understand we do not all feel the same, but have you experienced these things?"

He looked down, voice dropping into a non-threatening range.

"They're freaks," he said. "But no, they haven't hurt us. They'd probably be in a lab back home."

Asa studied Grace's posture and face, then the man's.

Grace gave the child to Dawn, who remarked on the child so clearly asking for food.

"Haven't understood but a few words from you, you little scamp. You wanted to impress our visitor, didn't you?"

The child leaned her head into Dawn's shoulder, patting her. "Cookie?"

Laughing, Grace made her goodbyes, suggesting she'd visit soon to divert them from asking to visit her. All but Derek waved as they left. He silently sat next to the boy.

To leave for shopping seemed painfully frivolous—until they came to the village square, she'd waited so long to see. She almost squeaked in delight. She spent the next hour keeping Asa on her toes, darting from shop to shop, and vendor to craftsmen.

She breathed it all in without caution or hesitation.

The villagers knew of her. The first Guardians emerging from the Keep had spoken of her and word had quickly spread. The Prefect had Mated a Human. Yes, she was respected and thought well of—different but not strange. There were no unkind words spoken of her by the Guardians. That was enough for many in the village to accept her. For a Human to be Mated to a high-ranking Fae… Gunnar was touched when Asa reported these things.

Grace had pocket money and she freely used it. Sampling food of every kind, laughing with vendors, complementing their skill, praising their use of spices. She was carefully unobtrusive in how she 'shared' with Asa so it could be scented first, a condition she had promised to obey.

Then came bookshops and craftspeople. She bought pens and sheafs of paper, books of history and folklore. A calendar of holidays. Beautiful containers of horn and carved wood for writing implements, boxes to hold her papers. Several pockets from the tanners to go on her knife belt were next. Finding child-size archery vambraces to fit her small arms made her smile.

Down the street were clothiers and feminine sundries. A simple linen tunic for the warm weather outside the Keep, a soft robe, a pretty scarf. Floral-scented hair soap—each purchase engendered polite, sometimes wary, often effusive greetings and small talk.

Grace looked to Asa. "I can't think of another thing. Can you?"

Asa thought it over. Grace had chosen no luxury clothing, no jewelry, none of the finer things her Mate would happily give her. Her choices were Grace-like. Books, writing things. Simple necessities.

"I've no idea, Grace. Of all the things we've discussed, shopping has never been one of them."

"Help me think of something for Gunnar," Grace urged. "He's so Spartan, it's near impossible to think of a gift. I'd like at least one surprise."

Asa thought Gunnar would say Grace was all he wanted.

But not wanting to disappoint her fun, she pointed down the street. "You might find something in the second shop to the left. But I'm warning you," she said, "when we get back to the Keep, I'll have to check it."

Grace understood the warning when she stopped in front of the shop. It was lingerie. She gave Asa a wicked grin as she went in. She did manage to find a few things, smiling all the way back to the Keep.

The three Dark Ops Guardians sighed on the return trip. They would not hesitate to guard Grace with their lives, wherever she went, but that last shop? It was worth the trip. Their perception of Prefect Gunnar needed revising.

Again.

It was not a particularly taxing day for Gunnar. He had received an update from Arundel with the welcome news that his mission was nearly complete. He would be returning to the Keep within the week. The message's arrival relieved his mind, though there was much sad news, and more reports of Mors.

He sent a return dispatch reporting all was calm in their district, and strongly worded details of the Western Protectorate's stance on their treatment of Humans. Every protocol in the Northeastern Protectorate that proved successful was shared between the Central Commands of other territories to use if they saw fit. All, save one, had incorporated some or all of the protocols.

The Western Protectorate was not sympathetic toward Humans, creating internment camps and treating them as a threat. The other territories made formal complaints against these actions, pointing them out as unjust and uncivilized on every level, citing their own positive results. The Western Protectorate had closed communication on the subject.

Finally, desk cleared, he headed home. As Asa departed he caught sight of a tiny twist at the corner of her mouth. Maybe Grace was extravagant. He wouldn't object in the slightest. His wages had been piling up for centuries. He would give her the stars if he could. He opened the door. Grace's voice stopped him.

"Wait! Close your eyes and put your back against the door." Surprised, Gunnar obeyed.

He could feel her warmth as she approached just beyond arm's reach away.

"Open them."

Grace was wearing—definitely not a night shift. She spun in a circle. Four floating, black gossamer panels flowed almost to the floor from a soft band at her throat. They were as wide as his hand and hid absolutely nothing. There was a tiny silk tie joining each panel just beneath her breasts. She swirled in the opposite direction, looking over her shoulder.

"I got you something…"

She had not finished her spin before his hands captured her hips, holding her in place. He was on his knees before her, hands sliding over, then exploring under the fabric. Lifting his chin, she bent to speak against his lips.

"I could challenge you to undo these ties with your teeth…"

He could wait an hour or two to hear about the village.

17.

HUNTER RISING

MORS' ARRIVAL ON Oberon during the Pulse was unique. By his own accounting, he was the only returning Fae. He'd been absent from Oberon some eight hundred years, since the previous catastrophic Pulse.

From his birth on Oberon, he had been linked with darkness. He'd violently emerged from the blackness of his dead mother's womb, his twin appearing to forfeit its life and any Gifts to him during the birth.

Warriors and training masters from his village watched carefully as he grew older, acknowledging the child's cruelty and apathy, traits unheard of in one so young. No specific Gifts appeared to be visibly manifesting, but he was a twin; unique ones would come. They waited in trepidation to see what they might be, wondering if malevolence itself could be a terrible Gift.

No matter what methods were used in attempts to train and educate him, the young male remained completely amoral. If a Seer-Gifted Fae had not predicted him gone in the near future, they might have killed him to prevent a potential threat to all around him.

It would have been a great mercy to millions if they had.

The boy was twelve when the cataclysmic Pulse threw him from his home in the forest into a place that looked identical but was not. Writhing in physical torment, he could not move for days due to blinding headaches and seized muscles. It was another week before he could crawl, foraging from the forest floor, unable to keep down what little he found.

When he could get up, racked with nausea and weakness, he realized his home village had vanished, and there were only strangers who did not speak his language. Although his facial features and coloring were similar to theirs, he was very tall in comparison to his apparent age. His starved appearance and ears also marked him as freakishly strange. The people didn't know what to make of him; perhaps he was a demon.

The village wanted no attention drawn to them just then. They'd suffered a recent slaughter unleashed by the most powerful of local warlords. He had killed an entire neighboring Tatar tribe on suspicion that someone had conspired against him.

The warlord was swift to act on a whim in his butchery. The youth would most certainly bring focus to bear on them. The villagers took him deep into the forest and left him there.

Attacking lone travelers for food and weapons, he quickly realized he was faster and stronger than those around him. At home he had been in training, but here, he was a warrior grown, and they were as children.

The boy pondered the reaction to his ears. He did not

understand nor care why they were physically different. He would not have such an insignificant thing stand in his way.

Using a knife he'd taken from a slow-reflexed hunter, he sawed the points from both ears, imitating as best he could, the round shape of the Others. It was not neatly done. He incurred several cuts to the face as well, adding to his formidable appearance. He healed, albeit with heavy scarring in a week. He stole what he needed, killed when he desired. He was a wraith local villagers spoke of in hushed whispers, putting shamanist talismans in their windows and doors.

Wandering the familiar yet unfamiliar forests, looking for Fae like himself, he found none, only the Others.

They were sheep compared to him and died easily. He ranged more widely, covering long distances easily.

He began to note areas with razed villages, smelling blood from bodies still fresh; he felt certain what he was searching for approached.

He was thirteen when he surveilled a meticulously run, harshly-disciplined fortress. For several days he lay covered in grass camouflage, studying the coming and going of warriors. He watched the villagers supplying it, the many prisoners brought in, and the pieces of them coming out.

This appeared a place in which to learn fighting skills. He watched for a calm period, then left the hills to enter the gates.

Walking into the fortress, a sentry swore at him, striking his head with the butt of his spear. He understood the challenge. He grabbed the sentry's arm and twisted it, striking it with an elbow. It shattered; the sentry falling to the ground in pain.

Shouts rang out. The boy was swiftly surrounded by a ring of guards with spears and cudgels, yelling for him to kneel.

The boy stayed where he was, looking them over. He knew the spears were useless unless they stepped closer to stab him. They were too close to each other, to throw. The same with the cudgels; they had a very short reach. The warlord was now standing at the door, watching.

The presence of their commander spurred four of them to lunge with their spears. The boy spun in a blur, easily grabbing the spears from their hands. Still in motion he dropped two at his feet, firmly gripping one in each hand to lance the four through the heart.

His swiftness caught the startled second wave, repeating the process. Eight men lay dead at his feet. The archers on the fortress walls had arrows nocked, ready to drop him at the warlord's command. The warlord raised a hand to stop the archers. As the boy looked at him, a cudgel from behind knocked him unconscious.

He woke on the floor of a small stone room, arms bound behind him. For a time, he debated his options. Break his bonds to leave or wait for the warlord. He decided to wait and see how the warlord would respond. The boy was seeking purpose, not companionship.

Guards fetched him, putting him on his knees before the warlord's throne. The bodies of guards who were outside when he entered the gate were piled next to the warlord's golden chair. Both those the boy had killed, and those who had not killed him. The boy nodded at the dead. It was right to have it so. They had all equally failed.

The warlord's eyes narrowed, intrigued. He spoke to the boy, assuming from his appearance and fighting skills that he was from unfamiliar reaches of his territory but had rudimentary understanding. The warlord would free him if he harmed no one without command. The boy nodded and easily snapped his bonds to demonstrate he had stayed by choice.

The warlord indicated a guard at the door who had not joined the fray with the others. The boy turned, covering the distance in a blur, grabbing the guard around the neck before he could react. In the same motion he drew his knees up, dropping his entire body weight to swing from the guard's neck, causing the guard to flip over him and slam into the stone floor. The boy punched him in the throat, crushing his windpipe, then stood, watching him suffocate, writhing on the floor. He turned back to the warlord, standing still, every weapon in the room directed at him. The boy nodded to the warlord again, then dropped to his knees, bowing until his forehead touched the floor. He stayed there until the warlord told him to rise.

The warlord asked his name. The boy had no name worth keeping; he wanted the man to name him, strengthening their bond. He laid his hand on his chest, shaking his head and said, "No."

"You are Subutai," said the warlord.

Subutai faithfully served as a lowly servant and messenger for the warlord, Kahn, until his fourteenth year. He proved his loyalty by following the onerous tasks set to him without complaint, leaving the obnoxious men over him untouched because it pleased the Kahn. One day he was called to clean himself, dress in new clothing, and appear before the warlord. The boy lay prone before him, pledging his fealty. He rose in fierce joy. This was the one to teach him many things. He bowed before his Kahn, whose name was Temüjin. Subutai would one day lead his armies.

Brilliant strategist, brutally relentless, Subutai adopted

techniques and weapons from every army he conquered for Temüjin. He learned to control multiple, vast armies simultaneously with unconventional signaling techniques. Employing a massive spy network, he was virtually unstoppable.

Subutai would become one of Earth's most victorious and notorious generals in history, conquering thirty-two countries, killing millions. An estimated 11 percent of the world's population. For many centuries to come, powerful generals would study his tactics.

But first he must learn to masterfully ride a horse, then, to shoot a bow with deadly accuracy at a full gallop. Critical skills, and trademark of Temüjin, also known as Genghis Kahn, and his legendary warriors.

Soon he learned the subtle art of appearing to age. He took wives and concubines through the decades because it was expected of him. Most did not survive his attentions. Several lost their minds. Subutai considered them disposable, his Fae blood wasted on them, producing progeny that would die like a breath of wind over a field.

He was still leading armies at sixty-five. When the Kahn and his succeeding son pulled him back, just short of conquering the entire eastern portion of their continent, he was furious, done with serving them. He slipped away in search of new challenges upon improvising his death at seventy-two. With his lifespan, he had barely begun.

The world was rife with opportunity for those who grasped it by the throat. After changing his name to Mors, Latin for "Death," Mors roamed the Asian Continent, chaos trailing in his wake. Chancing upon another Fae, he feigned benign interest in the history of his race. After greedily learning all the Fae male knew of Gifts, life strength, and how they could be transferred, he tortured the male into surrendering his Gift of Voice. Mors could now speak to, and understand, anyone on Earth— unleashing him upon the world with a new hobby… hunting Fae.

He hunted them with singlemindedness, torturing them with the promise to end it when they gave him their life strength and Gifts. On Oberon, the number of Gifts Fae could receive were limited by natural law. Earth had no such law, and while hereditary Gifts were not at full strength, Mors' special Gifting as a twin, and the sheer number he was accruing from his Fae treasure hunt, appeared to have no limits.

It took several centuries to find a majority of them. Six hundred years after he appeared on Earth, he had covered the majority of four continents. He continued with enthusiasm, hunting one of the few remaining Fae, a powerful Seer. Once his Gifts alerted him to her presence, he dropped everything to pursue her.

Secreted in a remote area of a continent he had yet to explore, she had fallen in love with a Human, bearing him a child who not only carried her unique physical characteristics but bore her Gifts in its bloodline. When her mate had died, and their child grew to carry on her line, she felt fate release her to attempt escape from an encroaching darkness.

Soon she was running for her life, knowing it was futile. She could only prepare for the end. Mors found it an exciting chase, for she always knew where he was. Until he acquired a strong Shield who had surrendered surprisingly quickly.

He tortured the Seer for weeks. He greatly desired her Gift, reading in her near-broken mind that she had made kings on Oberon. He also saw there was another Pulse coming. It would return him to Oberon where he would lead an army, the future of the planet balancing in his hands. He continued to rip knowledge from her, narrowing the timeline to the years immediately before the Pulse, when he carelessly released her hands. She sobbingly clawed open veins in her throat.

He held her torn neck together with his Healing Gift until she finally broke and looking into his insanity-filled eyes, pushed her Gift into him. All but a fragment he was unable to see. A blind spot, fate's fail-safe, waiting in her bloodline for this exact moment. It was a place Mors, with all his Gifts, could not see. Created to lie dormant, it would awaken when Mors was in close proximity to her descendants. He would be unable to See or feel to hunt them with his Gifts. Only in direct line of sight would they be visible.

He dropped her on the floor to bleed out, having enough life strengths. The blind spot disappeared into her child's continuation of her line, a continent away.

Mors worked his way to the location he was to await the Pulse. It was so simple now, moving between continents. He had watched mankind move from the High Middle Ages through the Cold War.

Time was spent familiarizing himself with the designated area. A New England prison would be built on the exact spot he must be. Mors thought it fitting as he planned to free himself from Earth's stifling effect on his Gifts, to full power on Oberon.

He arrived in the late 1940s feeling a strange pull he attributed to the coming Pulse.

Mors found the visions nonspecific, showing only location and a vague impression of great impact to Oberon. He contemplated how it should be interpreted. His Gifts had yet to fail him. He paid attention.

Mors wandered through Boston, looking for a fight or two. Openly slaughtering people must wait. His Seer Gift gave a tremendous pulse, this time sharply specific. Two laughing young women walked toward him. There was a wavering edge of light glowing around a person-sized space between them.

He blinked and the puzzling vision was gone.

The next night he walked the same streets and saw the women. There were three now, and he felt curiosity toward the one filling the strange outline in the vision. She was young, perhaps twenty, walking with a girlfriend on either side, college books under their arms.

Mors Shifted into a nondescript-looking man. He followed at a distance. His target left her companions, entering a dwelling alone. Mors offhandedly wondered why he didn't feel her—as though she wasn't there. No matter. His only use for females was to use and break them. The vision flashed sharply, showing the girl older, then went dark. It was his choice to accept or deny the vision, but it was clear she was meant to live past these moments.

Mors considered for only a moment. The Gift was consistent and accurate, he would not question it over such a small detail. She would remain alive when he finished with her.

Moving to the back of her dwelling, he quietly broke the

door from its hinges. She was moving about upstairs, changing her clothing. Ascending the stairs, he turned off the small hall lamp and Shifted back to himself.

The girl's parents came home later that night. Seeing her bookbag and coat in their normal place, light out upstairs, they retired for the night. The next morning, the mother ran lightly up the stairs to wake her oversleeping daughter. Her screams brought her husband running.

Their daughter lay on the floor, clothes torn away, body severely beaten. She gazed through them, tracks from an endless night of tears leaving lines on her battered face.

Three months later, the girl's parents sat with her as a small-town doctor removed the cast from the girl's arm, gently probing to assure the break had healed cleanly. A close family friend, they had moved near him as quickly as her condition allowed, intensely grateful for his help through this horror.

Her physical wounds were healing, but he worried over her mental condition. She rarely spoke, living in an almost complete state of dissociation. It was the most brutal assault he'd ever seen. He could find no words to lighten the additional burden he must give them. She was pregnant.

The internal damage had been so severe he had hoped her lack of menstruation could be attributed to her body waiting to heal. Her parents were motionless as he told them. The doctor sat silently holding her hand, allowing them time to absorb the shock. Her mother wept. Her father sat stroking her other hand, staring into space, wishing there was something, anything he could do to take this horror and pain from her.

The girl sat quietly. She'd known. Almost from the moment the fetus began, golden threads wove through her heart and mind to comfort and soothe. Her entire world was internal. She squeezed the doctor's hand, moving to hold her mother's.

She stood up, pulling her parents up with her. "I want to go home."

Mors, released of any further visions for the time, drifted at will until he felt the approach of the coming Pulse. Returning to the northeast, he encountered an annoying, relentless tug, clearly separate from the Pulse, yet connected to his physical being. He decided to investigate. Using his entire arsenal of Gifts, he searched for the maddeningly irksome cause, mystified. Unlike his centuries of hunting Fae, he could neither see nor feel the actual source. Casting doubt upon his assumption of supremacy infuriated him. Nothing existed that could challenge him.

His hunting took on a different shape, using tactical search methods in addition to Fae Gifts, narrowing down location and gathering information by what he could not see. There appeared to be two sources, not far apart. He had less than a decade left in his window.

During a methodical narrowing of territory and paths, he found one of the sources in an unforeseen encounter, a direct, visual confrontation. A female. She shocked him as their eyes met by the prism edges faintly surrounding her, and a latent familiarity. An instantaneous flash of recognition appeared in her gaze which was unprecedented. He was enraged when she instantly chose death to put herself beyond his reach. He lashed out too late to stop her. There was no time to risk pursuing the second source. The search for this one had taken several years.

Viciously slaughtering unfortunates along his way, Mors put himself where his Seer Gift told him to wait, the MCI Maximum Security Prison, roughly four years before the Pulse.

The defiant, irritating torment did not lessen.

He spent the final three years in the cold darkness of solitary confinement, plucking threads from his fluorescent orange, death row jumpsuit, Seer Gift ceaselessly searching for the source. It was frustratingly specific to this location. Mors' logic finally overrode his rampant narcissism. This location—there must have been a final Fae.

The ability to evade his search incensed him. He would carefully comb the corresponding area on Oberon, certain any remaining Fae would also return.

Oberon and Earth were circling around this pivotal moment as the sun began to stir.

Grace was 14 miles away.

18.

TOWERS

A WEEK AFTER ARUNDEL'S return, Grace sat at her desk, examining blueprints of the communication towers. She zeroed in on a pattern in the placement of several on every second highest geographical point, even when adding small deviations from the main tower line.

Well done—not using the obvious high point.

She flipped to plans depicting only summit towers.

Hmmm—not marked with maintenance division's symbol. Also, much newer. No small tears around the edges—barely creased or discolored. C'mon guys, Black Unit fingerprints all over these.

Grace shook her head. Tsk. She would have ironed in creases and edge tears—tea-stained them to add age. Covert arts and crafts. She'd ask Arundel's permission to ask her Mate for a meeting with the lead Dark Unit engineer. She never circumvented security protocol.

In this morning's brief, she'd told Arundel the intercepted

rebel codes were too easy to break. A distraction. The rebels were undoubtedly hard at work breaking theirs. Grace felt an urgency to verify accuracy and finish her work.

She messaged Arundel with her Tower observations, requests to examine the network, and reasoning. An hour later she received a message from the Black Unit engineers to meet the next morning. They would take her to the nearest tower.

Grace reread the reply, absorbed in writing a checklist for the test when she felt hands slide under her arms smoothing down her robe to rest at her waist. Gunnar was busy nuzzling her neck. She *loved* working from home.

Drawing his hands up a bit, she surveyed her work.

"Well, someone appears to be slacking. It's doubtful I could be coerced into thinking my work can wait a few hours. Care to test my resolve, Prefect?"

Gunnar lifted his head, scanning the papers on her desk. "We can move that classified paperwork to a safer place, or we can move to the bed."

"Your call, Prefect Gunnar."

The papers magically disappeared. He lifted her from the chair, turning her to lie face up on the desk. Tugging the tie on her robe loose, he settled into her chair, hooking her calves over his shoulders. "Let's disrupt your thought process here, then test your resolve over there."

Grace sighed. "I'll never look at my desk the same way again."

Gunnar nipped her inner thigh. "I will."

Preparing for her tower inspection with the engineers, Grace reviewed her notes. Her test checklist was extensive. The possible solutions column was not. Cracking rebel codes was child's play compared to this. Mors was the unknown variable in every part of the equation. What did he know? What didn't he know?

How do we work around that? Intelligence has brought no answers, only more questions without answers.

She might be physically useless in a fight, but she would do anything to give them an advantage. Time to test the things she could control.

Escorted by two engineers, Grace verified a tower's signaling accuracy in transmitting her code, roughing out a backup plan if a tower in the sequence were taken out. She would not give Arundel an unproven network. Finished, she shuttered the mirrors to their original configuration and started down.

Midway down, she paused for a final line-of-sight check. It was perfect. An undignified cheer and fist pump threatened to surface with the realization it was the last verification needed to prove her network sound. She wrestled the urge into a smile, giving Asa a thumbs up. She was teaching Asa socially acceptable Human hand signs.

Twin arrows striking her shoulder and thigh were the first sign of attack; ripping her from the ladder to fall the last ten meters. The four Guardians permanently assigned to her outside the Keep were in motion at the sound of the arrow's release. The first Guardian, directly below her, took an arrow to the back. Refusing to move, he managed to break her fall as both of them went down.

Asa was flattened over Grace a split-second later, a slicing arrow skimming her spine, carving her ear and cheekbone, as it passed. Asa performed lightning-fast analysis. Disregarding her own injuries, she could not Travel Grace away without knowing if a critical bone break could puncture a vital organ. Grace's life signs indicated she was unconscious. It would take two jumps to reach the Keep. She needed a secure moment to check her over, and so remained motionless while fighting continued.

The lead engineer went down, throat ripped open. The second and third Guardians were on top of the two assassins before they could nock another arrow, cutting the throat of one, breaking the arms on the second.

The fourth Guardian sprinted for Grace. Seeing Asa's open wound to the spine, he eased her away to examine Grace for critical bleeding or trauma.

The live assassin was stripped of hidden weapons; minutely searched for poison, garrotes, hidden slivers of blades, anything used to commit suicide, The Guardians bound him for interrogation.

The second engineer had wisely dropped flat to let the Guardians do their job. Shakily regaining his feet, he climbed the tower, messaging the Keep of the attack and the injuring of the Prefect's Mate.

They were a forty-minute walk from the Keep at Grace's pace. A Tessera of Guardians arrived in ten, spreading over the immediate area in protective formation, searching for more rebels. They brought two battlefield Healers.

A Healer stopped to verify the dead engineer, moving quickly on to Asa and the Guardian who had taken an arrow in breaking Grace's fall. The second Healer went straight to Grace, fully briefed in her human differences.

He gently turned her onto her side so he could examine the arrows. They had either missed critical bleeders, or they held it at bay. He left them in place, scenting carefully for poison, swiftly examining her for other injuries. She woke while he was examining her head wound, disoriented by pain and confusion.

"There you are, Grace. Hold still for me. I need to finish looking you over."

Cracked ribs, concussion, severe bruising. The Healer stopped the slow bleeding surrounding the concussed area of her brain, the arrows, and the contusions.

He removed both ends of the arrows, wrapping her in a blanket slashed to accommodate them. He wouldn't attempt to remove the shafts in the field. A clean environment was nearby, especially important with Grace's risk of infection. She was healing faster than Humans but had not experienced injury of this magnitude.

Asa's Healer finished what could be done in the field, bandaging her back, cleaning face and cheek wounds. Asa struggled to remain still, angry not to have heard the assassin's approach, even with four other Guardians present. She'd been looking up at Grace. They must have been planted nearby.

She called to the Tessera lead Guardian to search for embedded, not moving, targets around tower bases. There must be more of them. They could not have known which tower Grace would be on. More to the point, how had they known Grace was on the towers? Or her location? Was the Keep under surveillance? Thank the Mother, Arundel had returned.

Grace, now fully cognizant, ordered her volatile Guardians to calm down. None of her wounds appeared life threatening, though the Guardian who had taken an arrow to the back, had also broken several ribs and his arm in catching her.

The arrow appeared to have missed anything vital but the odds were not high of accurate assessment in the field. The Healer needed him to remain still. He continued to direct the others, dismissing the Healer's attention.

Grace ordered him to stop, asking two Tessera Guardians to assist him back to the Keep, rendering him unconscious if necessary. Although she had no official power, this was her operation and he subsided. She struggled to keep it together as adrenaline waned and she sank further into shock.

They readied to head back forty minutes after the first arrow's release, dragging the live and dead rebels. The surviving engineer shouldered his dead colleague. Tessera Guardians covered all sides.

Gunnar and a half-Century of Dark Unit Guardians arrived on the scene like an explosive shadow. Taking in Grace's condition with a battlefield commander's eye, then Asa's, he put his hand to Grace's face, reading. Between her and Asa, they would carry every specific he needed to know.

He apprised his warriors of exactly what they were looking for, embedded suicide units, strung through the line of towers, and surrounding area, warning the Tessera already in the field to be cautious in apprehending the rebels. Assassins were set to self-destruct. He wanted them for interrogation.

Then he turned to Grace, lifting her from the Healer's

arms. Careful to position her so the arrows were not shifted, his presence and touch were enough for her to stop fighting the painful wounds, worrying about her companion's vulnerability or calming the volatility of the protective Guardians.

His body against her lowered her blood pressure, which slowed bleeding. Silent tears of relief, pain, and shock wet her cheeks. He felt her tense body go limp in his arms, briefly pressing his forehead to hers as he made for the Keep.

One of the Healers with the aid of a Tessera Guardian was carrying Asa, who was bitching about her position, face-down across their arms, necessary with the spinal wound. Grace sighed, knowing Asa's wounds could not be terribly severe if she had strength to complain.

The terrain was rough. No matter how much care was taken there was no way to move quickly and smoothly at the same time. Somewhere along the way Grace mercifully fainted. Gunnar increased his speed, his rage at those targeting his Mate under rigid control.

He was piecing together a more chilling picture. The arrows wounding her were not meant to kill. Their precision-shooting carefully avoided major organs and bleeders and they'd allowed her to descend far enough to survive the fall. This was an attempt to capture her.

He needed Arundel to remind him of his duty or he would eviscerate every rebel he touched.

Awakening in the medical unit to a pounding head, throbbing wounds, and complaining ribs, Grace felt none of it mattered because Gunnar stood in the doorway, receiving a Guardian's progress report. Arundel had left moments before, following an initial debrief by Gunnar. He heard the change in her breathing, flashing to her side, fingers gently stroking her cheek.

Grace sighed. "We have to stop meeting like this."

Lips pressed to her forehead, Gunnar allowed a faint suggestion of a growl, pulling back to see her face.

"You made a funny. Asa?"

"She's already healed one wound; her back has closed over. No sign of impairment. The Guardians who carried her may never recover."

"And the Guardian who caught me?"

"He's asleep, raging until the last moment."

Grace made motion to sit up, prompting a louder growl. She obediently allowed him to ease her back to the pillow, her face white with pain.

"Mate, I will tie you down if I must. Drink this." Gunnar held a small cup to her lips. She readily swallowed.

"I want to thank him for saving my life."

"I have, profoundly. He's asleep," Gunnar patiently reminded her.

"What—happened—in the field?" Her heavy lids drifted down. The cup held more than a mild pain tincture.

"Later."

"Mors—coming…" she breathed, sliding into sleep.

Breath caught, Gunnar stared down at her.

Grace woke the next morning feeling much better. Her wounds still burned at the arrow sites, but to a greatly diminished degree. Her bruises and sore ribs from the fall—gone, as was her headache.

A young Healer came in just as she was pulling at the bandages. "Grace, please allow me to do that!"

She carefully unwrapped Grace's shoulder and thigh, checking entry and exit wounds.

"They're almost gone," she said. "They'll itch for another few hours, but all look well-healed."

She rubbed some salve into the wound sites and the burning disappeared. Grace inhaled deeply and released slowly, testing her ribs.

"I'll never get used to healing so quickly. Thank you. I'm grateful for your care."

The young female's face lit up.

"If Asa is outside, I think I'll go home."

She could guess where Gunnar was. It didn't bear thinking about. Asa was indeed outside her door, having healed a few hours faster than Grace.

Slipping into the room of her sleeping Guardian, Grace softly kissed his cheek, whispering to him, *"Thank you for catching me."*

As she left the room, he sighed, taking a small smile with him, sliding back into sleep.

19.

SLINGS AND ARROWS

GRACE REPORTED TO Master Oran soon after healing from the tower incident, ready to work. She would not be a defenseless target, a liability to her Mate. Able to heal from most injuries, it was time to reach for her limits.

"Master Oran." She nodded respectfully and waited for him to indicate where to begin.

She was clad in the training clothes the others wore. It made a substantial difference. This was a serious version of her favorite pastime, pitting herself against her best. Her reasons had never been so urgent. A gift she could give her Mate, lightening his cost in loving her.

No holds barred. Let's go.

Oran started her with a series of warm-up exercises. His manner acknowledged priorities had changed, accelerated. They'd had several sessions of strength training and two lessons with Gunnar's dagger, now living at her hip. But it was for emergencies, not a primary defense weapon.

Oran had marked her slight improvement at the end of her initial archery session. It should have decreased substantially from fatigue, due to the massively mismatched bow and arm pain from the bowstring burn.

Some of the performance rebound could be contributed to agitation at poor performance, but she had switched to walking toward the target, rather than shooting from a stationary position. He considered this an anomaly, deciding to explore it.

"Grace, the weaponsmith has finished your bow. He was particularly mindful with weight and draw."

Master Oran placed the longed-for bow in her hands. She felt a surge of familiarity flow through her muscles.

"It's beautiful," she said, closely examining it. "He's an artist."

He allowed her to shoot long enough to familiarize herself with the weapon, a full quiver of lighter, but deadly arrows at her back, watching her delight at managing a weapon engineered for her.

He started her walking toward him from the far end of the range. She missed a few targets but was steadily nearing the inner rings by the end of the row.

"Master Oran, may I experiment with it? It feels—natural in my hands."

"Follow your instincts," he said.

She centered herself on the range, then stood eyes closed, head down, breathing deeply. She appeared to be remembering, but he knew she had no experience with such a weapon.

She darted to the side, shooting until she hit several consecutive targets, then dropping to roll in an evasive maneuver, before quickly regaining her feet in the opposite direction. She hit her third target in the center, rolling again to shoot across the row, her placement improving toward the center, but within the three center rings on all targets. "What a difference the bow and lighter arrows make!"

Grace ran to gather her arrows, absorbed in her excitement over the weapon.

Asa and Master Oran exchanged a long look.

Starting from the far end of the range, she ran at a pace allowing her to pull and nock arrows every three seconds. She hit all targets within the inner two rings. Stretching, Grace caught her breath, a delighted smile on her face.

Standing with her back to the center of the range, she twisted to shoot behind her, firing from one end across the range until forced to turn and resume from the opposite side of her body. Her results were not as good, but far exceeded his expectations for such a posture.

Oran shook his head. Motion appeared to be the key, which puzzled the Weapons Master. Archers preferred a stationary stance for accuracy. Even in battle, they paused to shoot unless forced to move. Grace's accuracy appeared to improve with movement. He looked to Asa. She nodded, brows knit over the same details. With a few more running, rolling passes, Grace's accuracy was passing 80 percent.

The Weapons Master abruptly switched her to the throwing knives. Grace was reluctant to leave the bow, lovingly running her hand over it, but willingly turned to the task he set. Targets had been reset for knives, and Asa stood quietly, adding meticulous mental notes to a brief for Prefect Gunnar that was becoming more urgent by the day.

Grace faced the targets, working to remember the lessons from her first attempt. Body stance, distance, arm movement. After three throws striking the outermost rings, she walked to the target pulling the knives. Returning to the weapons board she picked up two more stacks of the same size and type of knife.

"May I, Master Oran?" She indicated the spot at center range.

He nodded.

Again she stood, eyes closed, head down, breathing deeply. Then she spun in a circle releasing knives only when facing the targets. Three of the nine struck the targets one ring out from center. The rest were scattered above or below them.

Master Oran scanned them, seeing a pattern.

If these had been Fae-shaped targets, every high knife struck average head height, the low, gut level. The ones missing the center did not miss. They are directly over the heart.

Her strength in gripping the stacks of knives would not allow heavy penetration but with exercise and a switch from practice to light, edged blades, they would. Master Oran had seen weapons prodigies, but this was something new to him.

Something else.

Grace was pulling knives from their targets. "Master Oran, my accuracy is terrible."

"Practice and time, Grace," he said

"Asa, the village leatherworkers, do you think they could make me a knife belt? I need it to run at a slight diagonal here." The belt description was completely different from any equipment on the weapons wall but familiar enough to her for detailed description.

"Grace, draw me a picture with approximate measurements. We'll take it to them."

They moved to the training mats. Grace had no surprises for them there. She tried some unconventional blocks to incoming blows but yielded in strength to every one. As she had stated in their first lesson, she had no muscle mass.

The Weapons Master did not share his thoughts aloud. She would never be strong enough facing a warrior, but the bow and knives could give her a chance.

Against a small number of adversaries, she would be a threat. He asked her to put away her weapons. Keeping the bow, he showed her how to strengthen her arms. Draw smoothly, hold to the count of ten, slowly return to first position. He moved to stand with Asa, angled toward each other so Grace didn't feel watched.

Under her breath, Asa questioned Oran. "What was that? Is it possible there's an unknown Possessor in the Keep?"

Master Oran shook his head.

"It appears to be muscle memory. Deeply ingrained muscle memory. It takes many years to coordinate complex assessment and response until it's automatic reflex. You must know this, Operative Asa."

He pointed out the pattern in the knives though they were no longer in the targets. "Head, heart, gut. Grace's eyes were looking at the ringed targets. Her muscles and reflexes were feeling the knives and their intended use." He looked grim. "A Possessor could only use her body with their personal reflexes. These techniques of bow and knife are foreign to me," Oran said. "They are the skills of a warrior, from nowhere I am familiar with."

Asa sent a message to Prefect Gunnar, requesting he observe Grace's next lesson. Some things must be seen, not read in a report.

Soaking in a hot, post-training bath, Grace heard Gunnar enter their rooms, knowing he would swiftly track her to the tub. She looked up to see him leaning against the door frame, eyes caressing her.

Impudently looking him over, she cocked her head "Prefect, you appear parched, in need of water."

She scooted forward, arms around her knees, gaze flicking over her shoulder to the open tub space behind her. "Reconnaissance appears warranted," he shrugged. "I'll finish these reports, then reassess the situation."

Grace threw a handful of water at him. Gunnar was kissing her before the last droplet hit the floor. His clothing quickly followed.

Grace leaned back against his chest, draping her legs outside his, pulling his arms around her as the rebounding waves settled. She tugged a willing hand a bit further south.

"I commend your reliability, Prefect."

Lips pressed behind her ear. A warm exhale shivered her wet neck.

"I'm not known to neglect my duties."

Resting against the sloping back of the tub, they relaxed into their favorite game, in which to surrender was to win. It was a struggle for Grace to avoid helplessly dissolving from the start. Her fingertips stretched to massage the back of his neck before combing through his hair, gently tugging the cowlicks she loved.

Her bowed body pressed her breast into Gunnar's caressing hand while providing his mouth easy access to her neck.

Thighs rising, Gunnar further spread her legs, aiding his reach below the waterline. Grace slid upward on his chest, dropping a hand to guide him beneath her. His slippery fingers withdrew, her settling glide onto him eliciting heartfelt sounds from them both.

They luxuriated in a rare combination of racing blood and breath in quiet bodies. Mostly quiet. Her involuntary tightening around him made it impossible for him to remain still. Grace inhaled sharply as Gunnar flexed his hips against her. His hand returned to circle against her as he repeated the movement, harder. When he readjusted his foot placement as an arm slipped around her waist, Grace wisely surrendered.

Gunnar stroked into her, hand teasing, knees holding her legs open against the tub as he rose and fell. In moments he felt her body tense precariously on the edge, her speeding breaths hot against his neck. Moving with increasing intensity brought a breathy cry and drove her gathering muscles into stretching release.

He held her close, not letting up in touch or stroking until her body's throes and the splashing waves of water subsided.

He nuzzled her neck, scenting her pleasure.

"Mate, the water is cooling, let's move to the bed."

Gunnar on his knees, toweling her dry was decadent. His gentle roughing with the linen towel sensitized her skin to the lightest brush of lips and fingers. Somehow, she missed her share of drying him.

He drew her to the bed, coaxing her to relax face down. Reclining on his side, head resting on a raised hand, the other kneaded and stroked her shoulder muscles, working down her back, prompting undignified grunts of pleasure.

"Between training and you, I had no idea how many muscles I have."

Gunnar leaned to kiss the nape of her neck. His wandering hand dropped lower to slip between her thighs, encouraging them to part. Two fingers entered her swollen softness, slick from their pleasure in the bath. Grace's hips rose to meet their movement.

"Warm-up is an often overlooked part of training," Gunnar said, pumping slowly in with three.

When she moaned, body tightly gripping his hand, he withdrew it, rising to lift her to hands and knees, nudging her legs further apart. He lightly pressed between her shoulder blades, encouraging her to rest her cheek and forearms on the pillows.

Kneeling close behind, he ran his thumbs up her spine, feeling her relaxed exhale at his hands firmly smoothing over her ribs. Dipping under to squeeze her breasts, he continued back along her flanks. He loved the tender place between belly and thigh, resting his fingers there. Grace's breath froze on a deep inhale as he pulled her to him while stroking in. And in. Gasping, she bucked against him, grasping at the sheet to leverage into his stroke.

Letting go of her hips, Gunnar stretched over her, curling her hands inside his, resting loose fists on the bed for her to push against. Face pressed in her hair, he thrust again with a bone-deep groan of pleasure at her ear. After several deepening strokes, he hoarsely spoke against her throat.

"Is it too much?"

His movement dragged a breathless "No—" from her. She urged him— "Let go…" Gunnar's eyes closed at the feel of her body quickening.

She pushed harder against his hands, increasing the power of every movement in a synergy of intensifying sensation. Their guttural cries and rasping breaths multiplied with the increasing force of spiraling pleasure. Grace was fighting to hold onto her orgasm, wanting Gunnar to come with her. A wildness was growing, spreading through her muscles, nerve endings, scent. Gunnar's lips were next to her ear. "*Now*, Mate."

Low notes in his rasping voice released a visceral response. As he moved fiercely in her, her back arched powerfully against his chest. From deep within came a low-pitched, escalating snarl as her climaxing body contracted hard around him.

Her scent and sounds instantly changed Gunnar's stance. Arm tightly encircling her body, his cheek brushed her hair aside as he bit the back of her neck, to hold, not hurt, answering her with a possessively thunderous growl rumbling through his body into hers.

Feeling her body's muscle and bone rippling alerted him. The movements weren't in climax, Gunnar's centuries of trained self-control instantly surfaced. She was Shifting. Letting go of her neck, he pulled her with him to drop to their sides, locking his body to surround hers in an iron grip, each heaving, growl-edged pant slowing as he concentrated to stop her body's reaction and control his answering Shift.

The bedding beneath her hands was shredded. He quickly turned her face toward him.

"Grace, open your eyes."

He watched her vivid gold irises fade to their normal color, pinpoint pupils expanding to human dimensions, knowing she was seeing the same in his.

Did she understand what had happened? He laid her back on the pillows, pulling her more tightly against him, wanting only to keep her safe, in control, as they calmed. Grace's body relaxed, then sated and seemingly unaware, she drifted into sleep.

"Mother and Father Above," Gunnar whispered.

In a breath he had moved from wild exhilaration to fear. Why was this happening to her? What did it mean?

He needed answers.

20.

CLEAR SIGHT

ASA'S MIND REFUSED sleep.

Prefect Gunnar had stood without movement at the back of the training rooms, minutely observing Grace and her inexplicable display of weapons skills. Dispassionately analytical on the surface, she could see him attempt to control a flicker of fear for her.

Asa had never seen him make an unsuccessful attempt at anything. That she could discern it at all communicated its magnitude. He asked for her overarching, long-term assessment, not her regular weekly brief.

Leaving her bed, Asa dismissed her unfinished notes and began writing stream-of-thought, emptying onto the page. She would edit and put things in order when it felt complete. As she finished, she wasn't sure which emotion was stronger, relief at having broken the dam or fear at the unknown ramifications.

Many noted observations hadn't coalesced until recent events pulled the entirety into sharper focus.

PULSE SICKNESS

When Gunnar first read her in Central, Grace's memories told of her pain and confusion in losing consciousness when the Pulse struck her down on Earth, arriving on Oberon with the effects of Pulse sickness fully manifesting. Her recovery time was similar to Fae. No other Human was reported to have experienced physical symptoms from the Pulse.

SEER

Grace's dreams upon arrival contained people, places, and relationships she couldn't yet know. She had repeatedly mentioned dreams of the village.

1) TELEPATHY

Grace spoke of receiving glimpses of Gunnar's thoughts.

MATING

Prefect Gunnar's body triggering the Mating mark response to a Human.

HEALING

Two days later, Grace demonstrated rapid healing from an arm injury. Presently, she healed from two arrow wounds, cracked ribs, and a head injury in one day.

WEAPONS SKILL—Unknown Gift

Demonstration of expert, foreign skills with bow and knives in training; Note: Master Oran suggests this is muscle-memory of a foreign style and technique. Grace appears unaware of the change, seamlessly incorporating the skills into her routine training.

EMPATH/POSSESSION

Empath Gifts were observed while Grace spoke with Humans in the village. She appeared to use Empath, and possibly Possession, to control an agitated Human male.

VOICE/EMPATH

A Human child in the camp attempted to communicate while upset, in an unknown language. Grace picked the child up, stroking her hair. The child immediately calmed and began speaking the common tongue.

ANALYSIS

Grace demonstrates plural Gifts. There are no documented cases of any appearing in Humans. Logic suggests Grace is of a high percentage, Fae.

Questions:

Possible explanations of plural Gifts? Unknown

Are there hybrid Gifts? Unknown

Theories to explain these observations? None to date.

Additional Anomalies:

Grace has spoken of widespread, active interest by Humans in Fae. She cited anecdotal use of the name Oberon in connection to Fae by a historic writer, references of Oberon military terms in Earth's history.

Research of Humans on Oberon: Reports of most recent appearance of Humans were estimated at eight hundred years ago, coinciding with a cataclysmic illness among Fae. Hypothesis: a possible Pulse.

Hypothesis: If historical humans on Oberon originated from Earth, they would have died of natural attrition due to lifespan. Human-Fae progeny may not have been easily detectable or were possibly hidden. If Fae were transferred to Earth, lifespan and possible descendants could account for active cultural presence.

Question: Could Fae/Human blood be a factor in transference triggered by a Pulse? Timing of immediate evidence could substantiate this theory.

End of report.

As she reviewed her notes, Asa decided urgency warranted Prefect Gunnar reading them in rough draft form.

Tonight.

Gunnar stared at Asa's list, running through triggered thoughts. First instincts were often correct. Some notes were familiar, but he had not focused his attention as he should, not zeroed-in as Asa had. His thoughts grew fragmented, jumping from one incident to another.

Her fear of the Door, was it Seer-led? Did fate drive her from the Bunker for the Pulse? She was comforted by my presence while delirious with sickness —as though she knew me.

Hands scrubbing his face, Gunnar pondered the two flashes of terrifying darkness he'd seen—one in her memories on Earth, one on Oberon while ill. *Was her latent Shielding aware of Mors searching for her? She had said, "Mors coming," as she fell asleep in the Med Unit.*

And—Healing—Mother Above.

His eyes closed. Such an immense relief of an egregious

worry, and the hypothesis had been sound—more sound at the time than leaping to the conclusion that a Fae trait was surfacing.

Gunnar rose to pace, struggling with anger over his blindness as he forced himself to focus.

Telepathy—she's sharp in how she sees and analyzes—it's easy to think she just knows. She recognized my Jaguar when only Arundel knows—but—I told him of its existence...

He stopped pacing at the wall.

Empath—she reversed the panic her trauma triggered the first time we were intimate—more quickly than natural subsiding of strong emotion. Did she pull comforting emotion from me? But Shifting—there's no supportive logic without Shifter bloodlines...

Gunnar laid a hand against the wall, resting his forehead on it.

Her eye color and vocalization—they're mine... Father Above. Can she manipulate Gifts?

He would take each point as truth unless they proved otherwise. They were defensively readying for war against an unquantifiable enemy. Had Grace a predestined part in this? How could he protect her without answers?

He had never before been truly frightened.

He was now.

21.

THE WALL

HAVING MOVED FROM Gunnar's arms in the grip of a disturbing dream, Grace stealthily returned. She relaxed as Gunnar tucked her back into his embrace. She didn't know he woke if any of her life signs changed in sleep. He stroked the curve of her hip, unable to resist moving upward to cup her breast. "You're awake early," he whispered against her neck.

He planted an open-mouthed kiss below her ear, breathing against it just to feel her shiver, her nipple peaking under his hand. She turned over in his arms to bury her face in his chest.

"*You* are irresistible to wake up to. It can make it difficult to sleep at all," she said.

"You were restless during the night. Unpleasant dreams?" Gunnar gently lifted her chin, searching her eyes.

Grace never admitted her bad dreams, an ingrained response from home. She felt it wrong to burden others with her near-constant stream of them. The dreams had abated upon Mating Gunnar and only recently begun creeping back in. She felt it was a personal flaw that they were returning.

"Unpleasant memories."

She pressed him to his back, scooting up to lie in her place of comfort, ear over his heart. The strong beats overcame anything wrong in her world.

In a little while, he moved her up, head resting on his shoulder at eye level. He caressed her cheek.

"I've never before seen eyes like yours. Only you and your sister shared them? I've few physical traits that I'm aware passed from my family. I know very little about them, but I know even less of yours."

Frowning slightly, Grace considered his words. She nestled into him.

"I've left it behind. My family feels insignificant in this place."

Feeling his questions forming, Grace tried to mentally retreat. If he didn't use his Telepathy, she could keep them at bay.

They've never existed here. I don't want to let darkness into my light.

"Mate, they created you to become a part of me. They are not insignificant."

He felt her stiffen. Thought fragments drifted to him.

It feels so long ago—leave it there—I had to change worlds to escape it.

Her agitation was rising. Gunnar scented the beginning of panic. Just as he moved to speak, she exhaled forcefully, and her expression changed. She'd accepted his request for answers. He paid close attention to her body language and words. Her voice was flat.

"You already know I killed my mother during birth. They took Ellie from her after she was dead."

Mate—no.

It was a struggle for him not to correct this terrible notion—so brutally put. But to stop her now would divert her flow of thought.

"My father followed her several years later. We rarely saw him. He drank, never looked after himself. Never looked at us." Grace paused. "Never forgave her death. Grandmother Lilli raised us. Mostly me. Ellie left so soon once we began school. They'd never seen someone so gifted."

Gunnar monitored every inflection, heartbeat, muscle twitch. There was a moment of warmth when she spoke of Ellie.

"Ellie's comprehension—she could see answers to questions or problems faster than they were given."

Both of them were Gifted. Her sister manifested to fit her surroundings.

"My grandmother—her stories…"

Grace twisted to curl up in his arms, voice sliding toward monotone.

"In her stories, I was special. She said I was like Ellie; we just had different purposes. If we did, I certainly couldn't see it." Grace rubbed her eyes, curled her body a little tighter.

"Grandmother got sick when I was fifteen. Old enough to get my Emancipation papers. They declare you a legal adult. I took care of everything, for all of us. Grandmother died."

A tremor entered her voice.

"Then Ellie died—it almost killed me too. The car—Mate, she was so afraid of fire…"

Her body was shaking in his arms from the tension of clenched muscles. Pain of mind and body radiated from her.

Gunnar couldn't bear it, he diverted her with a question.

"What did you know of your mother?"

She forced a deep breath, thoughts shifting.

"My mother was something of an enigma."

Gunnar highlighted everything that leapt out at him.

"My grandfather abandoned my grandmother, before my mother was born, which was shocking in an old Boston family. Growing up, there were no pictures of him. I never once heard anyone speak of him, least of all my grandmother."

She readjusted her cheek against him.

"I asked about him once. She waved it away and said everything important lay ahead, not behind. Most of all, I was to trust what my heart saw. Honestly, I didn't understand half of what she told me, but perhaps she meant you. My heart saw you before I did—I just had to catch up."

Grace uncurled, pulling up to kiss him. Gunnar's fingertips traced her face, gently keeping her at bay as he continued his questions.

"You must have your grandmother's strength."

"I hope so. She radiated calm. Such a contrast to her terrible scars."

Confusion crossed her face. "I don't remember ever hearing how she got them. Isn't that strange…"

Her tone changed as she shifted to a different thought. "She had an answer to everything. I would understand when I was grown—our strength came through our family lines— it made us sound like we'd been bred, like horses. Such an Old Boston family way of thinking."

Gunnar was having difficulty keeping himself in check.

It's not possible.

He could feel agitation rising in her.

"I hate my last memory of her. She was napping on the parlor chaise. She was restless and I was afraid she'd fall to the floor. So I went to wake her. When I touched her, she screamed—"

Grace froze. Her scent shifted instantly to utter shock. He felt an electrical pulse in her body jolt her heart.

Gunnar swiftly moved to hover over her, ignoring the pain that burned him in response to the tiny pulse, running his hand over her, listening to her heart.

She looked through him, barely breathing. He slipped into her thoughts, seeing her frail grandmother, restlessly moving. At Grace's touch, her scarred arms crossed protectively in front of her face, knees curling in.

"Mors!" she screamed.

Gunnar fiercely pulled Grace to him. Heart hammering, his mind ripped through facts, occurrences, comments. Final pieces falling into place.

Asa's report.

Her Grandmother.

Her Gifted twin.

The Gifts on Earth.

Her dreams.

Her Gifts.

Her Gifts.

Her Gifts.

Mors, possibly the most Gifted, vicious Fae in Oberon's history, was her grandfather. It was his blood—her grandmother had responded to Mors' blood in Grace. His arrival matched hers.

There was no escaping the logic.

When Grace did not respond to Gunnar, remaining deaf to his words, blindly staring into space, he threw on his clothes and shouted for a Guardian to get Ahma and Arundel. He held her, wrapped in a blanket, cupping her cheek to monitor her thoughts. She was locked in the moment of touching her grandmother.

Ahma and Arundel arrived together. Ahma already examining Grace as Gunnar laid her down. He looked to Arundel, searching for words—how to explain. He gave him Asa's report.

"Prefect, may I give her sleep to ease her until we know the cause? I'm concerned this—this shock is harmful to her mind and body. Her life signs are erratic."

Gunnar paused, weighing unknown factors against the overwhelming pain he'd felt jolt through her.

"Do it," he said.

Arundel read Asa's report, pausing over several points.

"There's more," he said.

He looked to Ahma as she smoothed the cover over Grace's sleeping form. Nodding, she silently left.

Pulling two chairs together, Arundel led Gunnar to sit. Gunnar realized he was shaking with adrenaline aftermath. He began running through the report, adding additional points he had not put together until now.

Gunnar went through the morning's questioning of Grace, carefully covering her memories of her grandmother, almost verbatim. Until she'd reacted with such shock that Gunnar had entered her mind to see the memory Grace could not finish.

Gunnar ran through his analysis and laid out his

conclusions and fears, shining with sweat. Faced with a problem logic could not solve, his Jaguar was fighting to Shift, wanting to physically protect Grace.

Arundel anchored Gunnar— as his brother countless times had done for him—while he processed Gunnar's analysis. He called for the Guardian outside the door. Moments later the door opened to admit a female Gunnar knew was his most powerful Shield. Arundel pointed to Grace, then indicated the perimeter of the Keep. The female nodded, retreating just outside the door.

Gunnar dropped his head, hands scrubbing his face.

"You would think I'd have covered that in the first moments."

"Brother, you're in shock. Who would not be? A Shield will remain with her day and night." Arundel looked thoughtfully at the report in his hand. "She might give us insight into him. Light illuminates Dark."

Arundel looked up as a ferocious sound ripped from Gunnar. He twisted out of his chair, voice changing with his body until words were gone.

"No! Darkness—overwhelms—Light…"

Papers scattered as Arundel blurred, shadow talons raking to hold Gunnar's shoulders, even as claws grazed his own. "Brother—do not give in. You cannot help her in this form—pull back."

Breathing hard, both stilled, bodies settling, bloody fingertips, still grasping the other's shoulders. Gunnar's head lifted, gold eyes fading. The snarling edge left his calming breaths. Arundel gave him a grim smile.

"I will not leave her or you alone, Brother. We will fight this battle as we always have, together."

Alone in their rooms while Grace slept, Gunnar's mind was stumbling under the repeated blows of his inability to protect Grace, his failure to recognize what was happening, his logic's inability even now to give solutions—or even plan ahead…

What did this mean—that such forces surrounded her existence? He stopped pacing, vision shaking with his heartbeats. He slid in next to her in the bed, curling around her so he could feel her breathing. Hear her heartbeat.

He touched the scar from the arrow on her shoulder. Her ephemeral existence sliced through him like a blade.

He would do anything to protect her. He lay for hours, arms around her, cheek resting on her hair, trying to control his panic because her mind was now completely blank.

There were no thoughts, no memories, only a featureless wall with no opening, or light. It had to be a form of protection from the shock. He could think of no bearable alternatives.

Hours later, Gunnar awoke from the light sleep he finally allowed himself, instinct telling him something was wrong. He could feel by Grace's breathing that she was awake.

He gently stroked her cheek. "Mate?"

There was no response. He forced himself to remain calm, counting her heartbeats, her breaths. He knew her rhythms to the second. They were dropping, already below normal. Her body was limp, unresponsive to his touch.

He vaulted from the bed to yank open the door, dispatching the Guardian to summon Ahma to the medical unit. Throwing on his uniform, he told the Shield to follow as he ran with Grace to the medical unit. Ahma was searching for a cause when Arundel arrived.

"Prefect, the sleeping tonic is completely gone. It waned some time ago. This is something unknown to me."

"Then why are her life signs slowing?"

Gunnar turned to Arundel, trying to hold his composure. "Arundel, there is a wall in her mind, I can see nothing, feel nothing. I've never encountered such a thing."

Arundel looked to the Shield. She responded with a nod, indicating she had not paused. Arundel told the Guardian at the door to send for an Empath and Possessor.

Gunnar watched closely as the Possessor stepped forward, settling his hand lightly on Grace's shoulder. His eyes closed as he felt for another Possessor's influence.

After several moments, the Possessor looked to Arundel, then Gunnar.

"The wall comes from inside. There is no trace of another presence. I have seen weaker forms in trauma victims. Never anything like this."

"Can you get through it?" Gunnar asked. "Break it?"

They could hear her heart rate continue to drop.

"Prefect, I tried. She's holding it together. She's incredibly strong."

Gunnar's voice cracked, "I *know*."

Her heartbeat was now half its normal rate, dropping fast; her breath becoming a whisper.

Arundel felt his exhausted brother's crippling despair. His voice sharpened, inciting Gunnar to act. "Brother! *Talk to her.*"

He motioned the Empath forward.

The Empath put a hand to her forehead, one over her heart. Gunnar spoke to her.

"*Grace*, you cannot do this. Whatever is happening, *fight*."

Gunnar's pain echoed through Arundel with all the intensity of his own loss. He reached toward Gunnar, then let his hand fall. He would have resented an intrusion when Etana was fighting for her life.

The Empath lifted his head, speaking to Arundel. "She feels —responsible for some terrible event. Her death will lessen it, saving many."

He looked to Gunnar.

"There is hatred of self, to have brought this to Oberon. To you."

Gunnar roughly pulled her shoulders from the table.

"*No!* You may not decide this for us both. *Mate*, do not do this! Break the wall—now—or I forfeit my life with you."

Grace's heart lurched violently, arcing her off the table, throat choking at the sudden intake of breath. Gunnar felt the wall in her mind implode, gasping for air with her as her body shuddered, heart staggering.

The moment of her grandmother scream had opened the floodgates to her bloodline, releasing memories of Mors' entire existence through her. The wall sealing off her mind had protected Gunnar from this. With the wall destroyed, she could no longer keep it from him.

Gunnar gripped the table edge as he fell to his knees, absorbing centuries of images and emotion as he was pulled through eight hundred years of Mors' monstrous life. The enormity of it—how would Grace bear it?

Gunnar, struggling to recover, spoke sharply to the

Empath. "Can you build a defensive block, a division—any-thing to protect her?"

The Empath considered carefully. He asked for the other two Empaths in the Keep. It took several hours to build a block of the sort Black Ops used to remain detached during torture.

This allowed Grace to see but not feel Mors. To keep the horror of him separate from herself.

The Empaths had to work in rotation. The evil in his memories affected even the Dark Unit warriors. They paced the room while recovering, grim-faced and sweating.

Arundel watched, willing himself to remain still. Like Gunnar, he felt the danger surrounding them, but had nowhere to attack.

Arundel's heart, safeguarded by the golden threads of his family, grieved for Grace, surrounded by Gunnar's love, yet determined to leave it to protect them all.

The Empaths confirmed they could go no further. The horrors were muted; she could turn away from them though they would not leave her. Gunnar cradled her limp body to move her to a nearby bed. He was stricken at the emptiness he felt in her, as though a candle had been put out. Her only reaction during the long hours had been an endless, silent trail of tears, while she lay blindly gazing upward.

"Mate, I'm here. Can you sleep?"

She nodded once. Closing her eyes, she turned away.

A Shield and Empath stood nearby while she slept.

Arundel and Gunnar sat in the adjoining room. Gunnar had never experienced such despair. He could not shield her from this horror. The war in her heart was not over. He bent over his knees, hands laced behind his head.

Arundel sat beside him, searching for a way to lighten his brother's burden. Only the Chimera actively manifested Gifts.

He could help Gunnar more…

"Brother, let me read the memories. It will help us both to find a way through this. Come, the training room may be large enough."

Arundel walked with Gunnar to the training room, closing the door.

22.

INSIDE OUT

GRACE KNEW WHAT was to come, what Mors wanted, and she could not tell them. If they had let her die quickly, the devastation of Oberon would have been halved. Many would now die in vain, while she left them by degrees. But Oberon would continue. That would have to be enough. That her end would come sooner, sparing her from seeing the rest unfold, was the hardest thing to bear.

Sitting at the conference table, Arundel was unsurprised by the empty seat at the far end. The other Northern Protectorate Commanders had the allegiance and intelligence to attend; their Command Centurions standing behind them in the near-full room. To his right was the Commander of Central Protectorate. Her territory shared Arundel's western border. Whatever the Northeastern Protectorate faced, hers would be next. She was a tested veteran commander who put her people before all else. She was also an ally who trusted Arundel implicitly, knowing their shared boundaries strengthened them both.

The Commander from the Central Western Protectorate sat to Arundel's left. He was not an aggressive leader concerning matters outside his borders. His territory suffered incessant catastrophic weather and drought. His primary focus was by necessity, maintaining food supplies and stability for his people.

The chair belonging to Western Protectorate's Commander was defiantly empty. Not even a representative was sent. Perhaps declining to engage in the certainty the other three territories would blunt any enemy attack before it reached his lands. Following his closure of communication regarding treatment of Humans, this did not bode well.

Combined Intelligence reports showed significant, unauthorized troop movements below the entire Northern Territories. There were also unverified reports of troop movement in the Northern Wastes.

Contact had also been intermittent, indicating Shields were in use. The ability to completely Shield what was surmised to be full Centuries on the move was particularly sobering.

Prefect Gunnar's briefing held a concise breakdown of Mors' known actions to date. He outlined his extreme Gifting, and without revealing the full history they now had of him, a brief hypothesis of how such a thing was possible. Mors' unknown base of operations was a strategic handicap.

The projection from each territory's reports on missing patrols and hostile actions in their territories suggested preparation by Mors to attack the collective Northern Territories. He appeared to already control a large number of rebel factions in the South, whether through alliance or Possession.

Gunnar's summation concluded with his analysis of Mors' goal for his first phase: occupy the Northern and Southern Continents. Phase Two was hypothetical: conquer the remaining continents.

The room was silent as each participant struggled to absorb the magnitude of this information. It was far worse than any were equipped to handle. None questioned its veracity, in light of their own intelligence networks and their trust in Arundel. Each had detected troop movement; all had lost intelligence Operatives or scouting parties without explanation.

The Central Commander responded first. "What do you need from us? We will immediately increase our Northern and Southern border strength, but we offer whatever assistance you need in this next stage."

Arundel thanked her for her commitment to the alliance.

They would continue planning, knowing they had her support. The two commanders shared signifiers confirming they would discuss this further in private, for security's sake. He would also brief her on Grace's codes.

Central's Commander rose from her chair, walking to the large wall map. She studied it for a moment before picking up a pencil from the tray below. Starting from the bottom of Arundel's territory, near the First Contact fishing village, she drew a line across the south of their territories westward, moving up through the center of Western Territory Protectorate, across the Northern Waste back down into Arundel's territory. "Mors lived in territory similar to this"— she tapped the Northern Waste— "on Earth, waging war for a century from it, down into lands such as ours, conquering almost two score countries and killing millions?"

"Yes."

"It is also comparable to his native land on Oberon?"

"Yes."

She put the pencil down and returned to her seat, saying nothing more. She didn't need to. Slander was a serious thing. But no one in the room could look at the map and not see that the Western Protectorate was a wide-open corridor for Mors to encircle the whole of their continent.

Western Territory's absence; was it more than arrogance and pettiness? Was it because Telepaths and Seers were present? Arundel silently allowed a long moment for his fellow commanders to chew on the possibilities.

Closing the meeting, he offered time for each of them to meet individually or in groups as they saw fit. They all felt the pressing need to hurry.

Asa now guarded Grace inside their quarters. As she came out to meet him, the shadowed defeat in her eyes confirmed there was no progress. Without a word, he understood the day was a repeat of the previous ten. Grace had eaten little, forced herself into shreds of small talk, managed a threadbare pretense of normalcy. No spark, no humor.

Her light, fading.

Gunnar stood at the door for a split second, hand resting on the handle, feeling an unreasonable flash of fear that he would open it to an empty room. But her scent was there, spurring him to enter.

Grace tried to keep everything that was killing her buried deep, Shielding so Gunnar couldn't read her.

Thank god it's only me. You're all safe.

One day, for one moment, her self-control slipped. Asa was in the next room while Grace washed her face.

Her glance fell on Gunnar's contraceptive tonic. Hope for the future that might have been, vanished. Looking into the mirror, Grace found it empty.

Puzzled, she realized Asa was holding her bleeding hand. The smashed mirror and shattered contents of the shelves were scattered across the washroom floor. But she couldn't remember…

"Grace. Don't move."

She watched, as though from a distance, as Asa rinsed glass fragments from her hands, carefully brushing them from her before carrying her from the room. Asa glanced at her face while bandaging her hand. Grace knew her body was there, next to Asa; she could read Asa's concerned thoughts through her touch, but her mind insistently moved farther away.

Gunnar felt only shadows of her pain; Grace refused to share it with him. Daily he entered the room to see her in the corner chair, an unread book open in her lap, waiting for him. He could barely breathe from wanting to ease her pain.

He lifted Grace in his arms, afraid to hold too tightly lest he hurt her.

His anguished heart whispered his thoughts lest she hear them.

You weigh nothing. You do not cry quarter. Mate, I will give anything, please… I cannot bear this.

Settling into the chair with Grace curled against his chest, Gunnar stroked her hair, swallowing the thickness in his throat. He tried to dredge up something interesting to share that did not involve his near-frantic work to save her from Mors.

It was their pretense: Grace pretended she could not read his every thought, and he pretended his attempts to slip past her Shield were not in vain. Their hearts met in the middle but could not speak. When she felt him winding down, she stood and pulled him up from the chair. She reached up to unfasten his tunic. He caught her hands, holding them in his.

"Tell me what you need… I'm—lost."

"Please, come to bed."

"Mate—"

"Please."

He obeyed, as he did every night. Her plea always the same. She was too exhausted to eat, to talk, to do anything but lie in her place of comfort.

He set her gently on the bed, stripping his clothing, letting it fall to the floor. Grace removed her shift, baring the slow ravages of lost weight. Gunnar slid in next to her, and lifted her to lie, ear over his heart, counting his heartbeats.

"It will be alright," she whispered. "Everything will be alright."

As he struggled with his powerlessness to save her from despair, Grace sent her Possessor and Empath Gifts through him, relaxing his body, soothing his mind. She would not do this while meeting his eyes, knowing he would see her barely holding on. When his mind and body eased, he felt her, limp with exhaustion, slide into sleep.

Gunnar watched over her throughout the night. Grace was so deep in the pit she had forgotten what his life's work had fitted him for, centuries before she came to him. Though Grace would not share the future, he could guess. She knew the narrative of what was to come, and he could not help. Grace would not give him a problem he could not solve.

And Gunnar felt a little more of himself die with her.

In the small hours of the night watch, Arundel sat alone in the conference room. He stared at a map depicting Mors' movements. Seers across the northern borders were confirming detection of incremental Shield coverage in motion. Enough to comprise another Legion, strung across the far North. Never had a war of such scale been waged.

Certainly not under a single command.

Searching for insight into his seemingly omnipotent opponent, he forced himself to review, yet again, Grace's memories of Mors. There must be an essential piece he was missing. Focusing on the first Fae killed for his Gift and life strength, he moved forward. In Mors' final two centuries on

Earth, he no longer took life strength. He didn't need them, he was immortal.

He reached Luma's sacrifice. It devastated him to watch Etana's sister suffer, but to turn away defeated the purpose of why she had allowed it. Arundel felt Etana give a great pulse, flashing the memory of their childhood meeting in the meadow.

In it, she was telling her sister Sola that Arundel would see Luma one day, as *they* saw.

Etana prompted him as he watched the terrible memory to understand what Luma had done. The moment Mors greedily took Luma's Gift, she pierced his arrogantly careless guard, using the power in her bloodline to craft a Gift concealed in her Human descendant's line. It would quicken and hide them, when Mors was near.

Arundel rested his head in his hands, trying to think through how this connected to them here, today. Another pulse from Etana's thread. Then each of the children after her. Three.

Again. *One, two, three… One. Two. Three.*

Arundel's head lifted, concentrating.

Lives? Contributors? One. Two. Three.

Etana and Luma were powerful Seers from their line.

His and Etana's twins were Seers of the line.

The Chimera was a Seer from the line.

Etana, the twins, the Chimera. One. Two. Three.

Arundel pulsed more brightly.

Etana's sister Luma was a Seer—with descendants on Earth… Arundel was running for the door from the conference room to the adjacent auditorium with a sharp order for none to follow. Barely making it through before he Shifted, the Chimera crouched as he flung out his Gifts, searching for Luma's bloodline through her Human descendants. The flow of images stopped in a flash of prismed light on Grace's grandmother, the first descendant encountering Mors. As with Etana, her grandmother was the continuation in a line to the twins, Grace and Ellie. The last to awaken the Gift.

Luma. One. Grace's Grandmother. Two. Twins Grace and Ellie. Three.

Luma's Gift, the creation of a place where Mors, in all his power, could not see. A blind spot. A memory fragment came alive within the Chimera; a child-Etana's voice said, "He will see Luma," as a dying Luma looked past Mors into Arundel's Chimera eyes. The Chimera sent a shockwave of awareness across time into Luma—surety that her purpose was achieved as she surrendered with a relieved sigh and died—closing her circle of their bloodline.

Arundel Shifted back to his Fae form. The silence was deafening. Grace's bloodlines had come through both Luma and Mors. With that simple truth came terrible realization; Arundel understood why Mors hunted Grace. The purpose of the war.

Mors had somehow discovered her while on Earth, tracing her to Oberon.

Mors couldn't see her with his Gifts past the blind spot, so he would set the world on fire to bring her into the open, visually find her. The Northern Legions and most reported in the Southern Lands were ghosts; Shield cover over nothing. Illusions to misdirect any threat to him while he drove her out.

By taking Grace's Gifts, his Gifts, manifesting again in

her, he would double his strength. Be like a god. Oberon would be his, without a war.

Grace was alone, locked within herself. She understood the consequences of him taking her alive. It was killing her.

23.

SHATTERING

ASA WOKE GRACE with a gentle hand, helping her to dress. Signing *silence*, she led her through the Keep. Gunnar was standing inside Dark Unit's doors looking at a report, an adjutant standing by. Gunnar did not acknowledge her presence. Grace asked no questions. Answers would come.

Arundel had spent the morning with his brother, explaining his breakthrough. Every move must be treated as though Mors and his Seers, likely stronger with his power Possessing them, were searching—even within the Keep. His eyes couldn't see Grace, but using them he could extrapolate from the actions of those around her.

Asa gave a nod to Gunnar. He returned the gesture, then turned back to the report. Taking an elevator down several floors, Asa brought her to the interrogation holding rooms, a place Grace had never been. In the Bunker the computer drives had been housed there. As Asa opened a door, Grace was startled to see Arundel seated at a table. There were Shields, Seers and a Possessor in the room.

Asa picked up papers from the table and left.

Standing, Arundel looked to the Possessor.

"Now."

The Possessor took the sight and hearing of everyone, including himself, leaving only Grace and Arundel untouched.

Grace turned, with a questioning look, too exhausted to work out the reason for these actions.

Arundel took her hand, leading her to sit with him.

"Grace, I'm sorry I could give you no warning. It's safe to talk—" Grace jerked to life, disbelief and anger coloring her voice.

"Arundel! No!"

"Grace, I know. Your knowledge of Mors' plan. Your attempt at death to stop him—all of it."

White with shock, Grace slid from the chair to her knees. Ugly, twisted sobs full of weeks in despair wrenched from her. Arundel knelt, silently holding her. Father Above, he couldn't fathom how she had borne it.

Grace struggled for control, desperately hoping for rescue from her solitary prison. But—*no*—what if—

The panic crossing her face dictated Arundel's next response.

"Mors can't see you Grace, no matter how strong his Gifts." Seating them both, Arundel held her hands. "When you received Mors' memories, you saw Luma, the last Seer he took?"

Grace nodded, face tightening in pain over Luma's torment.

"Luma and my Mate, Etana, were sisters, from the most powerful of Seer bloodlines. Fate has used their family's line repeatedly, over millennia, to help prepare and defend Oberon from threats.

"Luma, at her death, created a Gift, hidden within her bloodline, waiting dormant to protect her descendants from the threat her line sought to destroy. Her *Human* bloodline. It's in *you*, Grace."

Brows drawn, Grace searched Arundel's face.

"I don't understand. Mors is my grandfather. I have his Gifts. He's hunting me for them." Her voice rose. "How can I have both? How can he know of me if I'm protected?"

"In Mors' memories of your grandmother, his vision showed two women walking with an empty space between them."

Grace sifted the timeline of memories. "I see it. There's an edging around the space, like a prism."

Arundel felt his way—following the thread.

"He was drawn, but he couldn't see her until she was physically before him. He knew only that she was somehow involved in his future."

His gaze snapped up to meet Grace's.

"Since the memories stop with her—he didn't know he sired descendants—couldn't know his Gifts were uniting with a bloodline he could not see."

He sat back.

"We don't know how he discovered your existence. Your Gifts may have begun to surface, and in a place without Fae, he felt them. He'd successfully hunted down Fae for centuries."

"But Oberon is Fae, I'm the exception, not the rule," Grace said.

"True, but you're the exception in both places for the

same reason. Your Gifts. To have them at all on Earth—to have them in such quantity and strength here… with all his power, his arrogance, he can't locate you as the source. He must be furious."

Rising to pace, Grace tried to grasp the magnitude of events taking place, like a chess match between worlds.

"Gunnar believes the attack on the tower may have been a shot in the dark. An attempt to capture you, to have a look. He's been collecting Humans since arriving. It's doubtful he knows what you look like, or even that you're female. What may have drawn him, or his spies—is a Human protected by Guardians.

"These Shields and Seers are here because we will not be careless. I've only now understood the scope of your part. I know you're overwhelmed, Grace, but there's a critical piece I must share before we continue."

He led her to the empty adjacent room, placing her close to the wall. "Asa taught you the legend of Chimeras?"

"Yes, the stories say they haven't existed in thousands— *oh*—in times of great need!"

"I've been waiting for his time. Now it's time you met."

Grace watched Arundel walk to the center of the room and Shift. The Chimera crouched, shaking out his mane. He was stunningly beautiful. Crossing the room, Grace leaned against him, fingers buried in the rough fur of his chest, feeling his strong heartbeat. He settled on the floor, one enormous paw curving around her, his strength flowing into her exhausted spirit, mind and body, his thoughts gently unfolding into hers.

You are not alone, Grace. We were made for this place, this time. Together, we will be stronger.

Arundel Shifted back, supportive arm around her, the Chimera's words echoing in him.

"We were made for this…"

Are there legends of her? Have we overlooked them—lost them? Grace released a long breath.

"I don't know what to say. Even if I lose—we'll win."

"We *will* win, Grace. We'll stop his search for you by drawing him to a battleground of our choosing. You and I are an unknown threat to Mors. He underestimates you and knows nothing of the Chimera." Arundel took her hands in his.

"To Shield the others only the two of us may know. Mors cannot target Gunnar if he knows nothing of our plans. Thank the Father and Mother he loves us both. But it will be hard for him. Asa has a stronger grasp. She loves you, but understands to her core, that these things *must* happen."

Grace was still stunned—but—*hope*—.

Arundel watched this play out on her face, feeling how painfully close to death she'd been.

"It's easier for me," he said. "I lost everything I loved at my transformation. For me, my people have taken that place and it's been a time of waiting. I am deeply sorry that it's the opposite for you. You've just found everything, and now it's in jeopardy. I will do all I can to see it preserved for you."

Grace sighed deeply. "It's enough. If we must fight I'm grateful it's you. I've trusted you from the first moment I saw you."

Solemnly, he raised her chin. "I realized—in your memories—you have Luma's eyes." He smiled and rose from his chair, drawing her to her feet. "We have much work to do. Shall we begin?"

24.

BATTLE PLANS OF
THE HEART

"CAN THE CHIMERA be detected in your Fae form? When you're upset, and fighting the Shift… forgive me, but I have seen it in Gunnar's thoughts."
Arundel looked up to see Grace's apologetic expression.

"Never feel concern over things you see. Every Gift you have is one of his. Push them to their limits. Make them yours." Arundel leaned forward, stretching his back.

"The question you ask is wise. I suspect there's a power surge, though far less than a full Shift. It's unlikely there'll be other Shifting on the field, so it might stand out."

A sheaf of paper lay in diverging lines over the table's surface; a flowchart, addressing what must occur in minute detail along each possible line in order to reach the desired outcome. Both worked backward from the end goal. It often felt an impossible task.

She was able to spend more time working on the plan

than Arundel, making their time more productive. He could look over her timelines with a fresh eye, discerning which segments he thought would work, rather than starting from scratch.

Arundel was drawn to her reasoning. She respected his strategies. Together they made a compatible, formidable pair. But this was by far the most difficult strategic problem Arundel had ever encountered, and Grace could only guess at her role on the field.

He watched Grace as she worked; resting on her elbows, stretched over the table to ponder a segment, a slight scowl on her face. She was too frail from her time of carrying the burden alone. He must find a way for the Chimera to strengthen her. He refused to let her go into this weak.

Arundel thought of Gunnar. Their closeness had required no explanations as Arundel's profound respect for Grace had grown in depth and shape, and now, in the crucible of the war room, his growing awareness that he loved her. Her courage and willingness to give everything for Oberon. So like Etana.

Gunnar explained this dynamic was unfamiliar to Grace. She would need reassurance their love of her was expansive not divisive—they were different in nature; Gunnar was her Mate. Most importantly, its expression was hers to shape. Both agreed speaking of it must wait. They would not distract her.

These thoughts underlined his struggle as they worked on the timeline. Grace had the most difficult portion by far, which went against everything in him. It became more apparent with every line they worked through; he must help her walk into extreme danger. Her death was a variable in several plans. He forced his mind into another path, or the very reaction she feared might happen on the battlefield would be proven.

Yet there she stood, casually talking about some life-or-death element. Arundel's heart clenched painfully. He had to turn away, pretending to reference a wall map.

Etana, you would love her. She pulsed vibrantly within him, soothing his heart with her warmth.

"You can't fight me on this, Arundel. Using the tower to send Mors' reserves chasing our own ghost legions—Mors will be focused on me; he won't stop them—it will substantially decrease our casualties. It works in almost every timeline." Grace would not back down with so many lives at stake.

Arundel's hands spread on the table to prevent him from clenching them. He scanned multiple timelines, knowing she was right, but also what it meant.

"Grace," he said, "how will you cross an entire battlefield after he's injured you bringing the tower down?"

She jotted a note, refusing to look at him.

"You know he won't kill me. He can only incapacitate me enough that I can't run. And he won't *allow* anyone else to kill me."

Arundel cleared his throat. Grace interrupted before he could speak, tapping another line.

"If Mors has a significant number of Humans on the battlefield…" She snorted, with a dismissive gesture. "If I were him, I'd flood the field with them to occupy our Guardians, then have his archers kill them all so we have to fight over the bodies."

"It's a sound tactic if you can approach from flanking

position, but to drop so many in one spot will blunt the speed of his second wave," said Arundel, letting her lead him to a new topic. "It would be difficult to maneuver his own troops over so many casualties early in the battle."

She nodded, humming to herself. Arundel moved to her side of the table to scan the particular timeline she was addressing. Underneath the notes she was jotting, were the lines he most wanted to eliminate. The scenarios she was posing to him were not related to them.

"Grace. You cannot hide these from me."

She gave him an exasperated, what-are-you-talking-about glance.

"I'm only working on minor elements. I promise to share them if they look promising."

She swiftly pulled his attention to other thoughts.

"Last night I was sifting through our history's more surprising battle tactics. It prompted a memory that might be useful. An ancient city, Constantinople, hadn't been overthrown in a thousand years. Until someone left a small door in an exterior wall unlocked. The enemy quietly flooded in and sacked the city. Arundel, under certain physical conditions, if I could find a way to open and close a door in the blind spot, I could allow Mors to see or feel anything I choose. Pain, despair, anything to make him think he's overcome my defenses and I'll surrender. As long as I have my wits about me, I could manipulate him. He has no understanding why it even exists, so it's unlikely he would guess I controlled it."

Arundel met her eyes. She meant 'severely wounded, close to death.' His expression stabbed her heart. She quickly dropped her eyes, changing subjects yet again, rambling on. Hoping he would think she'd missed his pain.

She couldn't—wouldn't allow his feelings get in the way of this. The closer they moved toward a final solution, the more she steered conversation away from what was becoming an inevitable outcome.

"Knowing I'll get to ground zero, I'll have my bow and a very full quiver of arrows. It'll be a pleasure to demonstrate the evil of genetics to Grandpa."

Grace stopped talking, looking away.

"You're exhausted. Arundel, you mustn't worry about me. It diminishes your focus."

She smoothed a paper.

"This gives me significance. I was born for this. On Earth we'd say it's my superpower. I get to help save the world just by distracting him. It's worth it."

She laid a hand on his cheek. "You're worth it."

Arundel turned his face into her palm, then straightened.

"Grace—there must be—*something*."

"Regardless, I don't have the hard part," Grace continued as if he hadn't spoken. "I won't have to deal with Gunnar if I'm gone—you will. I know you'll take care of him for me. I'm deeply grateful you love each other so."

Grace reached out and pulled him into a hug. The first contact of its kind since Etana.

"I'm sorry to ruffle your fur and feathers. Allow me some lax discipline under pressure." She squeezed him hard, rocking from one foot to the other.

Just once.

Brightly looking up at him with a smile, she quipped as she stepped back, "At the very least, we can have a couple of

Dark Unit's best archers in the trees, to take me out quickly if things go sideways or he decides to play very nasty. I'd never know."

Arundel pulled her back against him in a crushing grip, his lips pressed to her hair. Only a long moment, then his face turned away, and his arms dropped limply. He swiftly left the room, two Shields falling in line behind him.

She went back to work on the timelines.

25.

ONE

THE FINAL NIGHTS before the battle, in the privacy of their rooms, Grace and Gunnar blocked their Gifts, keeping only Grace's Shield. They wanted no shifting Seer visions pulling at them, nothing in their world but themselves. The hours were few, but Arundel took time to cover or delegate tasks to protect their time.

Grace lay with her ear pressed over Gunnar's heartbeat, legs twined with his.

Cheek resting on her hair, Gunnar stroked her back, listening to her soft breaths. Both were easing away from the day's frenetic preparations. It was growing more difficult with the swiftly passing hours.

"The first day I explored these rooms, I stopped to look over your battle armor. We've spoken so often of ethics and philosophy. I never asked what you think about—when you step onto a field. Your courage never wavers."

Gunnar shifted her to see her face.

"Courage is not lack of fear. It's taking action despite fear. Fear of losing the thing you cannot bear to lose."

He was silent, carefully choosing words to honestly answer her implied question, but nothing more. He would not add distractions which might endanger her.

"The most worrying time is preparation. Strategy. Where legions are positioned, the order of battle. Mistakes bear heavy costs on the field."

His hand smoothed under her thigh, lifting her knee to pull her leg across him.

"Everything else disappears when I step onto the field. Calculations are finished. I respond to what is before me; my best, against my opponent's best." His arms tightened around her. "Don't worry, Mate. In centuries of fighting, I've always fought to win, but my heart has never carried such determination not to lose. You are my courage."

Tucking her head under his chin, she hugged him tightly.

"As long as my heart beats—your love is my courage."

Unable to see her face, he missed the difference in her words. Grace exhaled slowly, relaxing against him. Every touch, breath, heartbeat, allowed no sense of time to enter their enveloping peace and stillness. Languorous touch gave way to growing need and want. Gunnar lifted Grace from him to shift position, sitting back on his knees, guiding her to kneel astride him.

Her hands held his face as they kissed, hips slowly rocking. She gently tugged his cowlicks, then drew his head to lie over her heart, arms holding him tightly. He stilled within her, her heartbeat surrounding him.

He captured her hand, drawing it to rest with his, where their bodies joined. He rubbed his cheekbone along hers.

"My heart, my spirit, my body; you have them, they are joined to you as our bodies are joined. We are one."

She kissed him fiercely, pulling his hand up to wrap her throat. "Mate"—she struggled to swallow— "Mate, you are my miracle, my joy."

He moved to his back, stretching out beneath her, holding her to him. She pulled closer still. His hands cherished her body, hips lifting, stroking into her in small movements, slowly building until she tightened around him as she came. Gunnar's hand slid to the small of her back, pressing down as he followed her.

There was nothing left unsaid. One more day, one more night, until his heart would step onto that field with her. Grace lay, listening to his heart's steady rhythm. Praying her silent tears would not touch his skin.

An urgent knock sounded at the door.

Furious, with disbelief after shocking reports had revealed a terrible turn of events, Grace and Arundel scrambled across the cold, pitch-dark battleground, alone. After countless hours running scenarios, agonizing over small details that might change the timeline—one move may have shattered their plans.

Mors had stolen a march, silently moving his legions an entire day and night without stopping for rest. His army arrived on the outskirts of the conflict zone more than a day early, catching Arundel's forces still staging their moves into position.

Even civilians in the territory had been Possessed,

preventing them from raising the alarm as Mors' troops passed through.

His warriors would flood the field at dawn, seizing the high ground, positioning forces in optimal attack positions.

Gunnar and Stronghold Centurions were swiftly strategizing redeployment of their forces, organizing a column to push through to the field by morning. They had no option but to hold their ground until their larger forces arrived. Gunnar was certain to be in the Vanguard, sending intelligence to those who followed.

Grace felt betrayed by her Seer Gift. It had fallen oddly silent, prompting only physical movement. Giving up was not an option. Perhaps it was shifting for something they could not see. Something she had missed.

But our path hasn't changed. As though it were lifted and laid over different terrain. How is that possible?

The same new moon that covered their movements slowed their progress to a crawl. They'd chosen the field for its ground honeycombed with limestone sinkholes, useful to blunt the enemy's charges, and hindering movement for enemy troops.

Even without battle, in this total darkness it was sheer hell to navigate.

Grace was taking Arundel to his waiting place, critical to the plan's execution. Now, with major factors shifting, they could take no risks; he must be positioned at a far earlier time. Once she left him, there would be no contact between them. It would feel an eternity for them both while their timeline unfolded.

Her jerking heart would not settle, hands shaking in the few moments they were not silently groping their way over rocky terrain. She wasn't ready. She'd thought there would be battle chaos. Quickly said goodbyes. Brave sprinting to appointed tasks.

Arundel would lie for hours watching his people die, waiting for his critical time of action. Would Mors sense the Chimera in Arundel's struggle not to Shift? It had been an untestable concern. Grace could only Shield him and hope his control held.

They were little more than halfway across the field when violent, icy dread punched Grace's gut, forcing the air from her lungs. Arundel felt her reaction. Slinging his arm around her waist, he pulled her backwards with him into a pit, his body breaking her fall. He kept her pinned against him, sliding back until stopped by the curved limestone wall, beneath an overhang. The wall opposite was a cave-in of soil.

They heard Mors cutting through the field with his commanders, pointing out field placements. Even hidden in the pit, this was dire for them both. Having planned heavily around Gifts, now simple line-of-sight could take them down. Their command would order the field swept before placing their warriors.

Grace ran through dozens of scenarios at a lightning pace, listening as Mors and his officers moved about the field discussing the high ground. Feeling sick with frustration, she could see no alternate variations on the timeline. If she failed to save Arundel—unless—Arundel left her to save himself. He must. She twisted to hold his face, slipping into his thoughts.

You must go. Now. It's the only way.

Arundel's hands gripped her waist. *I'll Shift and attack. He's not prepared.*

No! You'll fall. They'll find me.

Her hand moved to her hip dagger. With her dead, Mors would still be a terrible threat, but he would not conquer Oberon. The Chimera would fight Mors in a later battle of Arundel's choosing.

Her hand still rested on Arundel's face; he had followed her thoughts.

Fly swiftly. He will scent my blood and the blind spot will vanish. Go!

She did not look at him as she broke his hold, sliding quickly away from him, dagger drawn.

Arundel yanked her back against him. *No. I'll fight Mors and return for you.*

Despair was draining the fight from her. *Then you will go and fall, and I will take my life knowing he will destroy Oberon.*

She turned her face away, bitterness at fate crushing her.

I should have died the night I first knew, eliminating this risk. You would have stopped Gunnar from following me.

Arundel shifted her to lean into him. If he took the dagger, she would find another terrible way. They'd known from the first, she could not be captured. Mors and his entourage were discussing the high ground, one hundred meters away.

Grace turned her face into his chest, speaking fiercely into his thoughts.

Then I will give you my Gifts now. It is the only other option. Arundel—I won't have to die alone...

Arundel squeezed her painfully. *Grace, stop this; I will not take them.*

Instead of simply ordering them, Mors possessed four of his warriors to sweep the field for hidden traps. Their eyes were his eyes, with his Gifts. Now their discovery was a mathematical equation; the only variables were if one or both of them would die.

Arundel cupped the nape of her neck, lips pressed to her forehead. *I'm sorry, Grace. It is wrong for a commander to admit, but I want you to survive most of all.*

He exhaled quietly, head back against the stone. Rallying, his arms tightening their hold.

I will not leave you here to die if there is a single thread of chance our plan will work. We would feel if the path were wiped clean.

Grace angrily straightened, shrugging his arms loose.

How can you not let logic make this decision? If you will not accept my Gifts, leave my dagger and go, quickly!

She was shaking with panic at his refusal to leave her. It was the penultimate abandonment for her; the removal of purpose for her existence. Her inability to save Arundel nullified a thousand-year plan, and the meaning in her family's deaths. Both their families' deaths. There was nothing left to tear from her.

Mors' commanders closed in. Frantic with fear at watching Arundel die, Grace fought ghosting away. She and Arundel were one in this purpose and now her failure would pull him down.

Gunnar's visual of them united as one body, one heart, flashed through her mind. Could—their Gifts merge while both lived? Such a thing had never happened. She and the Chimera shared one purpose. Fate created them with a singularity of purpose—they *were* of one heart.

The searching warriors were fifty meters away.

Eyes closed, Grace put every ounce of strength into

telling the Chimera within Arundel of their need to unite without death —link as though physically united in one body, allowing Luma's blind spot to cover them both.

Without waiting for an answer, Grace moved into action. They needed to be visually small to avoid the searchers' physical attention.

She twisted in Arundel's lap to face the cave-in's loose soil. She pushed his back to the wall, dropped her shins flat against the ground to the outsides of Arundel's legs, leaning out to scrape armfuls of soil toward them. Yanking Arundel's knees hard to her chest, she hurriedly pulled dirt up to cover them to the waist, throwing more handfuls to cover their drag marks.

He wrapped his arms hard around her; her cheek lay against his. Arundel's heart opened fully to her, as she spoke into him without ceasing, using every Gift, all her strength.

We are one mind; we are one body. We are one body. We are one body. We are one. We are one. We are one—

The warriors were standing at the sinkhole next to theirs. Grace crushed herself into Arundel's chest, trying to melt into him until they all but disappeared. Fae light shone into the pit's opening; she heard a warrior lean in, scenting, then back quickly as the edge began to crumble, dislodging loose earth and pebbles into the emptiness.

They moved on to the next one. Grace barely breathed; Arundel matching his breaths to hers. *We are one, we are one, we are one.*

She felt the words echo in him.

It took the warriors almost an hour to cover the area of the field close enough to demand their stillness. Grace's endless affirmations poured into Arundel.

Grace had just reached her hand to touch Arundel's face, when Mors' voice sounded only a few meters away.

She and Arundel, hearts pounding in their ears, had not heard him moving. She almost stopped her heart and breath completely.

Her hand fell to grasp the dagger. How could she use it on herself and get out of the way so Arundel could Shift? She must be dead, not injured before Mors could get his hands on her. She felt movement behind her.

We are one, we are one, we are one, we are one. Her mind was frozen around this final lifeline that her heart would not surrender.

Arundel shifted position. Grace allowed herself one second of limp relief that he was leaving. She gripped the dagger until it felt fused to her hand. One shot—and fast, she wasn't capable of striking twice. Eye—throat—heart?

I can do this—

Tears tracked her scraped and dirty face. She coiled her muscles, tensing until they must release. There was no ghosting from this.

Now.

Body jerking forward, she yanked the dagger point to her throat. Her last thought; Gunnar's loving touch there— not this.

Grace.

Lion paws wrapped around her, knocking the blade hand away. The Chimera had created a partial Shift in Arundel; wings cupped, cocooning her from all sound, paws holding her safe from the knife.

Grace shook violently in adrenaline aftermath, vision tunneling. She could hear nothing beyond the wings, only

Arundel's gentle breathing and heartbeat against her back, his cheek against hers. A resonant voice rolled through her.

Enough, Grace. The path does not end here.

A heavy paw rested over the dagger. She let it go, sliding into quiet darkness.

When Grace awoke, the Chimera was gone, and all was quiet. Her position had shifted. Her side pressed against Arundel's chest, his arms about her. They had kept her from Mors. She struggled not to weep in relief.

Dawn would come soon, and with it both armies. They would wait for them to flood the field and sprint for their positions, hoping no one took them down as they ran.

Arundel stroked her hair, pondering the depth of the miracle she had performed. She had indelibly changed him. But the Chimera had seen, so he had seen, her terror at the coming day—from which she would allow nothing to sway her. The Chimera had given her strength and reserves, such as a human body could hold. Arundel couldn't prevent the day, but he held her now, the affirmations of their oneness echoing through them.

He spoke softly. "Gunnar and I have long been of a single mind, a single heart. Physical expression was never needed. Only Etana held all three aspects in my life. It gives me joy to see the two I love most, love each other."

At his words, a ripple passed through her. Arundel lifted her chin.

"I never thought to meet someone with Etana's fire, passion for life, and most of all, courage. Such courage, Grace.

More than my warriors." He kissed her forehead. "I love you. I know you have felt it, but the words should have been said sooner. It is different than your Mate's love, as is right, but never doubt it."

He felt her struggle to swallow.

"I knew you cared—but I can't think—not before I walk out there. Asa told me, but I didn't understand. Until now."

She released a long breath.

"It's—Arundel, I'm not worth this. It's a relief the time-line has outcomes that will preserve you both. I need only for you and Gunnar to survive this day. And Asa."

He gave her a gentle shake.

"I can say with certainty how Gunnar and I feel about that. We three will talk when this time has passed. I know my brother's heart, but we need to reassure yours."

The approaching dawn diverted Grace's thoughts from love or her own survival. Fear was rising; at both the battle and of failing in her tasks. It was her curse. Everyone she loved died.

Arundel knew her thoughts.

"Grace. Believe. We will not leave you."

Their uniform jackets lay nearby. Glancing at the dark sky, he listened a moment, then laid her gently upon them. His touch took her away from her fears, cherishing her heart and body. The body she had repeatedly offered to death to save him. And would offer again when the sun rose. He did not let her think of the day.

Only this moment, this love, and the love to come.

26.

THE BATTLE

THE SIGHTS, SOUNDS and smells of the battlefield shocked Grace's senses. What she had envisioned from movies, books, or veteran's accounts bore no resemblance to the reality of it. Despite her military status, she was the lone person on the field who had no experience from which to prepare. It was the embodiment of Gunnar's definition of war.

The grunting clang from those wielding edged steel and heavy shields wove gruesome counterpoint with cries from wounds received and voices raised in reluctant death.

Arrows hissed and whirred, surgical blades amongst the ring and squeal of sliding weapons. Close-in blades were a life-ending surprise or distracting bite. The thud and thrust of spears into a body took a moment to feel or recognize. The unsteadiness of the dead and injured piled underfoot made movement difficult. And overlying it all—the horrible smell of dying; open and emptying bodies.

Grace had left her bow, quiver, and knife belt at the foot

of the tower when their plan had gone to hell. Warriors in pitched battle would instantly strike at any threat; her weapons would mark her as one—however small.

She had never been more grateful to be small.

Understanding there would be repercussions from the altered plan, Grace and Arundel's Seer vision had agreed; the desired final outcome was still in reach.

Occupied with bellowing at his troops, Mors missed the small power surge as Grace Shifted Arundel into a blood-stained, plain-faced warrior, dressed to blend with either side. He maneuvered into a shallow depression near the enemy high ground.

Grace laid the strongest Shield she could generate over him, begging the Mother Above that it carried the protection needed. It was the hardest thing to ask of him, to be still and wait. She laid a hand on him, holding his eyes in a final warning.

For me.

Her eyes lifted from him, searching through the chaos for her tower. With every moment she took, more of their people died.

There it is. Almost two hundred meters across open field. *So far.*

In the original plan she would have approached from behind, in the trees. She asked her Seer vision for a path. It showed where to run, almost in a straight line, low to the ground.

She sprinted, bent almost double. Because her speed was nothing to theirs, she caught very few eyes. Her size in the blur of battle, registered to most as no threat.

Her vision told her to drop flat, so she did, pressing

tightly into the ground as a spear, spent from distance but still deadly to her, went to ground inches from her. She scrambled back into motion, clawing at the ground and bodies with hands and feet to propel her forward.

Arrows zipped overhead and warriors fell, sometimes knocking into her as they came down. The vision steered her clear of any that would bring her progress to a full stop. It could do nothing to prevent her from seeing what was happening around her.

The shock of it all put her into a dissociative state that refused the emotion accompanying this full immersion into hell. She watched her acquaintances and fellow occupants of the Keep falling under sword blows, spears, arrows. She could not help them in any way but one. Finish her task.

Her vision told her to bear left. She wanted to resist anything that lengthened her path but obeyed. Her momentum slowed, forcing her to partially straighten upright or her body would dive into the dirt. She raised her head to see Gunnar. Her heart gave a shattering thump. He was with several of his Dark Unit, and they were horribly outnumbered but steadily bringing the enemy down. Her vision showed her to approach and stop, five meters from his right-flanking Guardian.

As she crouched there, the Guardian's eyes dropped to her and he ran forward to take up position over her. Gunnar felt his flank open and turned to cover the angle.

His eyes fell on Grace, crouched in the middle of the battlefield with no weapons. She was on a path she must follow, but he was stricken to his core with fear for her. She had never hinted she would be so exposed, defenseless.

Father and Mother Above... *Mate.*

She pointed up to the tower then back at herself. Gunnar gauged the distance. He felt his rear Guardian stumble against him and took a step forward. It was a hundred meters or more to the tower. Grace's face had shifted to shock, but his Guardian was still standing over her. Scanning the area around him for threats that had caused her fear, Gunnar saw his rear Guardian still fighting.

Then he felt the warmth in his side; twenty centimeters of spear protruded just below his ribcage. Gunnar shouted to his Guardian defending her to get her to the tower and parried the sword swing coming his way. He could not look to her to say goodbye. She could not wait. The Guardian gave her one of his knives and pulled her up, sword arm defending them. She let him yank her into motion.

They ran for the tower. Her vision took over, nudging him when a pit was ahead, pulling him low when a blade or arrow was passing over. They were ten meters from the tower base when her vision showed a split second before her escort took several arrows. She lifted her face, kissing the back of his guiding hand. He squeezed back with a grim smile, understanding her. He was dead before he hit the ground.

She scrambled the last ten meters on hands and feet, grateful it was uphill to the tower. Scrub bushes covered her weapons.

Thank the Father Above, they didn't burn this high when clearing the battlefield.

Grace dragged her weapons to her, turning for the tower base, only two meters away. Her vision told her to drop flat as a body fell over her. A sword had almost decapitated it. One of Mors'. Shoving hard to make the body roll downhill, Grace crawled to lean against the tower base, catching her breath. She couldn't see Gunnar or his warriors. She tilted her head back to look up the ladder. She was going to be the target of every archer.

"Fucking Coward!" she spit out.

She knew this was not her end. She had just watched her Mate take a spear through his body and continue fighting. She slung on her quiver, grabbing her bow. Checking her vision, she saw threats in two nests of archers, one to each side of her, and a path to take them out. She nocked an arrow, took deep breaths to steady her sight and heart and stood, spinning in the direction of the left-hand group. She took all seven down with arrows through the eye, throat, or heart as each turned their aim toward her. She spun toward the other nest, continuing to take out all enemy in her path until she reached them. Those in the second nest saw the path of warriors dropping from her arrows and heard her coming. Her vision told her to run toward them, then sideways onto the berm encircling them. They would be unable to draw an accurate aim on such a close moving target. She took them down without pausing in motion.

She slung her bow across her back, and turning, leapt to catch the bottom ladder rung, six feet from the ground. Pulling herself up, she blessed Master Oran for the upper body strength. Pouring on as much speed as her body could put out, she reached the swivel housing—covered until she had to move the shutter. Struggling to catch her breath allowed a moment for her heart to tear. Gunnar. *Mate.* She wanted to comfort him. But she knew Mors would feel it.

She would cut her throat rather than let him torture her Mate.

She forced herself back into action. Finding the

coordinates, she calculated the angle of the sun to send the code to Mors' army, redirecting them to meet the fictitious Legion. Her calculations done, she looked up to make sure everything was in place. The shutter mechanism looked functional but the mirror angle was turned almost 180 degrees off. Grace swore. It was a heavy mechanism, made for a Guardian. She began to climb.

Grace reached the capstan and scrambled into position. It no longer mattered if her back was to the field; she found the tread strips with her toes, threw her weight hard against the bar, and pushed. She felt tearing in muscles, joints popping everywhere, but it was moving.

She had to keep the momentum. The mirrored cone was flashing across the field as she forced it to the necessary position. She had forgotten to close the shutter.

Mors was scanning the battle, enjoying every kill that was not clean. Especially those turned into hacking matches with no finesse. A bright flash of light in his peripheral vision caught his attention.

Searching for its originating point, it beamed directly at him from a tower across the field. Mors scanned the tower but could feel no one there. Then his eyes caught a small figure struggling to reposition the signal light. He could feel nothing.

No thoughts, no Shield, no magic of any kind.

There was only *one* being in existence whom he could not "See." He began to smile. His entire world came together and his heart beat faster. She was here. So close he could see and smell her. Mors' Gifts were indeed morphing, as Grace's had done. He had only to lift a hand, and from across the field, beckon the tower. The tower base snapped and began to fall onto the field.

Grace felt the tower jolt, air stirring around it. It was falling directly over her. It was sixty meters tall; she was ten meters below its tip. There was nowhere for her to go. Too far to slide down the ladder, too far to scramble up to get out of the way.

The increasing angle of the falling structure threw her against the railing now beneath her. If she leapt to the side, perhaps could she swing out of the way before impact? She checked her Seer vision. No. Is there anything—?

No.

She lay against the railing, searching for Gunnar, hoping he was turned away. Just before impact, Mors stopped the tower, five meters from the ground. Hanging on through the jerking halt, a wild hope pierced her heart, thinking the tower had miraculously hung up on rough terrain. Grace looked up to meet Mors' eyes, sending a shockwave through the bloodline, ripping open a door in the blind spot, into him.

Blood pounding in recognition, their Gifts hurtled for each other, a single memory slamming into Grace as they connected.

Mors watching a car approach. Ellie was driving. Her eyes lifted, locking with his.

The unique eyes were not all Grace and Ellie shared.

Grace tore into Mors' strength, her and Ellie's Gifts pulling on the power of all three to reach into Ellie's miraculous, genius mind. Grace, the Pulse, Oberon, Mors, their bloodline's purpose with all its sacrifices, the potential future, exploded into Ellie's thoughts with instant clarity of comprehension.

I love you, Grace.

Ellie sharply yanked the wheel away from where he stood;

sure in the knowledge she must be irrevocably removed from the equation. The moment unfolded as it already had, the only change: Grace's understanding of Ellie's death. It was also a reminder; Mors had not foreseen this outcome: Ellie's blood also carried the blind spot. Grace watched Mors' rage as Ellie took herself beyond his reach, incinerating the car. Grace's eyes closed; Ellie's lifelong fear of fire.

Grace withdrew from Mors, closing Ellie's circle of their bloodline, her resolve to destroy Mors unstoppable as she fiercely swung her body forward to drop from the railing onto the field.

Mors dropped the tower on her. Her scream could be heard across the battlefield as the tower crushed her legs. There were three on the field who knew of or all of the plan. All of them loved Grace deeply. Their hearts were in utter agony.

Fighting back-to-back with another member of her Dark Unit, Asa felt herself weakening. She had been a good spy. She had served under the greatest of Commanders and Prefects, and she loved her charge and friend. She had held her own on the field, bringing down enemy, holding her place to protect those fighting at her back. A good life. She could Travel away like a coward, but she would rather die here with them. With Grace. With Gunnar. With Arundel.

There could be no better death.

Her heart took strength, as did her arm. She heard the zip as her rear guard took an arrow to the head. As he dropped, Asa knew she'd reached the end. She could not look away from the enemy before her to turn sideways to the archer behind, a smaller target.

Asa spit at her opponent as arrows tore into her neck,

back, and thigh; her body twisting as they cut her down. The soldier before her had already returned to the fray. Bleeding into the stinking mud, Asa selfishly wanted only to die before Grace screamed again.

Gunnar was on his side curved around the spear; it prevented him from sinking flat. Father Above, he wanted it pulled from his body. A cowardly thought, and he was physically incapable of doing so himself. Not one sword cut was a mortal wound; they'd only cut tendon and muscle, slow blood. Father Above, even the knife wounds missed anything vital. He should have drawn targets for the enemy. Pulling the spear would allow him to bleed to death.

He would not shame his Guardians by asking them to do it. The two guarding, fighting above him would not leave until he stopped breathing.

The Guardian he sent with Grace was the Juvenile he'd pinned to the wall for his base remark of her. He had felt he could never atone. He had more than done so. He was the first to cover her and had gotten her across the battlefield to her target.

Gunnar closed his eyes, attempting to will his heart to stop. Grace's scream. He had long since lost track of the battles he'd fought, the fields he'd lain injured upon. But—his Mate's scream—it was the worst sound of his life. His fault, selfishly refusing her a painless death in his arms. She had seen this future, staying only for him because he'd asked. She could not bear to have him die, no matter the cost. Father Above, please. He wanted to pull the spear.

Arundel lay still as death. Grace's scream had not been the sound of a broken arm or leg. He watched his outnumbered Guardians die. He saw Asa and Gunnar go down.

Now he could no longer feel Grace. But the Shield stood and there had been no indication the plan was void. He forced his emotions aside and focused on the plan, to keep from tearing the world apart.

Cradled in velvet darkness, Grace felt an insistent tug. It broke the comfortable silence with a high tone—increasing—until the world exploded into blinding pain, a living thing determined to kill her. Held fast, she couldn't escape it.

Mors watched from across the field, delightedly applauding. He'd been unable to see Grace and Ellie's connection. He dismissed the tugging irritation, and it had disappeared. There was only one thing of importance here, and she was within his grasp…

He Possessed a group of his warriors, marching them over to lift the wreckage and slide her out. It took them two tries to pull her body from under the chunk pinning her.

The male gripping her hands turned his face from her crushed body. She was so obviously not a warrior, her eyes burning with pain. Immensely grateful, she lost consciousness when he pulled at her. The moment the Possession command was fulfilled, he threw himself back into the fighting. Anything to get away from the sight of her. He welcomed the sword swing, a clean death, ripping through his throat moments later, sinking to the ground with his eyes closed, not taking the sight of her with him into death.

Mors stood reveling. Her scream was lovely. Surprisingly strong under the circumstances. He watched contentedly, monitoring her still body to ensure her chest still rose and fell.

He scanned the field for other amusements until she awakened.

He could feel a male marked as her Mate down. Impressively, still alive with a spear through him and many smaller wounds. He might allow her to crawl to him… Well, not crawl. Impossible with her legs. Perhaps creep.

He would assist if needed. Her sounds would be exquisite as he died in her arms.

Mors was no longer interested in the battle. These machinations, staged purely to draw her to him were done. He dropped his Possession of all Shields covering the mock Legions scattered around the continent, chortling in contentment. His horizons were about to explode. Perhaps he would savage other worlds. These two parallels existed, why shouldn't there be more? Grace moved a hand. Mors laughed.

"So feisty."

Observing closely, he could faintly see the prism-like edges around her.

"What *is* that?" Mors said.

His generals edged away at his tone.

It blocked his feel of her. Frustration did not breed mercy in him.

Where did that ability come from?

He wanted to know more of what he couldn't see, dissect Gifts out of her one at a time. Where did she come from? When their eyes met he felt a mirroring of his Gifts—then nothing, like the one who'd evaded him on Earth.

Mors' snappish impatience grew. Possessing a warrior in black, the male was directed to drag her by the arm across the field to her Mate. Grace looked up into the Dark Unit Guardian's face.

It was her Guardian. He had caught her, falling from the tower. He reached down to gently touch her face, moving his hand away to jerk upright against the command, his short sword under his ribs, pulled into his heart before Mors could stop him. He crumpled to the ground, smiling at Grace as his eyes emptied.

Mors shrieked in rage at the Guardian's defiance. Freed when Mors dropped mass Possession and seeing his visible descent further into madness, his warriors edged back from the battlefield, letting Arundel's forces drive them. Mors was oblivious to his Legion's rapidly dropping numbers.

Grace lay sobbing for her Guardian. His death, on a field soaked with death, tore viciously at her heart. It embodied all of the dying—payment they were all making to enable the task she was too weak to finish.

The Chimera's Gift released, washing through her brokenness with calm strength, an anchor to her purpose. Nothing could repair such massive physical trauma, but bleeding slowed, life signs stabilized. Rallying, she ghosted herself, distancing from the pain. Grace's mind was clear to act, not react. A pace away, she watched her body, prone on the field, shoulders twisting to rise onto forearms. Scanning the field, she bent, touching her own shoulder, Gunnar and Asa's locations leapt into focus. She opened her eyes, back in her body.

The change burned through Arundel as the Chimera sharpened his bond to Grace.

Her pain—her pain—

Awareness came through the bond of Gunnar, critically wounded—unable to help Grace—wishing for death—loathing himself for it. Asa too, unable to pull an arrow from her throat to escape from Grace's pain.

Arundel begged, too devastated to know to whom he implored. He lay protected on the field, surrounded by his torn people. Those he loved more than his life, dying. Never before had the threads of light within him been dark.

On the far side of the field, Grace began to pull herself forward. A spark ignited in Arundel's darkness. White hot, it burned, slowly devouring him, pushing aside his struggle. The plan was everything. His despair turned to rage.

The Chimera roiled beneath his skin, a thread of power flowing to Grace. With every fresh surge of pain from Grace, the rage grew.

Heart on fire to finish the plan, Grace dragged herself toward Gunnar. His flanking Guardians were dead. She cracked the door in the blind spot, allowing her suffering to trickle through to Mors. Pain of body and heart, her Guardian, the dead warriors surrounding her. She felt him zero in, feasting.

Grace eased the door shut as she neared Gunnar.

In this state, her Healing Gift could only manage blood-to-blood triage.

Mother Above, let it be enough.

Worse than his wounds, she could feel his broken spirit.

Blocking everything but her love, she spoke into his thoughts.

Don't speak or try to read me. Don't look.

A command, edged in Possession. She allowed no answering thoughts to reach her.

I'll pull you to me. I'll scream as though you've died.

She pulled herself against him. Dropped to lie, head over his heart.

Gunnar was in agony. His wounds were nothing. It was incomparably worse not to touch her, comfort her. He scented the full severity of her injuries and instantly fought the command.

STOP.

Full Possession froze him, a thing she had never done to him.

Please, Mate! Do this for me.

Grace's scream held all the anguish of his heart. She tore open the neck of her tunic, pulling his family dagger from under the flap. Mors correctly read the glimpse she gave him as she slashed above her breast. He savored the tearing flesh of the mourning gesture.

Grace fitted herself around the spear, her blood flowing over the worst of Gunnar's wounds. Her keening cry drifted across the emptying field. She laid him gently back, pressing her lips to his.

"For all that comes after," she whispered.

Turning, Grace dug in hard, hitching herself toward Asa.

She gave Mors a sip through a crack in the door. Her pain and anguish over Gunnar and Asa. She sent a thought.

No more—after I kiss Asa goodbye...

Mors immediately pulled the dagger to clatter at his feet. "I will not let you go with so little pain," Mors said.

Grace sobbed as she continued toward Asa, gently closing the door to Mors.

Her mind reached out to Asa, quickly flowing the images of how she'd ministered to Gunnar, instructing her be as still, so this plan could finish. Asa was lying with her back toward Mors, allowing Grace to do more. Grace assessed the arrow in her throat, which had missed the artery by mere millimeters. If it shifted, Asa would rapidly bleed out.

She cracked the door to Mors.

Let me give her a quick death.

She slammed the door, ripping the slash in her breast wider with her fingers, pulling the arrow. She rocked with Asa against her, bleeding directly into the wound, until she felt Asa's blood flow stop. Kissing her brow, Grace lay her down.

She turned toward Mors. Her ability to ghost away from her body's trauma was done, the pain overwhelming. She partially opened the door to Mors and let him feel that she was dying. Unable to cross the distance between them.

She lay her head down.

Mors threw out a hand and began dragging her over the terrible terrain she and Arundel had found difficult to cross on foot. Grace screamed without end. The shattered bones in her lower half were violently jolting apart. Her blood began to flow freely.

Grace opened the door wide.

The full weight and pain of her injuries crashed in on her and into Mors. She was in utter agony. She had nothing left to give. He would take her Gifts—know that she was his granddaughter—it was finished.

Mors' head snapped up and he ceased dragging her.

What? A granddaughter!

His mind put the pieces together—*Boston—I was to let her live—it would affect my plans here. Then she has all of my Gifts—and had morphed them into more— Is that why she can hide? Shield?*

Mors was beside himself. She could not die out of his hands. It was more than he'd dreamed.

He could hear her slowing heart weakly beating. Mors scanned for a last jolt of adrenaline to give her a few moments more. He beckoned to lift her above the rocks and bring her to ground a few meters from him.

He snarled at her. "Your grandmother surrendered easily, but you, you were a waste of my blood."

Grace opened her eyes and saw him standing with Arundel under his foot.

Mors had seen him on the near-empty battlefield. Arundel looked into her eyes with a bottomless apology at her pain—her suffering—so much worse than she'd let him believe.

Eyes locked on Grace to watch her scream, Mors reached down and cut Arundel's throat with her dagger. He dumped the body without a glance, flashing to Grace, who lay staring past him to Arundel's body—mouth open but unable to scream.

Hand fisting her hair, Mors dragged her from the ground into his arms.

Life seeping from her like water into dry sand, Grace

struggled to stop her heart. Mors read everything through the open door.

"No more time to play."

He raised her face to him.

Bellowing in rage, Mors flung her down, Grace rolling at his feet like a broken doll.

"You worthless Human! Where are my Gifts! I will shred you apart—*forever*…"

Mors roared at the heavens, face distorting, bones beginning to Shift beneath blackening, reptilian skin.

"YOU THREW THEM AWAY!"

She had not.

Huge wings blew a thunderous current of air against Mors, who turned in shock. He'd cut Arundel's throat— Mors looked back at Grace, feeling the truth through the open door.

Channeling her pain and despair had kept his gaze on her.

Her knife belt lay slashed on the ground, having shielded Arundel's throat. Mors, occupied with Grace, had no time to guard against the Chimera he had not seen.

Unleashing a roaring inferno on Mors, the Chimera reduced his arrogance into screaming confusion as gouts of oily stench billowed—his burning limbs curling upon themselves in the furnace.

Mors' brain fumbled among his hoard of Gifts, unable to wield them as the rage of the Chimera tore into his mind. Lion claws sunk deep into his body, slowly, slowly tearing burning limbs apart. Screaming, dying, Mors refused to meet the Chimera's eyes.

But he would.

Pulling final strength from the Chimera, Grace used Gunnar's dagger, dropped at Mors' feet, to viciously slash her hand. Pushing the bleeding mess into Mors' gaping shoulder wound, his body accepted his granddaughter's blood as his own. Mors' choked snarl of fury cut off as she Possessed him—tearing his Gifts and life strengths from him—pushing them into the Chimera.

Grace's eyes closed in relief, her ragged exhale leaving with her last heartbeat. Her circle in the bloodline closed.

The Chimera pulled Mors away from her, burning him to ash.

27.

AFTER

OSSESSION BROKEN, GUNNAR and Asa opened their eyes. Although Grace's blood had healed them enough to preserve their lives, they were too injured to rise. The Chimera would help them, but first he looked to Grace. He ripped a wound in his paw, placing it over Grace's breast wound, listening for a heartbeat. Grace's Human body could do nothing with his Fae blood, despite the Chimera's magic, but her heart began to beat.

Carefully taking hold of her, he took flight for the Keep. An awed hush fell as the Chimera landed. None present had seen Arundel in this form. There was no longer need to hide it. He gently deposited Grace with the Med Unit Healers, resuming his Fae form to dispatch messengers to all territorial Commands reporting Mors' death and of the ghost legions. Shifting, the Chimera returned to the field as his Centurions took command of the area and battlefield Healers flooded the field.

The following weeks were of necessity filled with healing wounded warriors and civilians. Arundel learned the difference between battlefield triage and careful restoration. He spent time with his people in both his forms, his people grateful the Chimera of legend, also their Commander, listened to their griefs, shared their sorrows.

He destroyed the networks of assassins and spies still sifting the continent for Grace, set up temporary unified commands in the Western Protectorate, freeing the Humans interred there. Finally, Arundel and his Guardians rested in the warmth of his territory's southern-most border along the sea. He had pushed them hard, and though all were willing and content in their task, they welcomed the chance to rest with their Commander.

He passed through the encampment, spending time with his Guardians, giving praise that would be held with pride for generations. As the exhausted warriors sought out their bedrolls, Arundel slipped away to a nearby beach.

For the first time in four centuries, Arundel Shifted, and the Chimera flew for the joy of it. Skimming the water's surface with his feet, climbing high to pierce a light layer of cloud, he looked upon the face of the moon. He felt the golden threads ruling his heart pulse with joy. He banked back toward land.

Toward his people.

28.

DAY OF GRACE

THE WORLD EXISTED solely in Grace's bed. Her heartbeats whispered in the silent room. Gunnar was completely focused on forcing them to continue. Between them he willed air to move, creating each shallow rise and fall of her chest. This fiction kept him alive.

Gunnar was anchored to her, rarely moving, despite his wounds. Healers had taken more than a day diagnosing her injuries. Crushed legs. Pelvis, arm, jaw, collarbone, broken when she'd been dragged, then thrown down. The jagged slash across her chest. She'd almost severed her fingers to make sure the final blood connection to Mors would be enough.

The massive blood loss was more grievous to her body than the hideous wounds. It prevented any recovery. Healers could knit most injuries with time, but they could not regenerate large amounts of blood. And Grace's blood was different.

Gunnar watched, growling with every breath, as they circled, not knowing how to work with such dire injury.

Gunnar twined a strand of her hair between his fingers, the only part of her he could touch without concern, listening to Healers whispering when they thought he could not hear. Only the Chimera's magic kept her heart beating. They agreed amongst themselves, her heart would not continue if the magic stopped. Gunnar watched her pulse. It was barely visible with so little blood pumping. Tissue and muscle atrophied incrementally every day.

Mate, I will love you all of my life, and for all that comes after.

The only thought he would allow while he waited beside her, week after week. Watching her body waste away, the thinness magnifying every horrific detail of her injuries. He rarely ate or drank. Only enough to maintain his task. He was afraid to touch her paper-thin skin. Every so often he lay his head on the bed and wept. For his Mate, for their lost future. For the unimaginable pain she had suffered.

Unlike Arundel, irrevocably tasked with protecting their world, Gunnar had no other purpose but her. She would leave him alone, empty. He would refuse life. He would go with her.

He waited, willing one more heartbeat, pulling one more breath.

Asa stared at the wall. Healers disturbed her at regular intervals with tinctures for pain, irritating dressing changes. She was both numb, and angry to the bone. The arrow in her throat would have killed her without Grace's blood. The others had struck organs that were now regenerating. It was utterly wrong that she should be here while Grace hovered, silently waiting for the Mother's arms.

The Keep's Medical Unit was not large. She heard Gunnar weeping. The most crushing sound she had ever heard. He would not weep so unless he were broken, had no hope. She wanted beyond anything to pour her blood into Grace. But how?

She did the only thing she could think of.

Arundel was still on the southern border, enforcing the truce until peace negotiations among the territories Mors had set against each other were accomplished. His adjutant handed him a note, just arrived.

It was a plea from Asa. Grace was dying. Asa wanted him to take her life strength and give it to Grace. She didn't know how to do it with Grace so close to death. She was sure the Chimera would know how. Prefect Gunnar was completely broken. If this did not work, his spirit would leave with Grace. Arundel folded the note. He spent ten minutes assigning Guardians to take over, then shifted, arrowing for the Keep.

There was not a time Gunnar had not sat in this room, his entire will focused on Grace, stitching himself to her so they would leave together. He, too, was wasting away. He allowed the Healers to change his bandages, but that was all. If someone looked clumsy in their care of her, he snarled and Shifted. He lay his head on the bed, Shifting back to sit in the chair, too weak to stand on four legs. They moved with care.

Arundel stood in the hallway outside the open door. He took everything in, stunned that no one had informed him of this.

Asa.

Because of the extreme situation, he entered Gunnar's mind without invitation, devastated by what he found. Asa was correct, his brother had shattered, was dying with Grace. He had left him alone with this terrible burden, not realizing it would not correct itself.

And Grace… his mind rejected what he saw before him, flashing to the war room, Grace hugging him, telling him she would be alright. Her body was unrecognizable. Words were foreign, impossible.

Gunnar felt a hand rest on his shoulder and Shifted, turning with fangs bared, staggering with a weak, feral sound. Arundel's strong grip held Gunnar as he Shifted back. His hand moved over his brother's forehead, stroked his temple, lay over his chest. Gunnar took his first deep breath in weeks, his body relaxing its stance in spite of himself.

"Brother—" Arundel swallowed. "Brother, I'm—there are no words. I will give anything, everything—."

Moving around the bed, Arundel reached to touch Grace's shoulder. He had learned much about his Healing Gifts these past weeks. His eyes closed, examining, visualizing her injuries. Arundel thought he'd known their severity, but this was so impossibly worse. All of this to shield him.

The Chimera was silent within him.

He could not fail. Gunnar wouldn't live without her.

I can't live without her.

Minutely examining her body, Arundel felt each biological difference between Human and Fae. The starvation of blood felt as though he had no air. He found the source, renewed the bone marrow. Tints of life blushed under her skin.

Gunnar watched, breathing his only movement. He saw the clear signs of blood returning to her system. Arundel's hand lightly cupped her broken jaw. Her face straightened, reshaped.

She looked asleep. The collarbone returned to a natural line. The shattered elbow pieced together, relaxing her arm into a natural position on the bed.

Gunnar's hands were gripping the mattress edge, head pressed into it sobbing in jagged relief. Arundel smoothed away the deep slash that had saved Gunnar and Asa. He gently lifted her hand in his. She had slashed it so deeply to finish the task— he needed to concentrate on the small ligaments and bones.

Arundel stopped moving, rooted to the spot. He'd felt an off-rhythm throb in his heart, a responsive recognition beyond their tie, jolting painfully under his skin. He fell hard to his knees, bending over until his head touched the floor, almost paralyzed with denial.

Grace knew—she knew as she pushed Mors' Gifts into the Chimera, that it was her last breath. She also gave him hers. There was nothing of her remaining here.

Gunnar caught glimpses of these thoughts through Arundel's shock, his brain plodding on. Perhaps it was why she had not healed. The lack of blood was a symptom, not the cause. Arundel had restarted her heart, but she had gone.

Gunnar had what remained of Grace. He had refused to let her last whisper leave him. Now with her body soon restored, he could watch her until he died without reliving every wound until insane. Now he could let go and not leave what remained of her alone, like discarded trash after she had saved them all.

Arundel's fists slammed the floor.

"No. No—this is not possible. She's Human. She doesn't have life strength to give." He rocked back on his knees.

"Brother, the Chimera—how was it not enough?"

Gunnar snapped at him. "Heal her body! No matter what comes, I cannot bear seeing her like this when you can heal her."

Arundel regained his feet. He reached for her hand, resuming the delicate work there. When he reached her fractured pelvis, he slowed. Gunnar felt him stutter there, then stop.

Looking up he saw Arundel's hand resting on her belly, but his eyes were on her legs. Gunnar had been absorbing the horror of them daily since they'd brought her to this room. Arundel was white to the lips.

"The tower—her scream."

"It's my constant companion," Gunnar said.

He looked to Arundel. His harsh laugh a broken knife-edge.

"I wanted to pull the spear from me to escape it. Then I remembered I forced her to live trapped, alone with the knowledge of this horror to come."

His voice steadied, now a razor.

"She pulled herself across the battlefield with her body like this to cut her breast and bleed into my small hurts so I would not die. She kept her wits about her, with injuries that would make a warrior weep, ordering me to keep still, to promise not to look at her, to keep *my* life."

Gunnar's voice escalated into a snarl. "It is fit that I should hear the sound of her scream. Every moment of every day and night, until my last breath. *I did this, to my Mate.*"

Arundel had no words in the face of such immense pain.

He reached out, taking consciousness from Gunnar, catching his body with invisible hands. Arundel laid him on the rarely used cot, healing the lingering wounds, relaxing his body into deep sleep, with no sounds or dreams to torment him. He turned back to Grace.

Arundel worked on Grace's legs and feet throughout the night. Crushed by the tower, pulled by herself to Gunnar and Asa, forcefully dragged over the terrible battlefield— they were liquid in areas. This would never leave him. He was meticulous in his work. Arundel paused, looking at the remaining damage.

Grace—Grace, forgive me.

His hands continued moving over the brutal evidence of her love for him. For them all. He would not leave his work until all was perfect. Then he would carry her outside, Shifting into the Chimera.

The Chimera will know what to do.

He would not give up. If the answer was his life, Arundel would ask the Chimera if it could exist as a separate entity or take Gunnar as host.

Arundel had seen a thing which changed everything.

Two tiny golden threads curled in Grace's womb. She was pregnant.

Conceived in the night before the battle. Fate had held them waiting for each other to begin. One was Gunnar's. The other was his. That they survived in this body meant fate had a plan, a way through this. It was on him to find it.

29.

RENAISSANCE

ARUNDEL HAD GONE over Grace's body carefully until he was certain it was fully healed. He checked on Gunnar, listening to his thoughts and life signs carefully to make sure he was in a Healing state. He kissed Gunnar's forehead, squeezed his shoulder. He might not see him again.

"Brother, I will give anything. Everything. Forgive me the suffering I have caused you."

Wrapping Grace in blankets, he carried her outside the Keep. Guardians ringed the area at a distance for privacy. Seated on the grass, Arundel held Grace, staring through the darkness.

He refused any reality that left his brother's Mate, this female he also loved, an empty shell held together with magic. A touchstone for his brother to hold, waiting for death to take him to her.

"Grace, I have done this before. Lost all that I love. I can't do it again."

Arundel did not know how to communicate with the

Chimera away from himself. It only existed as himself in another form.

He considered Grace's ability—*ghosting*. He'd felt her use it on the field. He searched his memories carefully to understand.

Laying her in the grass, Arundel moved away and Shifted. The Chimera returned to lie with his head on outstretched paws, inches from her, and let the Chimera's Gifts flow over her. The Chimera was so much stronger than Arundel—but he could feel nothing of Grace in her body.

Arundel formed the thought of wanting to ghost next to Grace so he could have contact with her and the Chimera. He was instantly next to her. Looking up, he saw the Chimera for the first time. He looked into the Chimera's eyes and saw a division had been created, a space for him to be his Fae self and communicate.

"Why were we unable to save her?" Arundel asked.

The Chimera spoke into his thoughts.

We maintained the body's spark; the human form could not heal alone from such damage.

"Why did I not feel this? Or Gunnar's state."

We were focused on our mission for Oberon. We may keep open as many threads of contact as we wish, we must only think of it. You did not know we could do this.

"What can I do to bring her back?"

She is not gone. She cannot return to the human body; it is too weak.

"I don't understand."

She pushed her Gifts into us. She is Human. The Gifts were a physical part of her, blood and bone, passed through Human bodies. They were not separate as Fae manifest. This is why her body would not heal. She pushed all that made up her Gifts, the life within her, into us.

Arundel was devastated. He could not live with Grace as a feeling inside of himself, taking her completely from Gunnar.

The Chimera lowered its head, breathing calmness over him.

She is here, everything is within us. Her Gifts are now too strong for a human body, unable to Shift.

Arundel struggled to form questions.

"Will my life-strength give her enough? I will give it. Can you survive without me? Shift yourself to her Mate? He is a worthy male."

No, Arundel. We were created together. We are one.

The last three words dropped his body like a spear to the heart. He felt the Chimera shudder in pain.

He whispered into the ground, "She is pregnant."

Yes. With her Mate's child and ours. They will be powerful for the needs ahead.

Arundel's heart nearly exploded. *Will be.*

He shakily pulled himself up to sit. "How will that happen? How will she bear them?"

Etana and your twins transformed you. Grace's strength from her twin and bloodline are now within us. This power is not meant for us. We will create another Chimera. Our lives will balance out.

Arundel struggled to understand.

"Grace and the children?"

She will have a Fae self, bearing the children. We will pass all of Grace's Gifts back to her.

Thinking of Etana and Grace's mother, his heart demanded another answer.

"Grace—she will live through the twin's birth? They will not die in the creation of another…"

The Chimera again lowered its head to Arundel.

Arundel, we are Seers. Look. *Etana, your children, Luma, and those in Grace's bloodline, died to impart the Gifts. They came through centuries to fulfill their purpose. Grace has died to fulfill her purpose—Fate has guarded the children for theirs. She will not die again in their birth. Her Chimera will not manifest until they are born. They are all the first of their kind.*

Arundel's fingers gripped the ground, anchoring himself. "How do we make a Fae body for her and the children?"

The Chimera stood, shaking its mane.

We see it, and it will be so. Come.

Arundel merged back into the Chimera. He stood over Grace's form on the grass. He closed his eyes, looking at Grace from inside her bloodline. He felt Luma, pulsing brightly.

Having gone over Grace so minutely during healing he understood the difference in Fae and Human biology. The only part of her, with the Gifts gone, which was and must remain Fae, were the children. They had waited for him to reach this moment.

The Chimera guided visualization of Grace's Fae body next to her on the grass. Strengthening, lengthening to accommodate larger lungs, heart, all the life sustaining differences of the Fae. But he did not change her natural shape. She would not become someone else, *something* else in appearance. He concentrated on all the things Gunnar loved in her physical self, pulling from Gunnar's memories.

This was not intrusion. Everything Gunnar loved about her physically gave her love of self; it must be the same. Her softness, her skin, her curves, her eyes, her smile. Her fierceness, her physical worship of him, and acceptance of his for her. The first area she had allowed herself to receive such love.

These things were different from Fae, much more intricate and deeply rooted. They were the wonder of Grace. He would not allow his brother nor Grace the smallest loss. The Chimera infused her Gifts, adding more to be handed down to the children.

The children.

The Chimera lowered his head over Grace's human body.

Come children.

Turning, he breathed over her Fae form.

In that moment, Grace's Fae heart began to beat, her lungs filled. In seconds, her blood circulated and her body was fully alive.

The human body vanished. Arundel Shifted to his Fae form. He had not expected her body to disappear without warning, leaving him bereft. He closed his eyes, seeing her human self smiling over some small thing, then turning the smile on him.

He was exhausted and in shock. He loved her, he needed to say goodbye. A hand cupped his cheek, he looked into Grace's eyes.

"I love you too, Arundel."

Grace leaned forward and kissed him.

Arundel sat motionless.

Grace pulled herself into his arms. She nestled her head against him, pulling his hand up to stroke her hair.

"So. How are we going to awaken my Mate and not kill him with shock? Then how do we explain the babies?"

She raised a brow. "Which brings a whole cascade of other explanations…"

Reaching up to touch his face, she spoke softly.

"Arundel, it will be alright."

Arundel's heart jolted painfully.

Grace felt the horrible echo of the last time she had said these words to him, telling him she would not suffer as Luma did—.

He didn't see her move, only knew he lay on the grass and she held his face in her hands.

"I'm so sorry, I didn't think— my words—"

Arundel's enfolding arms crushed her to him, anguish at the immeasurable pain she and his brother had suffered on his behalf, flooding him.

He struggled to speak. "*Grace*, I—"

Grace pressed fingers against his lips to stop the words.

"The sunrise is coming, you'll have much to explain if we're sitting here." She smiled, then grew serious. "I know your thoughts and what you passed through, healing my Human body. You and I will share that in private. But now, Gunnar is waiting for us."

She leapt up from the grass with the strength and speed of a newborn Fae. As she pulled him to his feet, Arundel heard a startled intake of breath.

Grace was grinning, fingers tangled in her hair. She pulled it back running her fingertips over her newly-shaped ear.

Arundel laughed. Yesterday he had been certain he would never laugh or breathe deeply again.

"Arundel, I would like Gunnar moved to our rooms. I need to think carefully how to awaken him."

Grace and Arundel stood over Gunnar in the med unit room. There was color in his face, his wounds were fully healed, and some of the lines had eased. Only food could help restore his weight.

Grace spoke into Arundel's thoughts.

He'll need exercise…

He tried to summon a serious face.

"You mustn't do that in public."

"I know. Soon I'll get back to the 'hammer in nails' Arundel mode."

"Where has this insubordinate side of you been hidden?"

"Well, the last time I checked, Arundel, I was Grace. You were not the boss of me…"

Arundel wiped his long-disused grin, as he turned to the Healers, giving them instructions to move Gunnar to their rooms, following any word Grace gave them.

He would need adjustment time as well. Father Above, he loved her.

"Arundel?"

"Yes, Grace."

"You're going to Asa? It's urgent — it must be now. She'll only listen to you."

"Yes."

"Without her—"

"I've had the same thoughts."

Grace sat on the edge of their bed, studying Gunnar. She had bathed him in the medical unit before moving him. He would sleep, until she called to him.

She watched him breathe. The worst wounds by far were in his mind. Arundel had healed his body. She'd been holding him asleep while moving him to their bed, to prevent his waking to panic and shock. She wanted control in explaining at a speed which would not overwhelm him—for him to be able to listen.

She brushed back his hair, taking a deep breath, easing it out.

"Gunnar."

She saw his eyes move under closed lids. She picked up his hand, cherishing it between hers.

"*Mate*, wake up."

Gunnar's breath came faster, pain lines in his face deepened. She knew it was not physical pain.

"You hear my voice, you're not dreaming. This is real. Look at me."

Gunnar cautiously opened his eyes. Grace was sitting there, holding his hand. She was naked, so he could clearly see there were no wounds, she was perfect…

His hands came up, covering his eyes, digging into his face. Grace could feel the torment in his mind. He thought he was hallucinating—that he had indeed gone mad.

Grace Possessed him, pulling his hands down.

Before he could fight her hold or let his mind defend, she opened his eyes, slowed his breathing and heart rate, calmed his mind.

"Mate, *Mate*, Arundel healed me. We're in our room. Mors is dead. You have not lost your reason, your mind is not broken, this is not a dream or hallucination. I'm only holding you to prevent you from harming yourself. Until you believe the truth. Tell me what you need to see and hear to prove these things." She freed him enough to look her over.

Struggling to hold emotions in check, his eyes moved over her. She was whole, healthy. The crushed, wasting—gone.

Everything cut viciously against his logic.

"This is a lie," Gunnar's rough voice broke. "You're—perfect—even his healing didn't—" Gunnar fought her hold, desperate to escape the insanity which had finally taken him. He'd believed nothing could be worse—until now.

He looked away, rejecting what he saw, still hearing her scream on the battlefield.

Grace uncovered him.

"*You* are still weak. The Chimera took over my care. Remade me."

She lifted his fingers to the place the arrow had marked her shoulder. "I have no scars. Look down at yourself."

Gunnar scanned his body. He saw the heavy mark from the spear. The new scars from his sword wounds; the numerous old.

"I will explain *everything*, let you read everything. But not until you believe me, so I can release you." Her voice broke. "I'm asking you," she said, giving him the words from their first night. "I will guide you where I want you to go."

She released all of him.

Gunnar lay still looking at her. Studying her face. Looking at her hand, stroking his. He tentatively turned his palm up to feel hers.

The instant he touched her, she lay covering him, pulling his arms around her, her ear over his heart. Sobbing, she pulled herself tightly against him.

Gunnar cautiously ran his hand down her back, feeling

her dips and curves, her soft skin. He allowed himself to breathe deeply of her scent—it was hers, but there were strange notes.

She pulled herself up and kissed him. She let him get used to her mouth, whispering soft touches against his. He was still holding himself.

Grace rolled onto her back, pulling him onto his side, pressed against her. Stretching out, she threw the pillow from under her head, bringing his hand to rest at her throat. She folded her arms above her head. She had so many things to say, to plead, to encourage… but let him set his own pace.

He cupped his hand around her throat, closing his eyes. His hand moved down over her soft skin to her breast, skimming over it to lay his palm on her belly. Grace tried not to hold her breath in hopeful anticipation.

Please…

Sliding down, he lay his head on her stomach, settling himself fully, his arm stretched across her hips gripping tightly. She brought a hand down to comb fingers through his hair, stroke his forehead.

"I love you. This is not a memory of the first time. This is now," Grace said.

Gunnar moved a hand toward her legs, then put it down. She did not interfere. He came up on his forearm and reached to run his hand along them. She raised one to bend at the knee, slightly open.

He dropped his head to her stomach, snatching back the hand, shaking with violent sobs.

"Your legs—"

"Gunnar. Feel my legs. My pelvis is under your head. It's whole, unbroken. Feel my feet. Look at my arm, my face.

Touch me, Mate. Or lie back and let me touch you. I need you. I want to care for you, as you've always done for me."

Coaxing him to slide up with a pillow under his head so he could see her, Grace knelt astride him. She raised his hand to trace fingers over the place of the broken jaw, slipping down over her collar bone, her chest where the cut had been, smoothing over her arm. She held her healed palm to him, fingers spread wide, and placed his against it.

She closed it, twining her fingers between his.

Then she took both of his hands and laid them on her thighs. She lifted slightly, sliding them to the silky inner sides. Her hands over his tightened their grip on her. She leaned forward and kissed him deeply, this time he opened for her questing mouth.

"You are not dreaming—*believe*. I know it's hard, Mate. If you still believe this to be a dream, fall into it. I will catch you."

She kissed him harder.

She could feel him responding. Her Fae ears could hear his heart speeding in a natural way. She slid down his body, licking and kissing her way. She nipped the dip where thigh met hip and he jerked. It tickled there and he always reached to stop her. His hand raised but stopped. She ran her tongue up the underside of him, his hips jerking up, his breath catching in his throat. Again. Again. She splayed out her hands, holding down his hips and gave him a wicked grin. He had no idea how strong she was now. She had not allowed him to see her ears, and he was too weak to have his full powers of observation for the rest of her.

Seconds later he believed he was awake.

Grace was gentle with him, as his every move with

her had been. She let him rest, giving him space to think things through.

Gunnar let his hands roam over her, scenting her every so often. He most often returned to her legs, running his hands over every bone, feeling something to be different but not able to say what.

After the fifth run up and down her legs, she spread them wide. He was going to feel that they were longer, stronger. She didn't want to flood him with everything at once, but the next step was approaching, and she wanted to be in control. Gunnar responded to her gesture. She could feel his heart begin to ease.

It would take time, but she would be patient. She woke several hours later to feel him moving restlessly.

He was spooning her with his arms wrapped tightly around her. She could feel him dreaming, seeing her injured. Her Gifts reached out, soothing his heart, calming his mind, replaying the first exploration of the night where his fears were soothed, and the physical affirmation of the second. He relaxed and the dream receded. When it was gone, she gently woke him.

"Mate, I'm going to the washroom. I didn't want you to wake and find me gone."

Cupping her cheek he kissed her.

"I *would* have panicked. I'm looking at you, touching you and I'm struggling still."

He let her up, reassured by the sounds of her moving around. When she returned, he was asleep. She slid in next to him, nestling into the curve of his body, monitoring his dreams.

30.

ASA

THE END BEGAN with pondering different manners of silence. There was the willing silence before extreme sacrifice. The despairing silence of a reluctant, final heartbeat. All forms of death, really, of the heart, the mind, the spirit. Worse, if the body did not follow—she was there now.

Asa lay unmoving, facing the room's blank wall, she would stay exactly there until her heart stopped. Her personal code would not allow a physical act to end her life unless in enemy hands, but her mind—she would allow it to accomplish what it could. A finely honed tool, it should be able to create silence.

She'd slowed healing to a halt, but still fought to escape the one silence she could not bear. The silence of those she loved more than her own life. The silence of those she had failed.

Battle was the opposite of silence. She had never shunned it. Never feared it. Then came Grace's unimaginable scream as the tower crushed her. She would have gladly taken a knife to the heart to escape that sound.

She could have saved Grace. Traveled in, and if unable to vanish her from the spot, pushed her out of the way.

If she had been paying attention.

Now she had the quiet of this room to re-examine every moment, every second. Quiet was simply hushed sound. Her heartbeat tortured her with every thump. She continuously heard the snap of the tower base and the screech of its fall.

Sight too, was involved. There were no visual memories she could recall, which had no sound attached. On this battlefield she had recorded the first. Grace healing her throat— she'd caught glimpse of her body as Grace put her down.

Her crushed body—silence had filled Asa's ears. It shattered as Mors pulled Grace from her—dragging her over that horrible field. There was only one way to stop the endless screaming ringing in her ears.

She directed the pain, like poison, to her heart. A beat dropped from its rhythm, then another. Finally. She forced her breath to draw shallow. Trained to fake death—it was strange that death could be faked, but not its silence.

Two more heartbeats. Her body, heavy as lead, sank into the bed, muscles limp. Slowly wiping her thoughts blank triggered a torture-resist training response, distancing mind from her body.

She had been avoiding these things until all had gone silent in Grace's room. It was time. She could be cowardly now, no longer facing her failure. The note to Arundel had been too late.

The report on Grace, she had left too late.

Numbness arrived, it helped so much. Her heart dropped several more beats, breath became a whisper. Relief took the last of her hold away. Her body drifted down to settle into life starvation. Silence slid toward her. It was Dark.

The body, no longer hers, shifted. Another beat dropped. Turned, lifted, pain from its dying tugged faintly. Another beat escaped, two left. Warmth seeped around her shoulders, a hand on her face annoyed her. She resisted, retreating into the silent darkness, blood pooling, lungs empty.

"Asa."

Moving from face to chest, the hand pulled at her heart, forced it to beat, rising, a beat every second. It pressed harder; a wisp of breath moved.

The silent darkness, so close, so close she nestled into it, the heartbeats vanishing. She would not stay.

"Asa. Open your eyes. Now."

Possession bit her. Tugged and pulled. It hurt.

She snapped the bridge between mind and body.

Hands grasped her face, then her throat, pushed hard against her chest.

"Asa. Now!"

Air flooded her lungs, full of razor edges. Falling into her body, everything was pain. Her heart thumped as though kicked.

The silence—was running, fleeing.

A whispered, angry, scream.

"No!"

Feeling returned to her skin. A hand rubbing her back and arms brought emotion rushing, enraging her.

Wounds were disappearing.

"No."

"Asa. Listen to me. Grace is alive. Gunnar is alive. You cannot go. They need you."

The words lied. They took Grace. Gunnar was gone.

Images ran through her mind. Grace laughing with Arundel outside. Perfect, healthy, different. Impossible.

Hands shook her, hard.

"Asa, open your eyes."

The command sent an impulse through her body; it was not a request. She let go of the trigger reflex, opening her eyes. Focused. It was Arundel. Control broken, silence fell out of reach, ripping her heart. She convulsed with sobs, her body curling in on itself. Arundel cradled her.

"Breathe, Asa. Let it go. It's not time. You could not have prevented any of it. You are not stronger than fate, Asa. Fate also wanted her alive. Grace succeeded, we succeeded. Mors is dead. Gunnar is recovering with her. We're going to leave them alone for a time, but you will talk to her soon."

Asa was still—staring at him—beginning to believe.

"Asa, you're catching up very slowly for a Dark Unit Operative. Do you think I hold all my Spies when they're hurt?" His mouth quirked. "Grace asked me to give you her love."

An enfolding warmth, calm and peace flowed through her.

It felt of Grace.

"Now that I've delivered Grace's message, here is mine." Arundel tightened his hold, looking past her. "Your message saved them both, thereby saving me. Like you, I could not have lived without them." He met her gaze. "Asa, when I left I thought she would heal. I was wrong. If you had not written, I would not have returned in time. You saved them." Arundel laid her back on her pillow, brushing back her hair.

"Sleep. Eat. Asa, you'll be back on duty, guarding Grace soon. She has news for you. You cannot be the weakest link. That's an order. Do you understand?"

"Yes, Commander," Asa whispered.

She took a deep breath, hearing it come in and go out. She could hear her heartbeat. She was not sorry to see the silence go.

Arundel leaned forward.

"Thank you, Asa."

Kissing her forehead, Arundel put her into a gentle sleep.

Standing, he smoothed the covers, watching her. Again. Again he was nearly too late. She had stepped from the precipice, was falling into the abyss when he touched her. He had to fight to pull her back. He could make no excuse. Now that he was fully manifesting Gifts in his Fae form, he needed to use them.

He went to Healer Ahma's office, closing the door to speak with her of Grace's future.

31.

REVELATION

TO GRACE'S JOY, Gunnar slept long, healing hours. She sat facing him from the bed's foot. When she'd arrived on Oberon, his face was the first thing she'd seen clearly. When he opened his eyes, it would be hers.

Gunnar was unwavering; love both tender and fierce, his joy taken in hers, her freedom encouraged, even while it terrified him. Running through memories from the moment his hand first cupped her chin until now, Grace realized the horizon was no longer fixed, the line stretching before her curved out of sight.

As long as my heart beats now shifted to Gunnar's declaration: *for the length of my life.* Her heart had stopped beating. He was her all that comes after. She would always love him beyond reason.

Stretching cautiously, Gunnar paused only a second before opening his eyes. Her feet were touching distance from him. He turned to his side, reaching a hand to rest lightly on them, fingers exploring, smoothing over them.

"Are you hungry?" Grace asked.

Gunnar's gaze caressed her face. "Yes. Ten minutes," he said, heading for the washroom.

He returned to her damp from the shower, roughing his hair with a towel. She made motion to fetch the food tray, but he carefully grasped her by the ankles and pulled her to the center of the bed.

He kissed his way up to her inner thighs. She hummed her pleasure. She was so sensitive; he had only to look at her with desire. Gunnar was contentedly focused, but Grace wanted him. Now.

Pulling him up to her, she left her legs on his shoulders, wanting to watch his face and his body in hers. He teased her, slowing and quickening. Close to the edge, Grace reached for Gunnar's hips, pulling him hard into her. Pushing him back, she pulled harder still. He needed no more encouragement. He drove in, letting go, losing himself in her. The world fell away. Grace arched hard against him as she came, her throes almost shaking him from her body, the strength of her pulsing grip bringing him with her.

As their bodies quieted, Gunnar reclined against the pillows —again smoothing a hand from her hip to ankle.

Grace stilled at the strange expression on his face. Not frightened, nor angry; something she'd never seen. For the first time, her nostrils flared as she scented him. Gunnar saw her reflexive action.

He nodded, looking back at her legs.

"Your ears are showing."

Grace burst out laughing. She rolled to her side, unable

to stop. The cumulative stress of intense emotion eased as peals of laughter rocked her. She held her stomach, gasping for air.

"I'm sorry—I wanted to tell you immediately but thought it too much, too soon. I would have told you this morning—but we were distracted."

She pulled up the sheet to wipe away tears, failing utterly to get her breath under control.

"My ears are showing!" She hiccuped, wrestling her laughter into submission.

"Your legs. I couldn't put words to it. They're longer, your arms, you can reach farther. And when you *came*… I could barely hold onto you."

His hands continued absently stroking her legs. She sat up, sobering, searching his face.

"I'm still me. The Chimera made me exactly myself. I'm never going to be a muscular amazon like other females, I'm just—me." Her voice was beginning to tremble. "Mate?"

Gunnar instantly turned to her.

"Grace! It's the answer to my dreams. I won't lose you—you'll heal—the list is endless."

"Then—what's wrong?"

"Grace—I don't understand—*anything*. There are complete blank spaces in my memory. I've never felt this way. It's—difficult for me. Who I am—I feel I've lost myself."

Sighing, Grace sat up, arms hugging her knees.

"Mate, I'll tell you everything. First, I had to get you back. I would have lost you. I need your help too—adjusting—to everything that's happened. *I'm Fae.* I've been in this body only hours longer than you've been awake."

Stunned, Gunnar tried to swallow, his throat painfully

tight. As was her habit, she carried the enormity of the burden alone, waiting until she thought him ready.

"Mate…"

The word staggered with the weight of his emotion. Pulling her to her place of safety, ear over his heart, he locked his arms around her.

Grace began to speak, then hesitated, wanting to address a thing that concerned her.

"… My decision to Possess you last night—I didn't know how to safely—contain you—while you went through the shock of it all. I would never… after all the horror you went through, I wanted to keep you safe. I—I ask your forgiveness if it—upset—"

She found herself flat on her back, Gunnar kneeling over her. She decided that his hands buried in her hair as he kissed her eyelids, cheeks, throat—was a good sign. He spoke softly against her ear, his cheekbone pressed to hers.

""After all I went through... After all I went through. Mate—I have no words. I will never have enough words."

He returned to his back with her covering him, focusing only on their breathing, their heartbeats. Grace lifted her head, chin resting on her forearms folded on his chest.

"You're ready for me to fill the gaps? There is so much."

"Grace, tell me all of it. Please, I need to hear."

She paused. "Shall I start with the easiest to understand, or most difficult?"

Gunnar considered her question. "When I work a difficult problem, I always begin with the most demanding element, when my skills are sharpest."

Grace looked down a moment, considering her next words.

"I'm so grateful we do this together."

Gunnar's finger brushed her cheek.

"I wish for you never to bear anything alone again. Mate, there is nothing you need fear to say."

Grace thought through a carefully edited version from Arundel's arrival to the medical unit, through her first breath as Fae. They were Arundel's memories, passed from the Chimera. She omitted only those parts that warranted a more detailed, separate revelation.

Lifting Gunnar's hand to her face, she let the images flow. She could do it without contact now but wanted him to feel some normalcy in this time of extremes.

He finished, pulling her hand to rest on his chest while he processed. It was so much information, such extremes. The torture of watching her—what he had become while waiting to join her—all Arundel had done. When Grace felt his attention return to her face, she spoke.

"I needed to take a portion of the Gifts from him. As a Chimera, I will not Shift for almost a year, then, maybe at will. I really don't know," she admitted.

Gunnar thought of her passion to meet whatever need lay before her, sacrificing all if necessary. Surviving the impossible. Of course she was a Chimera. A consuming part of him eased, knowing she could defend herself against almost anything.

Gunnar's brows rose. "This revelation is the most difficult?"

"Perspective is subjective, but I thought it might shock you."

"I love you beyond measure," he said, arms tightening around her.

"That's convenient, I feel the same."

With a smile she rested her cheek on his chest.

"You're well," he said.

"I am," she said.

"You're not in pain," he said.

"I most certainly am not," she said.

"You will live a long life with me," he said.

"Causing all kinds of trouble—for which I'm still not sorry."

Gunnar's eyes closed, hands feeling the softness and curves containing his heart, his life. Her words replaced months of fear and brokenness.

"I'm ready to hear the rest."

Grace's hands smoothed over his ribs, realizing afresh that he had also been dying as her Human body wasted.

"You are not tired? Hungry?"

Sneakily she appealed to his need to care for her, if not himself.

"Please, eat with me, I'm hungry, then we might rest. Your body and mind have been through so much. Do not compare it with mine."

"Let's continue while we eat, then rest."

Grace fetched a waiting tray of cold roast chicken, bread, and apples, pouring mugs of tea.

"Tell me of your relationship with Arundel."

As he ate, his thoughts returned to the beginning. He pulled her hand to cup his cheek, letting her read the memories of this critical part of him.

"As you see, it is unchanging. Until you, there was nothing that compared to it. You are different aspects of love, but equal in depth." He studied her face and saw nothing negative there.

"Does this worry you?" he asked.

"It brings me joy. And if I feel the same?"

Gunnar smiled, thinking of the decision made with his brother to wait until after the battle to tell Grace how they felt.

"I would be surprised, Grace, if you did not—you are the two I love most in all of this world."

"Arundel has said those exact words to me."

She showed him Arundel struggling to break open her suffering, finding her bloodline with Luma and therefore the blind spot—allowing her to live—not dying in Gunnar's arms day-by-day.

Arundel breaking in the war room, at her light attitude toward what she would face. Made even more difficult because Arundel could see most of it and could not stop it. Her suggesting it would be nothing like Luma's suffering — and the archers, shattering him.

Then Mors' tactical disaster that led to the terrible night before the battle.

Gunnar cherished her hand. Her act of saving Arundel was miraculous, though her levels of danger, frantic fear and panic throughout the night crushed his heart.

He and Arundel had been in countless battles, but Grace was Human, in an overwhelming situation. Arundel, fighting despair—and her desperation to take her life in saving him— had seen her fear. His love had comforted her. Gunnar had never seen love run so deep as that between them. It was not threatening; it was uniquely precious. Grace—the warmth and openness of her humanity—was the binding that made them unbreakable.

After pondering the rightness of these things, he saw

Grace's troubled face. "Grace, it is a precious thing to feel so." Her expression softened into tears.

Her miraculous Mate. She slid the tray away and launched herself at him, pinning him on his back, her ear over his heart, sobbing. The fear, loneliness, and anguish of the past months flooded through her.

Gunnar gently rocked her against him through the stormy release.

Sobs subsiding, she rested her head on his shoulder where she could watch him.

She gave him the last piece, gently unfolding the images directly into his thoughts.

"The last of it."

He saw why Arundel had stumbled while healing her pelvis. Arundel's purgatory healing her body, his determination to give his life strength—the Chimera's response to his plea— her transformation. The Chimera's prophetic words of the children.

She was still, listening to his heart.

Gunnar was also motionless while he absorbed the most profound revelation. Until he felt uncertainty grow in Grace.

Swiftly turning her to her back, Gunnar shifted downward to slide his arms under the small of her back. Eyes closed, he rested on the softness of her belly, breathing in her scent.

Not only was the Mated scent so strong it stunned him, but also the unmistakable scent of her pregnancy.

How had he missed them?

This was the reason she wouldn't Shift.

He whispered against her skin, "Tell me I'm not dreaming."

Grace held him to her belly, fingers tugging his cowlicks. "You've never been more awake."

Raising his chin, she chuffed a short groan to him, feeling his arms release her as she blinked. Half the mattress sagged alarmingly, and a welcomed heaviness lay on her belly, a rough warmth beneath her hand. Gunnar's jaguar rested his head there, body pressed alongside her legs. His nose skimmed her skin, yellow-gold eyes holding hers, mouth slightly parted as he drew long breaths; exhaled grunting hnnk, hnnk, sounds against her.

He shifted slightly to tilt his massive head, closing his jaws to repeatedly rub his cheek against her hip bone; the motions pushing back his upper lip to expose great teeth. Grace ran her fingers through his rough coat from cheek to ear, fur disappearing between them to become Gunnar's dark hair, cheek resting on her belly, eyes fading from gold to gray.

He listened to the three heartbeats telling him love had won.

NEW HISTORY

GRANDMOTHER LILLI'S STORIES of their mother's birth were outright lies. Lilli could not have known the birth's significance across worlds. She knew only of her nightmarish suffering.

The delivery had been a marathon of shock and horror. The baby's large head would not pass through the birth canal. The doctors, desperate to save the badly scarred, struggling young mother, performed an emergency Cesarean, forcefully pulling a black-haired, dusky-skinned infant back from the canal before killed her mother. After removing the child, the stunned surgeons realized there was not one baby, but two. Girls, different as night from day. Nurses cleaned the babies, laying them side-by-side. The astonished surgical team studied them in disbelief. None had ever seen such a drastic difference in twins. The first infant was not only black-haired, brown-skinned, and startlingly larger—but heavier-boned of body and face.

One surgeon, examining her face closely for signs

of deformity, noted with surprise that the child had the Epicanthic fold to her eyelids. A genetic trait not often seen in their area, its origins ranged throughout Northern Asia, up into Mongolia and across to the Inuits. The trait was not present in the other child. The second infant had the finely-boned, light-skinned features of her mother. He shook his head at the strangeness of it.

Lilli was slow in surfacing from anesthesia. Her waiting parents stood at the nursery window, numb with shock. There could be no doubt who the firstborn girl resembled.

When Lilli awakened, the nurses brought the babies. Her mother put her second daughter in her arms. Cherishing the small, embodiment of her heart, Lilli was flooded with gratitude; there had been purpose to her suffering. The nurse took the infant from her, placing the other child in her arms.

Lilli froze, caught in repellent darkness. The infant seemed to reject her touch, no longer having need of her. She was the image of her father, renewing Lilli's horror of his planting the child in her.

She wanted the child away from her, unable to stop her growing panic. Worst fears confirmed, her parents quickly took the infant, asking the nurse to give Lilli something for pain and rest.

While their daughter slept, they spoke of how to handle the impossible situation. The dark child would destroy their daughter—a constant reminder of the horror which begat her.

Frustrated, they could find no solution.

They baptized the infants while their daughter slept. Names from their family lines; Kara and Mary.

The following morning the somber-faced doctor came

in. He held Lilli's hand as he told her of Kara's death during the night. He couldn't explain it, she had been the more vigorous of the two. Their conclusion was sudden infant death syndrome. Lilli held Mary fiercely, weeping in relief at release from a lifetime reminder of Mors' torture.

Immediately after notifying her, the doctor's knowledge of Kara's birth slipped away. His memory, and that of all personnel present in the hospital had been wiped clean.

Mors, led by a vision-invoked curiosity, had looked upon the child Kara the night of her birth. Standing at the nursery window in the small hours of the night, he was surprised at the satisfaction he felt looking at himself in miniature. He considered Human progeny a waste of his blood. But this girl— this girl looked like a miniature Kahn, who would grow to lay waste to empires.

Mors Possessed a nurse to steal the infant. His Seer vision showed him the woman would raise the child in a harshly-disciplined, spartan manner. He implanted a command to take the girl to his homelands, the Daurian forest-steppe of Mongolia; his Gift of Voice enabling her to teach the child Mongolic tongues. His tribe would butcher her, taking the child. The girl looked and spoke as they did; it was fit she be raised as their own. Even her name, Kara, in the phonetic was a Mongol name. Qara, meaning "black."

Qara would travel with the Pulse to Oberon. That his progeny would wreak havoc in his birthplace, even as he did so on the opposite side of their world amused him.

Mors departed, wiping staff memories, implanting the doctor with a final order. He dismissed the child from thought; uncaring whether she fulfilled the vision or not. Left to fend for herself in discovering her Gifts, she was a feral thing, designed to live and die by the amoral code for which her genetics molded her.

The twin's purpose was written in their DNA. Mary carried the antidote to darkness, her dark sister, the obliteration of light. Both had Mors' blood and Luma's blind spot.

> "The dead can survive as part of the
> lives of those that still live."
>
> —Kenzaburō Ōe

ACKNOWLEDGMENTS

I've wanted to write books for as long as I could read them. Mostly because I'd get to keep them. Returning them to the library was a surrendered bit of my heart. Two beloved ones were so overdue I couldn't afford to return them. Still have them. Sorry, Banfield Elementary.

Eventually I bought books of my own, but the desire to write them remained.

Ironically, now I'd like to return my books to every library in the country, and into the hands of anyone who might enjoy my journey from there to here.

Gratitude given to:

My parents, who never minded that communication of any kind needed emphatic repetition to pry me out of the paper world I lived in.

My husband, for financing the many, many heavy boxes of books I finally got to keep—through many, many moves. Then generously opening his wallet for everything I needed to reach this book.

My kids, for not laughing in all the right places.

My sister Dawne, for more lovely things than I can list here.

Darreby, who gave me permission to stop dreaming and do it.

Wendy, my oldest friend on the planet "gotcha!".

My friends and relatives who heroically struggled through two years of horrendous drafts, before we reached simply bad drafts. I hope you deleted the evidence. Please, god. The best one, in signed hardcover, is on its way.

Brave, brave editors, Nicole Schuette, gifted, patient, brilliant, kind. Destyn Hehr, stunt-Proofreader extraordinaire. And the miraculous Lisa Nicole and Daren Swanson, who kept the book alive.

Maggie Stiefvater, for providing my daughter and me quality time wandering through every book she's published, and inspiration and encouragement in the writing seminars we globetrotted to. I told you I'd put you in here.

Meredith, Stephen, LeeAnn, Shelby, Alana, Sarabeth, Jenn, Dave, Karen, Lauren, Tinatin, Lisa, Matt, Jodi, Mingzhu, Chip, Lauren, Jane, Rebecca, Cindy, Dianna, and Dave.

Because it's a smutty book, last names were omitted for the squeamish. You know who you are.

ABOUT THE AUTHOR

J Z York is new to fiction writing, Pulse is her debut novel. An Air Force Veteran, she happily participated in the launch of women into all-male career fields. She is also a professional photographer, cat rancher, dog magnet, miniature horse breeder, and unlucky guinea pig grandmother (sorry Jenniva). Working in the film and television industry garnered useful anecdotes and a fervent dislike for high heels while crashing numerous Cannes and Telluride Film Festivals, and gold statue events. She loves things that zoom, above, or over the ground. This week she's residing in Southern California.